PERFECT

P. J. GUDKA

This novel contains themes of grooming, sexual exploitation, and abuse, presented within the context of a fictional thriller. These elements are depicted for narrative and thematic purposes and are not intended to romanticize or endorse such behavior. Reader discretion is advised.

Print ISBN: 978-1-964885-63-6
eBook ISBN: 978-1-964885-64-3

This book is dedicated to my mom, who upon reading my first book advised me to write something more positive and uplifting for my second one. Mom—my apologies in advance.

PROLOGUE

I OPENED MY MOUTH TO SCREAM FOR HELP, BUT HE QUICKLY wrapped his fingers around my throat, silencing me before I could make a sound.

I tried to scratch him, kick him, push him away. Anything to get him to loosen his grip.

"I'm sorry, Lily, but I can't have you messing up my life. I'm not going to let you destroy my future, everything I've worked so hard for."

His face was frighteningly blank as he continued squeezing my throat. I gasped for air, my lungs burning. I blinked rapidly. My vision was getting blurry, and I was starting to see spots.

ONE

SALLY

My mother always told me no one had a *PERFECT* marriage. Or a perfect family. Of course, that was usually after one of her partners did something terrible to her or to us both. Her acceptance of our pathetic situation made me angrier at her than any of the men who had come and gone. Instead of protecting me, she had spent her life moving me from one toxic situation to another. And I hated her for it.

By the time I finally left, I swore to myself I would do what she never could. I would have the perfect marriage, be the perfect wife and mother, have the perfect family, and live the perfect fucking life in suburbia. My mother never protected me, never put me first. But I promised myself that I would be different. I would always prioritize my children and protect them.

Good luck, Sally. That was all she said to me for years whenever we fought, and I told her I would be the mother she never was. *You'll always be trash*, she'd snickered in her drunken state. Drunk and miserable, that's how I will always remember her. Destroying everyone and everything in her path. Like a black hole, pulling everything into its field.

I stared down at my slender, pristinely manicured fingers as I expertly cut the vegetables on the chopping board before me.

On my left hand sat a beautiful diamond ring—both the size and design were impressive enough to turn heads, even years after I had received it. I smiled slightly, enjoying this little moment to myself. As I breathed in the aroma of the food I was preparing, I could not help but think about how far I had come.

I guess there is something to be said about living your life out of spite for those you loathe. Because my life turned out pretty well in the end. I married a man she would never have imagined me with and built a life she could never have given me.

I had an amazing husband who was always there for me, two sons who were both bright and kind, the most beautiful and intelligent daughter anyone could wish for, and, of course, a house in the suburbs. It was like something out of those ridiculously cheesy romance movies I used to love. The only thing missing was Colin Firth. Although with his boyish smirk, dark hair with a few grays scattered in, and big brown puppy-dog eyes, my husband was much more handsome than any English actor could ever be. Hugh Grant could never.

I always wondered why he was enamored with me, someone so plain and regular. Thanks to my mousy appearance, with straight, fine brunette hair, a pale complexion, thin lips, and dark brown eyes, I rarely got any male attention growing up. Most of the time, people seemed to look through me. But not John. He always made me feel special and seen. From the moment we first locked eyes, he had been nothing but incredible. Even after all these years, he doted on me. Telling me how beautiful I was every single day.

I finished preparing everyone's dishes and added lots of fresh vegetables to the plate. My kids never grew up hating their veggies. In fact, they loved them because I had never forced them to eat anything they didn't enjoy. Something my mother did to me often growing up. We never had home-cooked meals, which was actually a blessing because she couldn't cook squat. And when I got sick of the microwaved lasagna, I was forced to eat it or risk getting a beating from whatever loser she was dating at the time.

I yelled for everyone to come down to dinner and heard their eager footsteps coming down the stairs almost immediately. I couldn't help but smile at that. As the kids sat down, my husband walked in too.

"That smells incredible," he told me, kissing my cheek.

I smiled even wider as we sat down next to one another. My husband, John, was the kindest human being I had ever met. He was there for me at my lowest, and if it weren't for him, I don't know where I would have ended up. I certainly would not have had the happy life I have now. He saved me, and in return, I have done everything I can to keep him and our children happy.

"So, James… I was wondering if you wanted to invite Lily to Sunday dinner this week," I asked, turning my attention toward my eldest son.

Although James was almost legally an adult now, he would always be my little boy. Until his siblings were born, he had been the single most important thing in my life. Everything I did was for him. And he had been the most amazing child a mother could ask for.

He had been such an adorable kid and had grown into a very handsome young man. With thick dark hair, a sharp jawline, and bright, sharp eyes, he looked like a teenage heartthrob. He resembled me more when he was younger, but now his features are strikingly similar to his father's.

He had recently started dating Lily, a girl from his high

school who had moved here from New York. She was nice enough. A little plain, if you asked me, but her personality was fine. She wasn't too tall and was quite slender. She had thick black hair, slightly tanned skin, and observant green eyes. Other than her eyes, there wasn't much to her that was attractive, but James obviously felt differently. Still, she was sweet, had a nice laugh, and most of all, James adored her.

Although I didn't hate her, I hated that James couldn't spend more time with us because he was always off with Lily these days. Especially since he would be all grown up and off to college soon. But I had accepted that this was a part of life. They really do grow up in the blink of an eye. No one ever prepares you for how much it hurts when you wake up and realize your kids aren't your *kids* anymore.

"Um, I don't know... We sort of got into a fight after school..." said James, staring at his plate.

"Oh no, what happened?" I asked, more curious than sorry.

"It's complicated," James muttered, averting his eyes.

Now I was even more curious. It wasn't like James to keep anything from me. He stared at his plate, pushing around the peas but not eating much. Something was wrong—I could always sense it when one of my babies was hurting. But I had to play it cool. Nothing repels a teenager quite like an overly enthusiastic mother.

"I see. Well, if you ever want to talk about it, your father and I are always here to listen," I let him know.

"Yes, always," agreed John, lifting his head to give James a reassuring smile.

James gave John a curt nod in response but went back to staring at his plate. An argument we had a few weeks prior about Lily came to mind. He had been completely infatuated with her then. Could things have changed between them so quickly? Was that why he had been acting strangely these days?

"How was school, you two?" John asked Sophia and John Jr., turning his attention toward our two youngest and snapping me back to the present. Sophia was nine, and John Jr. was six. They were both very smart for their age, though. You would think they were little adults.

"Fine," they both replied in unison, too preoccupied with shoveling food into their mouths to care too much about the conversation.

John chuckled softly and continued eating.

Sophia and John Jr. (or JJ, as we affectionately called him) were carbon copies of John. They had his light brown eyes, his smile, and his dark hair. Other than being slightly more tan from playing in the sun all summer, like James, they resembled their father. And I loved that. I loved him too much to be mad about having mini versions of him running around the house. If anything, I was proud to be able to give him these wonderful children that we both adored.

Some women may judge me for that—being a housewife and mother isn't "in" these days. Sure, I could have had bigger hopes and dreams. But years of living through the worst imaginable had taught me a lesson that it takes most a lifetime to learn: to be grateful for what I have because things change at the drop of a hat.

I sat there admiring my perfect little family, smiling as I watched them enjoy my cooking. Everything had finally fallen into place for me, and I couldn't imagine life being any different from this. This was my heaven, and I never wanted this moment to change.

Right on cue, the doorbell rang, interrupting our bliss. I

frowned, annoyed at the awful timing. What could be urgent enough that it was necessary to interrupt our dinner? As I got up and walked to the door, for whatever reason, my heart began to palpitate. Something was wrong—I could sense it.

TWO

I OPENED MY FRONT DOOR SLOWLY TO SEE TWO POLICE OFFICERS standing there with their notebooks out. For a split second, I panicked, and my fight-or-flight mode kicked in. Well, for me, it was mostly a fight-or-flight mode—I wasn't one to fight. But I quickly recovered and put on a fake smile.

This could not possibly have anything to do with what had happened so many years ago.

The officer on the right appeared much older, his thinning gray hair and sunken eyes clearly visible even on our dimly lit front porch. The one on the left was a little younger. He had neatly combed blond hair, no grays, and a rather prominent forehead. His face didn't look old but rather mature. It was the face of someone who had lived a hard life. They looked somber as they stood there staring at me. My stomach was in knots.

"Can I help you?" I asked.

"I'm sorry to bother you. I'm Officer Smith, and this is my partner, Officer Jones. We need to talk to… uh… James," said the older officer, checking his notebook to confirm the name.

"That's my son. I'm sorry, what is this regarding?" I asked, trying to hide my surprise.

What could they possibly want with James? My mind instantly went to all the worst scenarios.

"Do you know a… Lily Johnson?" he asked me.

I nodded, still confused.

"Well, she was reported missing by her parents and was last seen at school with James. We would like to talk to him in case he knows anything about her whereabouts," he continued with a neutral expression on his face.

"Can you do this some other time? We're in the middle of dinner. And Lily's a teenager, she's probably gone over to a friend's place or something," I told them dismissively, trying to avoid the situation.

"Ma'am, we just need to talk to James for a few minutes, and then y'all can get back to your dinner," said Officer Jones, who had been silent so far.

He was taller and larger, and his voice, although quieter, was still authoritative—the kind of voice you wouldn't dare disobey.

"Fine," I sighed.

I moved out of the way and fully opened the front door, allowing them in. This was ridiculous. A girl doesn't show up for dinner, and suddenly the police are at *my* front door questioning *my* son.

"This way to the living room." I gestured with my hand. "Have a seat. I'll call James."

Taking deep breaths to calm myself, I walked into our dining room, which had now fallen silent. It was a shell of the happy haven it had been moments ago. They all stared at me with questioning looks as soon as I walked in. I told the younger kids to finish their meal, that nothing serious was going on. That didn't seem to satisfy their curiosity, so I promised them I would tell them everything when we were done, and that seemed to ease them for now.

I asked James and John to come with me and explained the situation to them in the hallway in hushed whispers before we entered the living room. I couldn't help but notice the scared expression on James's face.

"This is James," I told the officers, motioning to him as he stood awkwardly beside his father.

"Hello, young man. Mind if we ask you some questions?" asked Officer Smith in a chatty tone.

I knew that trick. They try to sound friendly to get you to talk. They try to make you feel a false sense of security so they can get what they need out of you.

"Sure." James shrugged.

He was trying to play it cool, but I could see how stressed he was. He kept playing with his hair, and his eyes were fixed on the officers, observing them.

"Do you know Ms. Lily Johnson?"

"Yes."

"And did you see her today?"

"Yes."

"And when did you last see her?"

"I talked to her out back after school ended, and then I headed home. She stayed at school because she had a violin lesson in the music room. That was the last time we spoke."

"Did you see her go into the music room? The music teacher, Mr. Live, mentioned that she didn't show up for her lesson, which, according to him, was unusual for her."

"I saw her head back into the school. That was the last time I saw her."

"I see. And what did the two of you talk about? Did she seem emotional or upset?"

"We... we sort of had an argument, and I broke up with her," said James quietly.

He quickly looked away, his eyes avoiding everyone in the room. He was playing with his fingers nervously.

"Hmm... and you haven't heard from her since? No phone calls or messages that may indicate where she is?"

"No, nothing."

"Are you sure, son? Her parents are really worried and say it's unlike her to disappear for so long without contacting them."

"I'm sure."

James continued to stare at the floor, pushing his hair out of his face.

"And when you spoke to Lily, were there any other students around who could verify that you two *only spoke*?"

I didn't like where this was going. Were they seriously trying to insinuate that James had something to do with Lily's disappearance? This was ridiculous—they're teenagers, and teenagers fight. They're almost a hundred percent hormones at that age. She was probably upset and acting out.

"I don't think there was anyone else there since we were outside and class had ended for the day."

"And what exactly was your fight about?" asked one of the officers.

A deafening silence filled the room. The ticking from the clock suddenly sounded much louder and more noticeable than ever before. I adjusted my hair, nervously tucking it behind my ears.

"Answer him, son," the other officer ordered more sternly.

"It's just... I felt like we had different priorities and goals for the future, and she was weighing me down... so we broke up," James mumbled.

"I see," the officer said, writing something down in his notebook.

"And where did you go after you two had this fight? Were you with anyone who can vouch for you?"

"My son had football practice after school," I blurted out.

"I didn't go to practice today... I was driving around, and then I came home," James admitted in a quiet tone.

I stared at him, dumbfounded. He *never* skipped practice.

"And you were driving around alone or...?"

"Alone."

"Hmm... Okay, well, that's all we need for now. She's probably upset and needs some time. We're hoping she'll show up soon or at least contact someone. If she does contact you, please let us know immediately," said the younger officer, abruptly standing up.

James promised he would, and they left after handing us their contact information.

I thought I would be relieved watching them leave. But there was this weird, lingering feeling in my gut that something was wrong. That something had changed. I blamed it on the fact that I'd never been comfortable around cops (to be fair, most of us aren't) and nothing more.

I had hoped to talk to James, but as soon as the officers were gone, he silently headed to his bedroom, completely ignoring his father and me. The way he slammed his bedroom door shut told me that he wanted to be left alone right now. So, I walked back to the dining room to talk to Sophia and JJ about what had happened. I owed them an explanation, even if it was a very watered-down one.

THREE

I woke up with the same weird feeling that had been bugging me since last night. I had tried my best to ignore it, but it just would not go away. I reached for my phone on the nightstand and saw that there were no new messages. It was around four in the morning, but I was wide awake. My heart was beating rapidly, thumping against my chest. As I lay there staring at the ceiling, John rolled over to face me.

"You okay?" he whispered.

"Yeah... sorry, did I wake you?" I whispered back.

"Kinda," he chuckled, wrapping his arms around my waist under the covers.

I lightly stroked his beard with my fingertips, smiling. He kissed my jaw, my neck, and my chest, and I sighed in response. Before long, the sound of our moans replaced the quiet of the night. I fell asleep in his arms and woke up feeling more refreshed. But that feeling of dread lingered in my mind, and I could not shake it.

James was the first one down, and I decided to speak to him about everything. I wanted to make sure he was okay. He seemed to be in a better mood compared to last night.

"I'm okay, Mom," he reassured me.

"Good, don't worry. Lily will turn up soon, and we can put all this unpleasantness behind us," I told him.

He smiled and nodded in agreement. I went back to my cooking, and soon, the kids and my husband were both rushing out to their destinations.

The rest of the morning started out normally. I cleaned the house and decided to run some errands. I stopped by our local store and bumped into Betsy. She was the mother of one of James's closest friends and was certainly not my favorite person to bump into. All she did was gossip, and it was exhausting—especially because I knew she gossiped about me, too.

I had definitive proof of it because she was stupid enough to butt-dial me while gossiping about me with one of her friends. Apparently, the liberal way in which John and I were raising our children was "concerning" and a bad influence on the kids. In my opinion, the only thing that was concerning was her damaged, bleached blonde hair, crying for moisture.

"Did you hear about Lily?" asked Betsy, trying to look concerned.

It would have been much more believable if the Botox hadn't frozen her face into an expressionless mask.

"I did. It's terrible," I responded, trying to walk away from her.

"It's a shame. They still haven't heard anything," she said, following me to the frozen foods section and running her fingers through her hair. She had long, brightly colored acrylic nails, and her hands were adorned with golden jewelry. Her blue eyes sparkled almost as much as the diamonds on her wrist. She was clearly enjoying the drama.

"Yup, real shame," I said, stuck between her and the freezer.

"I heard the police came to question James... and I wanted to let you know that if he says he had nothing to do with her disappearance, I completely believe him. I mean, he's *probably* telling the truth," she added.

There it was. That's what she had been wanting to tell me. She was hoping to get a reaction out of me—something to chat about with her stupid friends in their stupid yoga pants. How did she even know the police officers had come to our house?

"The police came to our house too," she continued, as though she had read my mind. "Apparently, Lily was supposed to meet Mark after school because he was giving her violin lessons. When she suddenly didn't show up... he was so worried. He came home and called her parents immediately, and they called the cops. And a few hours later, the police were at our doorstep. I just hope she's okay... that poor girl." She placed her hand on her chest, shaking her head.

Mark was Betsy's husband and the music teacher at the local high school. From my encounters with him, I could tell he was a kind and polite person. I felt bad for him that he ended up with Betsy. He always seemed somewhat embarrassed by her.

Their son, Ian, was about the same age as James, and the two boys were pretty much joined at the hip. He was what most people would imagine a high school football player to look like: blondish hair, broad shoulders, and bushy eyebrows. He wasn't the sharpest tool in the shed, but was smart enough to get by. And he was always polite when he came over, which I appreciated. Thankfully, I believe he ended up being much more like his father than his mother.

"Yeah, hope so," I responded, trying to figure a way out of the corner she had literally backed me into.

"I heard James was the last person to see Lily, and they had a big fight," Betsy continued.

How the hell did she know *that*?

"Mark told me he heard them yelling—the woods are quite close to the music room," she explained. "Apparently, Lily broke up with James, and he didn't take it well."

My face must have given away my shock because I could see the smug look of victory on hers. She had finally gotten the reaction she wanted from me. But at this point, I didn't care about Betsy and her mind games anymore.

James had lied to me. To us. To the cops. I couldn't believe it. He never lied to me. And to lie about something this serious. My heart pounded, and it became harder and harder to breathe. It was as if someone were squeezing the air out of my lungs. I needed to get out of here before I had a full-blown panic attack.

"I have to go, Betsy. Nice seeing you," I mumbled as I pushed her and her cart out of my way. I briskly walked to the register and somehow ended up in my car. I took a few deep breaths before turning the key and heading home.

Could Mark have misheard them? Maybe Mark thought Lily was the one breaking up with James, when in reality, it was the other way around. I mean, there was no way. James was an honest boy. He was a good boy. He would never, ever lie about something this serious. Maybe he was embarrassed, and that's why he lied. My brain was going into a frenzy trying to think of reasons why James would suddenly lie to me. I hoped that Mark had misheard them and that James was telling the truth.

As soon as I got home, I made a cup of chamomile tea to calm myself down. The cup shook in my hand as I brought it to my lips. I took a sip and inhaled deeply, trying to get rid of the tightness in my chest. I hadn't experienced any serious anxiety in years. Not even when the kids were little. But this brought back all the bad memories. All the pain. I couldn't stop picking at my skin with my fingernails.

No, don't go there. Focus on your breathing.

Just as I was finally calming down, I heard a knock, and my heart dropped.

I got up and went to the door, peeping out to see who it was. It was the police again. I opened the door and smiled at them, hoping to seem calm and relaxed. The two things I was furthest from right now.

"Lily's body was found in the woods behind the school early this morning. She was strangled."

FOUR

"WHAT?" I GASPED AS MY HAND FLEW TO MY MOUTH.

I couldn't believe what I was hearing. *Oh, God.*

"Lily's body was found—she was strangled," repeated the officer.

"You may remember us. I'm Officer Smith, and this is my partner, Officer Jones. Both your son and a number of witnesses confirmed that Lily was last seen with James. Is your son home? We have some more questions for him in light of the recent findings," Officer Smith explained.

I wanted to respond, but I couldn't. It was like my mind and body were two separate beings, and I was floating in the air, watching all this unfold. I couldn't believe that Lily was dead. That she had been murdered. The poor girl. James would be devastated when he found out.

That was the first thing I thought about. How James would react, what this news would do to him. But slowly, it began dawning on me that James's reaction was the least of my worries. He was the last person seen with Lily, and, even worse, they had been seen arguing. So many emotions flooded me all at once, but at the same time, I was numb.

"Ma'am, are you okay?" asked Officer Smith.

I nodded and motioned for them to come inside, hoping to buy myself some time to calm down. They walked into the living room, and I followed them. I sat down on the couch, trying to process all the information.

"I'm sorry, I can't believe this is happening. She's... dead?" I whispered.

"Yes, I'm afraid so," Officer Smith said gently.

"We understand if you need a moment to process this information," chimed in Officer Jones. "But if we could talk to your son for a few minutes..."

"Oh, I'm sorry, no. My son is at football practice. They have a game coming up, and my son is a major part of the team. I mean, I don't know much about sports, but that's what everyone says," I rambled.

In my head, I knew I should stop talking. And I wanted to. But my brain and body were still refusing to cooperate.

"I see. Well, we'll come back later then. What time will your son be home?" asked Officer Smith.

"He should be back after six," I answered.

"Okay, please ask him to stay home, and we'll be back after six," said Officer Smith, getting up.

"Wait, does he know? About Lily?" I asked.

"Probably not; her body was found at around 4 a.m. and moved soon after," Officer Jones answered.

"Oh... Okay," I didn't know whether to be slightly relieved or horrified. I knew that it would probably be better if it came from me rather than the police, but I hated the idea of causing James so much pain over a situation none of us had any control over.

"So, did you know Lily well?" asked Officer Smith, suddenly turning his attention toward me.

"Ummm, not really. They had moved here pretty recently,

and I only talked to her a couple of times," I stammered, surprised by their line of questioning.

"I see." Officer Smith's sharp eyes continued to focus on me for the next few seconds.

I wanted to look away, but was afraid it would make me seem guilty, so I continued to stare back. I knew I didn't have anything to be guilty about—I hadn't done anything—but his watchful eyes made me want to squirm.

"Anyway, we'll see ourselves out," Officer Jones interrupted.

I nodded, and soon they were gone.

I sat on the couch, not knowing what to do next or how to react. I sat there till I heard Sophia and JJ at the front door.

For years, I hadn't worried about the cops or about anything much at all. I had put all the worries behind me. I thought I finally had my happy ending. I was living in blissful ignorance, the boring, stagnant life of a housewife and stay-at-home mom. And I loved it. Every minute of it.

This was bringing back the memories I had hidden so well all these years. Memories of the police at my door, of being terrified and anxious every waking moment. Not knowing what was going to happen next. Before I met John, my life was never stagnant or predictable. Each day had been a battle. And I refused to go back to that.

Things will sort themselves out, I told myself.

Deep down, I knew this was not one of those problems that went away on its own. But if I accepted that right now, I was going to have a nervous breakdown, and I did not have the energy to deal with that. So, I kept lying to myself. Saying it was going to be okay. I got up and walked to the door to let Sophia and JJ in, a fake smile plastered on my face.

"Hi, Mom!" they yelled and ran inside, laughing. They headed to their rooms to drop off their school bags, then ran straight to the backyard to play. They were probably going to be there till dinner, which was something I was grateful for today.

I went to the kitchen and opened the refrigerator; I should probably start making dinner. I would wait for John to come back and talk to him before I talked to James. John was my rock and would help me calm down. I only had to get through the next thirty minutes. I prayed James didn't hear about Lily before he got home.

I mindlessly chopped the vegetables in front of me, heating some oil in the pan. I was completely zoned out until the smell of garlic burning hit my nose. *Shit*. I turned off the stove and tried to salvage what was left of the garlic. As I was doing that, I finally heard John's car pull up and rushed to the front door.

"We need to talk. Follow me to our bedroom," I told him as soon as he walked in.

He looked bewildered but followed me without protest.

"The cops came back, and they found Lily," I explained, nervously tucking my hair behind my ears.

"Oh, thank God," he said, relieved.

"No, that's not... I phrased that badly. I mean, they found Lily's body. She was strangled," I clarified.

"What?" asked John, horrified.

"They found her body behind the school in the woods, John. That's where she and James were seen fighting. The last time she was seen alive," I sobbed, finally letting out all the emotions I had tried to control all this time.

"Oh God," gasped John.

"I know—it's all so awful," I cried.

"You don't think he...?" asked John, very quietly.

"Of course not! We know James. He would *never* hurt a soul."

"You're right; you're absolutely right. There must be some other explanation for all this," said John, taking me in his arms and hugging me tightly.

I nodded in agreement. But Betsy's words echoed in my head. James may have lied to us. And if he had lied to us, what else could he be capable of? I thought about the fight James and I had, how he had defended Lily. I could tell he loved her deeply. There was no way he could have hurt her.

I shook my head, trying to get rid of the bad thoughts. A part of me wanted to ask John if we should get a lawyer involved. But I feared that would make James look guilty or make him think we didn't support him. And most of all, it would make this whole nightmare real. Too real.

"It's going to be okay, my love. It's all going to be okay," John whispered in my ear while stroking my hair. I couldn't tell if he was trying to convince me or himself.

FIVE

"JAMES, HONEY, CAN YOU COME INTO THE KITCHEN FOR A moment?" I called as soon as I heard James come in through the front door.

My heart beat faster as he walked into the kitchen. He smiled as soon as he spotted me and asked what I wanted to talk about. Thankfully, it seemed like he hadn't heard about Lily's body being found yet.

"James, the police stopped by this afternoon," I began.

I didn't quite know how I was going to break this to him. John and I had decided to be honest with him, but I hadn't told John about what Betsy told me at the store. And I didn't know if I should bring it up with James right now.

On the one hand, if it had been a misunderstanding on Mark's part, telling James would bring out the truth, and we could lay everything to rest. But on the other hand, I had this underlying fear that James would admit something to me. Something I did not want to hear.

"What did they want? Did they find Lily? Is she back?"

"The cops... They found Lily's body in the woods. She was strangled," I stammered.

James's face twisted in horror, and a few seconds later, he was kneeling on the floor, sobbing with his head in his hands.

His whole body was shaking as he sat there, wailing in pain. He sounded like an animal about to be slaughtered.

I quickly put my arms around him, holding him for at least ten minutes. I wish John were here right now—he would know what to say. But I needed him to keep the younger kids occupied. I didn't want them to see their big brother in this way. I didn't want them to see any of us in this way.

"How did this happen, Mom? Do they know who did it?" asked James between sobs. How was I supposed to tell him that he was probably their primary suspect right now? I couldn't do that to my baby.

"They don't know yet. They came over to ask you a few questions, and they'll be back soon since you were at football practice," I explained.

He sniffled and continued to kneel on the floor.

"Did you see anything or anyone suspicious in the woods when you were talking to her?" I asked, hoping... praying.

"No, it was just the two of us. Almost all the other kids had gone home," James answered hesitantly.

"Hmmm," I responded, not knowing what else to say.

He appeared confused at first, and then suddenly his entire demeanor changed. His eyes darkened, and his nostrils flared.

"Wait... Do they think *I* did it?" James asked angrily.

"Of course, no one thinks that. It's probably part of their procedure because you were the last one to see her," I explained.

"I would *never* hurt her! EVER! I loved her. I loved her more than anyone in the world! And she loved me!" James exclaimed with a pained expression on his face.

"So why did she break up with you?" I asked quietly.

James raised his eyebrows, his eyes widening. I was equally

as surprised that I had blurted it out. Usually, I was not a confrontational person. It just sort of slipped out before I could stop myself.

"I can't do this right now. I'm going to my room," said James quietly.

He slowly got up and walked away from me as I remained on the floor, still on my knees. I guess I had hoped he would answer me. That he would tell me the truth.

I was still staring at the ground mindlessly, lost in my own thoughts, when John walked into the kitchen. He rushed over to me, asking me if I was okay. All I could do was nod, assuring him that I was fine. He helped me stand up and wiped away the tears.

"What happened, Sal? Did you tell James?" he inquired.

"I did—he didn't take it well. He's in his room trying to process everything," I told him.

"Should I go talk to him?" John asked, concerned.

"I think he needs his space right now. I'm going to finish making dinner. Try to keep Soph and JJ occupied," I instructed.

"Are you sure? Do you want to order takeout or something instead?" John asked.

"I'm fine, John," I assured him.

"Sal, I know this must be hard for you… I mean, after everything that happened with—" John started, but I quickly interrupted him.

"Don't. Don't say his name. I don't want to talk, or even think, about him. Let's keep the past in the past and focus on dealing with this for now," I told him coldly before turning around.

I ignored his presence, even though I knew he was still

standing there, hoping I would change my mind and talk to him. Eventually, I heard him sigh and exit the kitchen.

John didn't grow up the way I did or experience what I had. He didn't grow up around dysfunction and chaos. He had a great childhood and was unconditionally loved by his parents. He still talks about them often and tells me how he wishes they could have met their grandkids. Unfortunately, his parents died in a car crash about a year before he and I met. He was still mourning their loss, and I was mourning some losses of my own. In a way, it helped bring us closer together.

But the one thing I hated was that he always wanted to *talk* about things. Our childhoods, teen years, relatives, and friends. When I told him I didn't have any relatives or friends anymore, he wouldn't let it go. I finally opened up to him about a few things, but it was never enough. He always wanted to talk about *everything*. I think he thought it would help me move past them.

But the thing that people like him don't understand is that there are some things you don't move past. Some things that stay with you forever, as though sewn onto the fiber of your very being. They haunt you for the rest of your life, no matter how much you try to run away from them. They leave your heart scarred, and there's no point in picking at those scars and reopening old wounds.

Just as I put the stew to boil, I heard a curt knock at the door. I had heard that knock enough times now to know that it was the police officers again. My heart sank, knowing what was to come next. I lowered the heat on the stove, wiped my hands, and headed to the door, but John beat me there. He opened the door for them, and I went upstairs to call James.

I knocked on his door and entered.

He was lying on his bed, staring at the ceiling. His mouth

was downturned, and his usually bright eyes were now dull and lifeless. All I wanted to do was hug him, hold him. I wanted to comfort my baby, but I knew he needed his space right now.

"James, the police are here to talk to you," I said.

"Do they still think I did it?" he asked sarcastically, continuing to stare blankly at the ceiling.

"It doesn't matter what they think because you didn't do it. You said you loved Lily and didn't hurt her, and I believe you. Your father and I are always on your side," I promised.

"Thanks, Mom," he sighed as he got up from his bed.

We headed downstairs together, and I heard John talking to the cops.

"They're still examining the body, but we'll get back to you when we have more information," said Officer Smith, whose voice I now recognized clearly. Everyone turned to stare at James as soon as we entered the living room. He silently sat down next to John, who patted his shoulder supportively. I sat down on John's other side and felt his other hand squeeze mine.

"Hello, James. Your father mentioned that your parents had already spoken to you about Lily. We're very sorry for your loss. I know it's a lot to process, but we were wondering if we could ask you a few more questions. We want to figure out what happened to Lily, and it would help if you were completely honest with us," Officer Smith said gently.

I appreciated him being gentle with James, even if it was probably only a facade.

"Okay," agreed James.

SIX

"WHEN YOU LAST SPOKE TO LILY, YOU MENTIONED THE TWO OF you had an argument?" asked Officer Smith.

He was staring intently at his notebook—I assumed he had a list of questions ready. Officer Jones was sitting silently beside him, intently watching James. Probably waiting for him to make a mistake or catch him telling a lie.

"Yes," replied James.

"And that argument took place in the woods behind your high school?"

"Yes."

"What were you two arguing about?"

"We… we were arguing about our relationship."

A vague answer, almost as though he was avoiding the truth. James stared at the floor intently, as though he was suddenly seeing it for the first time.

"What was the last thing you said to Lily?"

"That I hoped I never saw her again."

"And then you left?"

"Yes."

"Was there anyone else in the woods or nearby?"

"No, sir. Most of the kids had already gone home. I had stayed back for football practice, and she had stayed back for her violin lesson."

James cleared his throat and pushed his hair back, something he only did when he was nervous. Or lying.

"Did you know that she never showed up for her violin lesson?"

"No, she was always excited about her violin lessons. I tried to support her as much as I could, even though it took up a lot of her time. I loved her, and I knew playing the violin made her happy."

"I'm sorry you've lost someone you loved at such a young age. It can't be easy."

"Thank you."

It's never easy, no matter what age you are. This was not the first loss James had ever experienced. I was just eternally grateful he didn't remember the first one. I was terrified he would, especially when he was younger. But kids are resilient. They hide trauma, even from themselves. They do what they must in order to survive.

"So, you didn't show up for football practice. Why was that?"

"I needed to clear my head."

"Can you think of anyone who may have wanted to harm Lily?" asked Officer Smith, frowning slightly.

"No, I honestly can't. She was wonderful. She made everyone more comfortable. It's like you could talk to her forever. I can't imagine anyone wanting to hurt her."

"Are you sure you can't think of anyone who may have wanted to harm her? Perhaps a jealous ex or friend?"

"I was her first and only boyfriend as far as I know. And she didn't have any close friends except Patricia."

"You told us last time that you two were fighting because you wanted to break up with her, and she did not take it well?"

"Yes."

Was it my imagination, or did I see his face twitch ever so slightly?

"Well, we talked to Mr. Live, the music teacher, and he said that he heard the two of you arguing from the music room, and that you seemed to be the one upset because she wanted to break up with you. Is that true?"

"Maybe he misheard?"

James wiped away the sweat forming on his forehead with his sleeve.

"Are you saying that she did not break up with you?" Officer Smith squinted his eyes and leaned forward, his body tense.

"I … it was complicated, but I wouldn't say she broke up with me," James tried to explain, barely getting the sentence out.

"Son, we need you to be honest. Just tell us what happened," Officer Jones chimed in.

"I *am* being honest. We broke up, and that's all that happened. Are we done now?" asked James, clearly agitated.

The two officers glanced at one another and then at James.

"That's all for now. We'll be in touch," said Officer Smith, getting up from the couch.

James got up too, and in a few seconds, we heard the slam of his bedroom door. I was sure Soph and JJ must have heard it too and would have a number of questions. Thankfully, they were still in their rooms doing their homework, but they would be out soon enough. I needed to get rid of the cops before that.

I hurried toward the front door, hoping they would follow me, which, thankfully, they did. We quickly said our goodbyes, and I shut the door. I could already hear the two younger kids running down the stairs.

"I'll take care of this. I'll talk to them. Just finish making dinner," John told me, squeezing my hand. I smiled at him gratefully, giving him a peck on the cheek as I headed to the kitchen.

I stared blankly at the stew, which was still slowly boiling. The smell of the seasonings hit my nose, and suddenly, I was nauseous. I put my hand over my mouth and tried not to heave. I moved away from the food and quickly walked toward the sink. Turning on the tap, I filled my hands with the cool water, splashing it on my face. I stood by the sink for a minute or two as I waited for the nausea to pass.

For the rest of the night, I could not stop thinking about James and how he had avoided the question about the breakup. Why was he still lying about it or avoiding it? Did he not understand how serious this was? And worst of all, I knew exactly the person his lying reminded me of. The person I hadn't thought about since I met John.

"Are you okay? Do you want to talk?" asked John quietly.

He was rubbing my shoulders gently and kissed the top of my head. I knew he was trying to calm me down and put on a brave face, but his expression told me that he was as worried as I was.

"I'm fine, I promise," I assured him.

"Are you sure? Because you haven't turned a page in your book in almost five minutes," he observed.

He was right; I had been staring blankly at the book in front of me. I didn't even know which book it was. Usually, I cherished the few minutes I got to read before bed, but tonight I took the book more out of habit than anything else.

"I know," I sighed, turning to face him.

"It's James. I'm worried about him," I confided in John.

"Me too. I wonder what the officer meant about the breakup and Mark hearing them arguing. Do you think Lily really broke up with James and not the other way around?" asked John.

"About that, I ran into Betsy the other day, and she also mentioned that Mark heard Lily break up with James," I said, frowning.

"What? Why didn't you tell me that before?" John's face fell in betrayal.

"At the time, I assumed she was trying to get a rise out of me, but now I'm thinking maybe it's true. But why would James lie about something like that?" I wondered out loud.

"That's the thing—it's such a weird thing for James to lie about," John agreed, nodding.

"I don't know anymore, John. This whole situation, it's all so weird… and familiar," I admitted. "Do you think we need to start looking for a lawyer?"

I had been thinking about this more and more. Earlier, I had managed to convince myself that this would blow over soon, that they would find the real culprit, and James would finally have time to heal in peace. But after what happened with the police this evening, I wasn't so sure anymore.

"No, I trust James, and I think the police are probably going to realize he's innocent soon enough," John assured me. "And anyway, getting a lawyer right now might make him look even more guilty."

"You're right. I'm just terrified for him," I whispered, staring at my hands.

"I know, hon. But don't worry. James is a good boy. He's *our* son, and we raised him well. He'll tell us the truth when he's ready," John assured me, holding my trembling hands in his.

Hearing John say that was somewhat comforting. And he was right—James was a good kid. He would talk to us when he was ready to explain everything. I was probably overreacting and jumping to conclusions. I had to continue to trust him.

SEVEN

"STOP IT! YOU'RE HURTING ME—LET GO OF ME!"

I woke up in a panic, gasping for air and my entire body sticky with sweat. I blinked rapidly, shaking my head. My fingers were numb, and I tried to move them to get the blood flowing again.

It was just a dream. Just a nightmare. It wasn't real. I was fine. Everything was fine. *I was safe*, I reminded myself. I slowly turned and got out of bed, trying not to wake John, and went to the kitchen. I was surprised to find James already there, getting a drink from the refrigerator.

"Hey," I said softly.

"Hey, Mom," he replied.

We both stood there silently for a few seconds. He looked sad, the bags under his eyes darker than I had ever seen them. His hair was a mess, and there was a slight five o'clock shadow on his usually clean-shaven face. He finally spoke.

"Mom, I need to tell you something," he said quietly.

"Of course. You can tell me anything, honey," I told him.

"Mr. Live was right. Lily did break up with me, and I got really angry about it. I guess it was so unexpected, and she refused to tell me why she wanted to break up. And the last thing I told her was that I never wanted to see her again." James's voice cracked.

"Oh, sweetie," I said, putting my arms around him. "I know you didn't mean it, and I'm sure she knew too."

"I thought everything was fine, but a while ago, she started acting distant and weird. She was busy all the time, and she was on her phone all day. But I kept thinking it was going to be fine eventually. Then she broke up with me all of a sudden, and I couldn't handle it," he sobbed.

I held him tighter, wishing I could take his pain away. It hurt so much to see your child in pain and not be able to do anything about it. As a parent, you want to protect them from everything, every tiny little thing that could hurt them. And not being able to do that is the worst feeling in the world. We stood there for a bit, our arms around one another.

"You know what you have to do, right? You need to be honest with the police. I know admitting you were angry enough to yell at her makes you look bad, but lying to them will make you look worse," I told him.

"I know. I'll stop by the station after school and let them know the truth," James agreed, wiping his tears with the back of his hand.

I knew it. I knew he would never hurt anyone. We raised him well, and this was all going to work out. They would figure out who *actually* killed Lily, and James would grieve but eventually go back to his normal life.

The rest of the day passed by quickly, and I eagerly waited for James to come back from the station. I was still proud of him for opening up and volunteering to tell the cops the truth. Something inside me had shifted. I felt lighter; things were going to get better.

James finally came back, and I went to the door to greet him while John kept our other kids occupied in the backyard. I was expecting him to be relieved, considering he would no longer have to keep lying, but he looked utterly devastated when he walked in. He wasn't even this devastated when I told him about Lily. His eyes were puffy and red, and his face was flushed. I could tell he had been crying.

"What's wrong?" I asked immediately.

"It's Lily. They finished the full autopsy, and she … she was pregnant," he sobbed so loudly that I could barely make out the end of the sentence.

I had felt the word heartbreak a million times in my life, and I thought the worst moments of my life were behind me. I genuinely thought I would never experience this kind of pain again. But for the first time in a long time, I actually felt my heart break. Nothing seemed to make sense in my brain anymore.

I was bombarded with a million emotions all at once. I didn't even know that James and Lily had been sexually active. And to find out like this was crushing. No wonder James was devastated—he hadn't just lost his girlfriend. He had lost what would have been his first child.

And poor Lily. I couldn't imagine what it must have been like for her if she had known about the pregnancy. To have someone take away your life and that of your unborn child. Her last moments must have been hell. No one deserved that.

From the corner of my eye, I saw James walk past me to the staircase, and I heard him walk up the stairs to his room and shut the door behind him. But I couldn't stop him. I couldn't speak or even move. I just stood there. What could I have possibly said that would make him feel better anyway? Nothing takes away the pain of losing a child.

John must have sensed something was wrong because

eventually I felt his hand on my shoulder. He asked me if everything was alright. I wanted to respond and tell him everything, but all I could do was cry in his arms, slowly sinking to the floor. We sat there on the floor, my face buried in his chest until the tears subsided and I could finally speak.

"They told him at the station that Lily had been pregnant when she died," I finally revealed as my tears subsided.

His face paled. I watched his calm exterior slowly crumble. He looked like he was in pain, as if I had punched him in the stomach. He looked exactly like I felt.

"How? How did … I didn't even know they were …" he trailed off, his brain trying to make sense of it all as mine had been doing moments earlier.

"Did you know? That they were having sex?" he finally asked.

I shook my head.

"I can't believe this. I just can't believe this. Oh God, Lily. That poor girl." He shook his head in pity.

"And poor James. I can't imagine how he must feel. We should go talk to him," he continued, getting up and helping me get up too.

"You're right. We need to talk about this with him. You should have seen his face when he walked in, John. He was broken," I told him.

EIGHT

John lifted his right arm and knocked on James's door. There was no response, but we entered anyway. James was once more lying in his bed, this time with his back turned toward us. He hadn't even bothered to take off his shoes. He was just lying there, unmoving.

"James, your mother and I wanted to talk to you about all this," John started.

"We're so sorry that you're going through this. You don't deserve it. Lily didn't deserve it. This whole situation is awful," I continued.

"You were good kids. This should never have happened," John said.

"Good kids? You think I'm a good kid?" asked James slowly, his back still turned to us. "I told the girl I loved that I hated her and never wanted to see her again moments before both she *and* my baby were murdered."

"You can't blame yourself, James," I tried to comfort him.

"Who the fuck else am I supposed to blame, then? If I hadn't fought with her, or if I hadn't come home like an idiot, they would still be alive right now! I am so sick and tired of you two pretending like I'm the victim here. I'm not the victim. Lily was the victim, and my baby was the victim!" James erupted.

I instinctively took a step back. Hearing James yell made my stomach turn. I swallowed the bile threatening to rise.

"And you know what else?" James continued, fully facing us now. "I'm fucking sick and tired of playing happy family with you people. You always act like we're so great and we're so perfect, but guess what? I'M NOT! And neither are any of you!"

He was shaking with anger, and his face was contorted into a deep scowl.

"Do you think I couldn't tell that you were just pretending to be nice to Lily, Mom? Acting like she was beneath us. As though you didn't come from fucking trash! You're no better than her, and you *never* will be," spat James, glaring at me.

I couldn't believe what I was hearing. I had never seen James this angry. He never got upset, especially with me. We had a natural bond. This shook me to my core. And hearing him yell at me brought back too many bad memories.

I couldn't stand shouting or even loud noises. As soon as I heard someone getting aggressive, I shut down. It's a trauma response that never went away, even after all these years. Hearing someone yell immediately took me back to the place I barely escaped.

I stared at James for a few seconds and left the room. I didn't want him to see me break. He had already dealt with enough today. I hurried into our bedroom and shut the door behind me. I sat at the foot of the bed and began sobbing.

When James yelled like that, I couldn't see him as my baby anymore. Suddenly, he was the monster that hurt me beyond repair. The person I tried to never think about. And I knew I was projecting my past trauma onto him, but I couldn't help it. I knew he wasn't a monster. He was a good person going through an awful situation. But his voice, his tone, the anger in his eyes—it scared me.

Was he right about me? Had I pushed him to be perfect till he couldn't express his negative emotions around me anymore? Is that what I was doing to my family? Forcing them to be perfect?

I never wanted them to feel that way, like they had to be perfect for me to love them. I wanted them to be the best version of themselves; that was all. Especially James. I had tried so hard to make sure he turned out to be the best he could be. Not a mess like I was when I was his age. I wanted him to be good so badly. Because deep down, I was afraid that he wasn't. I was afraid that being a monster was in his DNA, and I was to blame for that.

I continued to sit on the bed with my face in my hands, only lifting it when I heard a soft knock on the door. John quietly walked in, and James trailed behind him. His now remorseful gray eyes were fixed on me.

"Mom, I'm sorry I snapped at you. I don't know why I said any of those things. I shouldn't have. You're an amazing mother, and I have no right to take everything out on you. I just... I can't control myself when I get angry," explained James.

This apology, this situation—it was all too familiar. Maybe because I had heard those exact words so many times before. My past was trying to take over my mind again. I closed my eyes for a few seconds, trying to push everything back down.

"It's okay, James. I know you're upset, sweetie. Come here," I said, holding out my arms.

He briskly walked over to me and hugged me tightly. I took a deep breath, trying to relax. *This* was my James. I was overreacting. I was letting my past get the best of me. I was right the first time—he was a good kid, and he would never purposely hurt anyone, ever.

"It hurts so much," admitted James, sniffling.

I continued to hold him tightly, trying to soothe him.

NINE

THE NEXT FEW DAYS WENT BY QUICKLY. WE DIDN'T HEAR anything more from the police for a while, much to everyone's relief. Maybe they had found other suspects to focus on and were getting enough evidence against them to be able to arrest them soon. I hoped that was the case. I couldn't wait for this ordeal to be over.

The one thing I was most afraid of about this mess was that it would permanently scar James. I could tell that it had already changed him as a person. He used to be funny and playful and energetic. Now he was sullen and quiet. He spent all his time in his bedroom, barely speaking a word to any of us. It was like a part of him died when Lily did.

The only positive thing was that he continued to play with his younger siblings during his free time and even smiled sometimes when he was with them, which I took as a good sign. The majority of his time was spent with friends and at football practice, the way it was before all this happened. I hoped that eventually he would move on and live his normal life again.

Personally, I was doing better now. John suggested I speak to a therapist because of all the stuff from my past this was bringing up. But I wasn't a fan of shrinks. The kind of trauma I had wasn't the kind that shrinks away. It was the kind that follows you around, even when you think everything is perfect.

Just as we were all beginning to breathe easy again, the police came knocking at our door. They confirmed that James was, in fact, the father of Lily's child. They had taken his DNA sample at the station the day he had stopped by. Unlike the last few times they were here, the questions were much more direct, and their friendly disposition had quickly been replaced by icy stares. It very much felt like they were trying to get James to confess.

"Your fight with Lily wasn't the first angry outburst you've had at school, was it?"

I was completely taken aback by their question. What did they mean by that? James had always been incredibly calm. He rarely fought with his siblings, and even when he did, they made up quickly because he generally apologized first. We never had any complaints from any of his teachers or his principal. If anything, his teachers always spoke positively about his behavior and grades.

"I don't know what you mean," muttered James, crossing his arms.

"Well, we have reason to believe that you and Lily had quite a few heated arguments recently. And you had also been in an altercation with a classmate named Brian," accused Officer Smith, tapping his pen on his notebook.

James's face turned white almost instantly. He shook his head a little but didn't answer. I wanted to interrupt and ask him what the hell they were on about and how John and I didn't know anything about it, but I kept my mouth shut. I didn't want to make this situation worse than it already was.

I glanced at John, expecting to see the same surprise on his face as mine. But instead, he had an emotionless expression plastered on his face. Almost as if he was purposely trying not to give anything away.

"It's true that Lily and I got into a couple of arguments recently. But that was all they were, stupid arguments. All couples fight. We had our problems. Everyone does," James admitted eventually.

"And what about Brian? Didn't one of your arguments leave him with a bloody nose?" asked Officer Johnson. "And I believe the argument had to do with Lily."

"Yes, but—that—it's not what it sounds like!" cried James, his eyes frantically darting toward John.

"It *sounds* like you have a history of violent behavior, and your family has been covering it up for you, so it kept getting worse. And now we have a dead body on our hands," Officer Jones fired back.

"No, I'm not a violent person—I just get angry sometimes. Having a bad temper isn't a crime. But I wouldn't hurt anyone. Especially not Lily! I loved her!" James defended himself.

I couldn't believe what I was hearing. James had a history of violent behavior? How was that even possible? This was literally the first time I was even hearing about any of this. None of it made any sense. My head was spinning.

I looked at James. He was seated rigidly, and his lips were pressed together into a tight line. I had tried so hard to make myself believe that James was not an angry or violent person. That he was not like the monster I had spent so much of my life trying to get away from. That not all men were monsters. But it was getting harder to believe it.

"You claim you would never hurt her, or anyone, yet we have multiple witnesses who saw you physically assault Brian and yell at both him and Lily. If you loved her, as you claim you did, why would you behave like that?" Officer Smith continued.

"It's because I was jealous, okay?" yelled James. "I was jealous because I thought Lily was cheating on me with Brian," he repeated more softly, burying his head in his hands.

"What made you think that? Tell us everything," urged Officer Smith, more gently.

"When Lily and I first started dating, everything was great. But recently, she wasn't herself. It was as though she had one foot out the door when it came to our relationship. And she was always on her phone talking to Brian," James explained.

Officer Smith jotted something down in his notebook and nodded, urging James to continue.

"It was always Brian this, Brian that, and I started to feel like a third wheel in my own fucking relationship," confessed James.

"So, I confronted him. But he kept denying everything, telling me he had no interest in Lily. And something inside me snapped. All the frustration I had been holding in came out. I know I shouldn't have hit him. I know it wasn't the right way to deal with the situation, but you don't know what it was like for me."

James's voice cracked. His eyes were desperately fixed on the officers, hoping they believed him—hoping they understood his frustrations.

"And this was a couple of weeks ago?" asked Officer Smith.

"Yeah," whispered James, his head still in his hands.

"And that's what you and Lily had been arguing about that day, too? You felt that she may have been seeing someone else behind your back?"

"Yeah."

"You said you snapped and felt out of control when confronting Brian. Is it possible that the same thing happened when Lily broke up with you?"

"No. I mean, yeah, I did get angry, but I didn't hurt her. I swear I didn't lay a finger on her," James promised, sounding defeated.

The two officers looked at one another and left shortly after. However, before leaving, they asked James to go down to the station to talk to them, as they would have more questions for him. He promised to go the next day, which was a Saturday. I sat on the couch while John walked the officers to the door and let them out. I was too stunned by James's revelations to do anything. I didn't know what to say or how to start the conversation.

This wasn't my James. It was like there was a stranger sitting beside me. Somehow, he had stopped being my little boy and turned into someone else. Someone I didn't recognize. And he had hidden all this from me. Never once confiding in me. I thought he trusted me. I thought he told me everything. And if he hid all this from me, what else was he hiding?

I was also baffled by John's reaction to all this—or rather, his lack of a reaction. He had sat there the entire time, staring blankly ahead, completely avoiding me.

"What the fuck is happening?" I finally whispered as John entered the living room.

Both he and James seemed shocked by my language. I didn't swear much, and never around the kids. But I couldn't help it tonight; I felt like I was about to lose my mind. James and John both looked at one another and then at me.

"Sal, I think we need to talk," John told me.

Yeah, no fucking shit.

TEN

"So, you lied to me this entire time? For all these years?" I glared at John in disbelief.

Hearing him admit it felt like he had put a knife through my heart and twisted as hard as he could. I was an idiot, a fucking moron. How had I been so blind? How had I not noticed that my own son and husband were lying to me? That James was struggling.

"How could you do that to me, John?" I questioned further when he didn't respond.

"It's not Dad's fault. He was trying to protect us both. He knew it would hurt you if you knew the truth. That's why we tried to keep everything from you," James interjected.

"I can't even look at you right now. Go to your room, James," I instructed harshly.

"Go to your room, James. Your mother and I need to talk," John told him more gently.

James appeared as if he were going to argue, but eventually sighed, got up, and left without a word.

Apparently, everything in my life was a lie. Everything in my perfect little life was as imperfect as it had always been. John had simply gone out of his way to keep me in this little bubble, so I never knew the truth.

How could someone do that to their own spouse? He was

supposed to be the one person I could always rely on to be honest with me. We were supposed to be a team. And now I find out that he and James had been lying to me all this time. They had even gone out of their way to make sure I never found out the truth.

John finally told me the truth as we sat on the couch. Apparently, James had been having angry outbursts for a couple of years now. And they had gotten worse after he and Lily started having relationship problems. Eventually, it turned into a physical fight with Brian.

John had been called to the school and was able to smooth everything over without me ever finding out. He had asked the principal not to say anything to me because I was "emotionally vulnerable" due to past trauma. John's words, obviously, not mine. James was physically assaulting some kid, and I was the "emotionally vulnerable" one?

This was crazy. It was like I had suddenly woken up in a different life where everyone looked the same but were completely different people. Was I in an episode of *The Twilight Zone*? James wasn't the sweet and innocent young man I had raised. John was not the honest and loving partner I thought he was. What else had they kept from me? At this point, nothing made sense anymore. Everything was upside down.

"Sally, please calm down. This isn't James's fault," explained John. "I asked him to keep this from you because I knew this is how you would react."

"Don't you dare," I whispered, my voice dripping with outrage. "Don't you dare make me the bad guy here. How the fuck else am I supposed to react to finding out that both my husband *and* son have been lying to me, *for years*, about something this important?"

"We only lied to you to protect you. I know you think you're strong, Sally, but I've seen you at your worst. And I could not bear to see you in pain again." John tried to hold my hand, but I quickly pulled it away.

"It's all about *you*, isn't it? *You* couldn't bear to see me in pain again? But what about me? What about how I feel? What about the fact that I would have wanted to know about something this serious even if it was painful for me?" I retorted, angry tears threatening to fall from the corners of my eyes.

John sighed, his shoulders slumping.

"You're right. I was being selfish. I should have been honest with you. But, Sal, you've done so much for this family. I wanted to let you keep believing it was perfect," John said, reaching for my hand again.

"I'm not crazy, John. I know we're not perfect. Why does everyone think that I need them to be perfect? I don't *need* perfect, John. I need the truth. I need to know what's going on with my son. I need to know if…" I couldn't finish the sentence. Even in anger, I could not say out loud what I was thinking.

"Say it, Sal. Just say it."

"I need to know if my son is capable of murder. I need to know if he hurt Lily," I confessed.

"He's going through a rough patch, Sal. That's all. No matter what he's been through, no matter what issues he has, I really think deep down he's not a bad kid. He wouldn't have hurt someone he loved," John said gently.

"That's what everyone thinks, John. No one thinks they're capable of murder until it happens. And you know our past, John. It's filled with violence. It's in his DNA!" I cried, tears streaming down my cheeks.

"No, it's not. He's *our* son, and we raised him well," John assured me.

"I don't know if I believe that anymore," I mumbled.

John sighed and held me tightly in his arms. We sat there in silence till we were interrupted by John's phone ringing.

"It's Paul," John told me as he stared at his screen.

Paul Johnson was Lily's stepfather. I hadn't ever spoken much to either of Lily's parents. I did not know them well, and to be honest, they never struck me as people I wanted to get to know well. They were not bad people from what I saw, but they were very traditional and had strong opinions that I mostly disagreed with. So, naturally, I avoided them as much as I could. I had spoken to them maybe twice the entire time James and Lily were together.

However, I had reached out to Lily's mother when we first heard that Lily was missing. I had promised her that I would let her know if Lily contacted us or if we heard anything about her whereabouts. I called her again when I found out about Lily's death, but she was barely coherent. She was weeping violently for a few minutes, repeating Lily's name again and again till Paul took the phone from her.

It was understandable that she was so distraught. She had lost her only child. I would be inconsolable too, had I been in her place.

Paul sounded sad as well, but spoke to me anyway. I told him that we were all sorry about what happened, and if there was anything we could do to please let us know. We spoke about Lily for a few minutes, what a great young girl she had been, how much potential she had. He promised to contact us again if they found out any more information about what happened to her. That was the last time we had spoken.

John came back to the living room, phone still in his hand.

"Paul wanted to invite us to Lily's funeral," he said.

"Oh, right. Of course," I responded.

The funeral—of course, there was going to be a funeral. I had been so preoccupied with James that I hadn't even thought about Lily's funeral. I instantly felt a pang of guilt. When did I become such a self-absorbed person? Someone had been murdered, and all I could think about was myself and my family.

ELEVEN

"Are you cheating on me?" he yelled.

I was curled up on the floor in the corner of the room, covering my ears with my hands and crying. My entire body was shaking violently. My hair was covered in sweat, and my hands were full of angry purple bruises.

"Of course not. I love you. I swear I would never do that," I promised him, still sobbing.

"I don't believe you. You're a lying fucking bitch and always have been. Fucking slut," he spat the words at me.

I sat there on the floor crying, not knowing what to do. I hated when he was this way.

"Shut the fuck up with the crying. You know that guilt-tripping shit don't work on me," he said, grabbing my arm and forcing me to stand up. "I'm asking you one last time—are you fucking him?"

I shook my head, sobbing.

And then I heard it, a slapping sound and a burning sensation on my cheek. It took a few seconds for my brain to register what had happened, even though I was used to it by now. I was on the floor again, clutching my cheek.

"Please... please, I'm pregnant... please, don't hurt the baby," I pleaded.

I woke, gasping, fingers grabbing at the bed covers. It took me a few seconds to realize where I was. I lay there, taking deep breaths, trying to calm myself down and slow my heartbeat to a normal pace.

"You okay?" asked John, sleepily turning his head. I must have woken him up.

"Just a nightmare. I'm fine," I assured him.

He turned around and went back to sleep. He was used to this.

The first few years we were together, I had nightmares almost every single night. Eventually, they became less frequent and then went away almost completely. But I still have them once in a while when I'm stressed out or anxious about something.

And today, I had a lot to be stressed out and anxious about. It was Saturday, which meant that James was supposed to go down to the station to talk to the police. I would drive him there, since John had work, but he would be questioned alone. I hated the idea of him being all alone in that little room.

And tomorrow was Lily's funeral. John had talked to James about it since I was still not over his behavior and the fact that he had lied to me. John told me that James confirmed that he would come to the funeral with us. He wanted to say goodbye to Lily one last time.

We left the house at about ten in the morning and reached the station pretty quickly. Before we went into the station, I told James to be honest and promised him I would be waiting right outside if he needed anything. He nodded, his eyes sunken and hollow.

John thought we needed to begin searching for a lawyer now, and I agreed with him. He was frantically trying to find a good one, but it was hard to find someone this quickly. It wasn't like the movies and the books where they appear out of nowhere. There were appointments to be made, if they had the time to see us, that was. And even then, we had to find one that was a good fit for us.

I hated myself for not listening to my gut and hiring a lawyer much earlier on. I shouldn't have let John talk me out of it.

The interrogation lasted about two hours. I sat there fidgeting with my phone, mindlessly scrolling through social media in an attempt to distract myself. I had left Sophia and JJ with Mary, a friend of mine who lived close by. She had a son who was about Sophia's age, and they got along great. I knew they would be fine there.

James emerged from the interrogation room about two hours later. Unlike earlier, he now had a pale and sickly appearance. I wasn't sure what they had asked him, but I knew it could not have gone well.

"Are you okay?" I asked as soon as he got close enough to hear me.

"Let's just go home," he muttered, looking at the floor.

We were silent throughout the car ride, and he briskly walked to his room as soon as we got home. I was extremely curious about what had gone down at the station, and I wanted to ask James about it immediately, but I knew it would be best to wait till John got home. After last night's revelations, I wasn't sure he would be completely honest with me if John wasn't there.

It was awful, knowing he didn't trust me enough to be honest with me, his own mother, but I was trying to be more understanding. I did my fair share of lying as a teenager, too.

And what James was going through right now must be a lot to deal with. I didn't really blame him for lying to me anymore. I was just disappointed that he felt the need to hide things from me.

I did blame John, though. Although I hadn't said anything, I was still mad at him. But I knew this wasn't the right time for that. So I held everything in and tried to get through the day. John got home later in the afternoon, and we decided to speak to James together once he had freshened up.

I knocked softly on James's door and went in. John asked a few questions that James answered briskly, and it felt like we were getting nowhere. Until James finally asked something I had been dreading for years. Something I had hoped he would never ask.

"Are you my real dad?" James asked John, looking him dead in the eye.

TWELVE

We both stood in stunned silence. Neither of us knew how to answer this question. For years, we tried extremely hard to make James feel like he was fully part of the family. That John was his father. And in every way that it counted, John *was* his father. *Just not biologically.*

"James, of course, John is your father. He raised you, he took care of you, he—" I tried to explain, but James cut me off.

"You know what I mean. Is he my biological dad?" His voice trembled a little, but he didn't back down.

James didn't appear to be angry—more downcast than anything else.

"Why are you asking that all of a sudden?" John asked, still flabbergasted.

"At the station, they said you weren't my biological dad," James informed us.

Those assholes. That's fucking low, even for them. I had worked so hard to shield James from his past, from our past. My hands shook, and I took a deep breath to calm myself, afraid I might collapse if I didn't. I was less prepared than ever to have this conversation with James. I blinked and ran my hand through my hair, trying to clear my head.

"James, biology really doesn't matter that much…" I started.

"So it's true, he isn't my real dad? Who is my real dad? How could you keep this from me all this time?" James asked angrily.

"It's not like that. Your father died when you were very young, too young to remember any of it. And then I met John. And we never wanted to make you feel like you weren't our son or like you were an outsider. So, I gave you John's last name, and we raised you as our own," I explained.

"I need to know more than that. Who *was* my real dad? How did you two meet? How did he die?" James's eyes were bright with anger.

"Your biological father was called Trevor. We met when I was seventeen, and he had recently finished college. You were a toddler when Trevor fell off a ladder and hurt his head. He died almost instantly," I explained.

"That's what the cops said, too. Thanks for telling me the truth, Mom. I needed to know you wouldn't lie to me again," James told me, sighing.

"Of course. You're old enough to know the truth, James. And we would have told you at some point, anyway. We were just waiting till you turned eighteen," I admitted.

"And no matter what, I love you as my own. You will always be my son, James," John added.

"I know, Dad. I love you, too." James got up to hug John and me.

"If you ever want to talk about anything else, you know you can always talk to us. I'm sorry I kept the truth from you, but you were young and innocent. I wanted you to think of John as your father and bond with him. But you're older now, old enough to have questions and understand the answers," I said to James, my face buried in his hair.

"Thanks, Mom," James replied.

Of course, the cops would have known about James not being John's biological son. And about Trevor's death. I had called 911, hysterically begging them to send help. However, when the cops finally arrived, it was too late. He was already dead. I was sitting by his body with my son in my hands, both of us crying inconsolably.

"Sal, I think we should talk about James," John told me as we prepared to go to bed.

Here we go again with the talking. I sighed, slightly irritated, but turned my head toward him nonetheless.

"What do you want to talk about?" I asked.

"Why did you lie to him again?" asked John.

"I didn't lie to him. Trevor did die when he was a toddler. I may have left out some unseemly details, but they were things he didn't need to know about," I replied, annoyed at his line of questioning.

"Things he didn't need to know about? Have you ever considered, the reason he acts out is because he doesn't know himself, and you've forced him to repress the first few years of his life? Kids don't understand too much when they're young, but they're not stupid. They see things, and they understand enough for those things to have a lifelong impact on them," John stated.

"He's acting out because he's a teenager, and that's all," I said, pursing my lips.

"Oh, really? Weren't you the one who was concerned that

his anger was genetic only a few days ago?" John questioned, raising his eyebrows.

"I was wrong, and even if it were genetic, telling him everything isn't going to help. He'll only be more confused and continue to act out," I retorted.

John sat down at the edge of our bed, sighing in defeat. Deep down, I knew he had a point. But I could not do to James what my mother had done to me for years.

She had always unloaded all her trauma onto me. She would tell me things about the men she was seeing that no child should hear. Every time they fought, she would come running to me.

That's when I first started having anxiety and panic attacks. I was holding in all this information with no one to talk to about it. I was too young to even understand most of it. And every day, I would be terrified there would be something new to worry about. A new problem, a new fight.

I couldn't do that to James. He could never know the truth about his father. Especially not right now, when he was already going through all this. It was better for him to think he was loved and cared for than to know what a monster his biological father was. From the moment he was born, I knew I had to protect him. Do everything I could to keep him safe. And this was me keeping him safe, even if it meant keeping him in the dark.

"If you think keeping the truth from him is the right thing to do, I'll support you. But I still think you need to be honest with him and tell him about *everything* that happened between you and Trevor," John finally said in a low voice.

"I know what you mean, but I don't think this is the right time for that," I said.

"It's up to you." John shrugged and got into bed, turning his back toward me. I did the same, looking forward to not having to think for a few hours. I had taken a sleeping pill, which I hoped meant that the nightmares would leave me be for tonight.

THIRTEEN

I woke up with a dry mouth and a headache on my right side. It was a struggle to get out of bed, but I knew today of all days, I needed to be alert and on my A-game. Today was Lily's funeral, which meant that I needed to be there for James emotionally and physically. This was going to be a difficult day for all of us, but particularly for him. It would be his final goodbye to the young woman he had loved deeply and wholly. Nothing was more difficult than losing someone you loved, even if your relationship was not perfect.

The weather was dreary, almost as if Mother Earth knew the unfortunate circumstances of Lily's death and was mourning too. The clouds were gray, and the cold wind blew harder than usual. The leaves and branches on the trees were moving back and forth, creating a soft melody. It was drizzling, but the pitter-patter was neither relaxing nor calming as it usually was. Instead, it had a much heavier aura today. Like the drops of rain were dripping onto my soul.

I stared out of the window while quickly washing the dishes before we headed to the funeral. I was lost in my own world, yet every nerve in my body was hyperaware of what today was and what it meant for James and our family. Lily's death had broken our life beyond repair—what were once minor cracks had since evolved. Now we were left with shards of what was once our happy family.

"You should probably get ready," John softly suggested as he walked into the kitchen.

"You're right. I should," I agreed.

I turned off the tap and went upstairs to our bedroom.

Everything was still a haze. I was numb from the anxiety and was barely going through the motions, trying to get today over with. I did not feel the kind of sadness where you cry. It was the kind of sadness where you don't have the energy to cry or even grieve. The kind of sadness that hurts badly enough that your brain never really processes it. So you hide it in a corner of your mind, hoping to never have to revisit it again.

On the bed lay the black dress I had picked out for the funeral. It was an old dress. I don't wear black often anymore, and I wear dresses even more rarely. The dress was almost new. It was the first thing I had purchased after Trevor died. I bought it to wear to his funeral. I had spent the last few dollars we had on it.

He and I may not have always been on good terms; there were even moments I truly hated him, but in the end, I still loved parts of him deeply. He may not have been the man I had fallen in love with before he died, but that man was still inside him.

I knew he had no other friends or family that would attend his funeral. Even his parents and sister wanted absolutely nothing to do with him. Not after he borrowed a large sum of money from them, promising to use the money for university, when in reality, he had invested it in a shady business that went under in a few months. He barely had any real friends, and the company he did keep was not the kind that would care to attend a funeral.

James had been young then, barely three years old. He didn't know what was happening or why Mommy was crying. Why we had to move to a much smaller apartment, where roaches crawled around as we slept. But he was content enough.

At first, I thought he would eventually ask for his dad or at least about him, and I would have to explain everything to him. But he never did. He didn't mention him once. If anything, he seemed relieved. In many ways, I was too.

I put on my black stockings and then the dress, trying to keep the memories at bay and concentrate on the present. Slowly, I curled the bottoms of my hair and put on a simple silver necklace. I tapped the bare minimum amount of makeup onto my face and finished with a deep red lipstick. Looking in the mirror felt like I had gone back in time.

"Are you ready? We need to leave," John let me know, popping his head into the room from the doorway.

"Just finishing up. I'll be outside in a minute," I told him.

I took one final glance at myself in the mirror and left. John held an umbrella over my head as we walked to the car. The silence in the car was deafening—even Soph and JJ knew to behave themselves today. We had talked to them about Lily's passing, but had spared the gory details.

"Are you okay, James?" I finally asked, breaking the somber silence in the car.

He was sitting beside his siblings, staring out of the window, lost in his own thoughts. He had a detached expression, as though he had tuned out from everything.

"Yeah, I think so," responded James quietly.

We parked the car and got ready to go in. A number of cars

were already there, and I recognized Lily's parents' car parked close by. It was supposed to be a small funeral, at least that's what Paul had told John on the phone. Just close family and friends. I also recognized Betsy and Mark's car in the parking lot, along with a few other cars belonging to parents of students who went to school with James.

It had been a long time since I was inside, or even anywhere near, a church. Neither I nor John were religious, and we had given the kids the freedom to choose their own beliefs. When I was younger, we went to church every Sunday until I was eight or so. I did enjoy those few hours of peace, but as I got older, my belief in God wavered and eventually faded. No father would want their children to suffer, and yet it seemed that all humans ever did was suffer. Even when we had done nothing wrong. When our only sin was to exist in the imperfect world He had created. Where was the logic in that?

We walked up the stairs and into the church. Everyone turned to face us, except Lily's parents, who were seated at the front. Almost immediately, I could hear their whispers. Their accusing stares like daggers. I lowered my head, avoiding their eyes, and kept walking toward the coffin. It was a closed casket, for obvious reasons. Beside the coffin was a picture of Lily in a beautiful floral dress with a big smile on her face.

I inhaled deeply, trying to hold back the tears. Although I had believed at the time that she wasn't the right person for James, I was still incredibly saddened by her death. No one deserved to have their life taken from them. She never got to say her final goodbyes, never got to experience her dreams, never got to achieve her goals. How could anyone be cruel enough to hurt an innocent young girl?

As we got to the coffin, Paul got up to speak to us, but

before he could utter a word, Jen, Lily's mother, rushed toward us. I moved back a few steps, surprised.

"How dare you?" she screeched.

FOURTEEN

"How dare you come here? You fucking murderer," she continued, glaring at James with hate-filled eyes.

The church was now silent—you could have heard a pin drop. I could feel their eyes burning a hole in the back of my head. I peeked at James, trying to make sure he was okay. But he didn't even seem fazed by Jen's outburst. He simply stared blankly at her, his eyes devoid of emotion.

"Jen, please," said Paul, rushing to her side.

"You dare to show your face at her funeral? You took my baby away from me!" She pointed at James.

"Jen…" Paul tried to calm her down, his hands on her shoulders.

"I didn't hurt Lily. I loved her," James replied, surprisingly calmly.

"Sure you did, you fucking little psycho!" said Jen sarcastically.

"Jen, I invited them. Lily loved James, you know that. Please don't make a scene, not right now," Paul explained to Jen.

She went back and sat down on the bench, defeated, sobbing silently. Her usually well-maintained blonde hair was messy and uncombed; her skin was flushed, and her fingers trembled as she brushed away the tears. She looked like a shell of the woman she had once been.

"I'm sorry about that," Paul told us quietly. "Jen… She's taken this really badly. I don't think she meant what she said. I don't think she even knows what she's saying. But I think it might be best if you say your goodbyes to Lily and leave. I don't want to upset her any further," he confided in us.

I nodded, and we walked toward the coffin.

We stood by the coffin for a few minutes and then stepped back, letting James have a moment alone. I noticed both JJ and Soph seemed upset by Jen's outburst, so I told John I would take them outside to get some fresh air, and he could meet me at the car with James when he was done.

As we turned around, I once more felt the glaring eyes of the people in attendance. It was clear what they were thinking. They thought my son had killed Lily. And we were the monsters that had the audacity to still attend her funeral.

I could see Betsy's stupid, smug face in the crowd. She must be loving this. This was another reason I never attended church —the people who claim to be the most nonjudgmental are usually the most judgmental people you will ever meet.

"Are you guys okay?" I asked JJ and Sophia as soon as we got outside.

They both nodded but still looked a little upset.

"Don't worry about what happened. She was just sad because Lily isn't here anymore. Things will get better over time," I explained.

"Why isn't Lily here anymore? Why did she die?" asked JJ.

"It was a really sad accident. I'll tell you about it if you're still curious when you get older, okay?" I promised.

"Okay," said JJ.

After a minute or two, both he and Sophia were playing in the parking lot. They were running around, chasing one another and hiding behind cars. I checked my phone to see if I had any messages or notifications. While I was staring at my phone, I felt a sharp tap on my shoulder and turned to see Betsy, Mark, and Ian standing behind me. They were all dressed in black, Mark and Ian in suits and Betsy in a tight dress with a large matching hat.

I absolutely did not have the patience for her today.

"Hi." I smiled politely.

"Hey, Sally. How are you holding up?" Betsy asked, with a pitiful expression.

"Just tryin' to get through the day," I muttered.

How did she think I was holding up? What a stupid question to ask someone at a funeral.

"Yeah, it's been tough on all of us. Ian says the atmosphere at school has totally changed since they found Lily's body," Betsy continued, conveniently refusing to get the hint that I wanted no part in this conversation.

"Yes, one would assume so," I responded.

"If you guys need anything at all, let us know," chimed in Mark.

"Thanks," I said with a tight smile.

Please, just go away.

"And about my statement to the police ... I never meant for James to get into trouble or become their main suspect. I told them what I saw and heard because I assumed it would help them find Lily. You know how teenagers are. I thought she might have run away or was staying at a friend's or something. I mean, who could have imagined something so horrific could have happened ..." Mark whispered the end of the sentence, a haunted look in his eyes.

I honestly didn't blame him. He had told the truth. It just happened that the truth made my son look like a murderer.

"It's okay, Mark … we don't blame you—" I started.

"And right next to my classroom … If I had just been paying attention, I might have seen who did it or even been able to help Lily. I can't sleep at night knowing I could have done something, but I happened to go to the teachers' lounge to grab a coffee before the violin lesson—" Mark continued as if he hadn't even heard me.

"Mark, it's really alright. You did the best you could. You had no way of knowing what was happening outside," I assured him.

"That's what I keep telling him. *He* has nothing to feel guilty about," Betsy said pointedly.

What is that supposed to mean? Was she insinuating that James *did* have something to feel guilty about?

"You okay, Ian?" I asked, trying to change the subject.

Ian was their son and a close friend of James. He was quietly standing behind Betsy, staring at the ground. He used to come over more often before, but hadn't since Lily went missing. I assumed Betsy had something to do with that.

It was Ian's girlfriend, Patricia, who initially introduced Lily and James. I saw her seated next to her parents inside the church, too. She looked so upset. Her eyes were now red from crying, her blonde hair was in a messy bun, and her delicate body slumped with the weight of her grief.

I was sure this situation had shaken up all the students. Especially because there could be a murderer among them still roaming free.

"I'm okay, Mrs. S. Thanks for asking," Ian said quietly, smiling a little at me in reassurance.

I gave him a tight-lipped smile in return.

"Well, I should probably go wait by the car," I said, backing away.

"Of course, and just so you know, even though *everyone* else thinks James did it, we're on your side. No matter how much evidence they've found," Betsy commented, her voice like nails on a chalkboard.

Fucking cunt. She couldn't let me leave in peace. Evidence? Everyone? I knew she was searching for some drama. People like her feed off it. They can't bear their own stagnant, pathetic lives, so they say stupid shit to get a rise out of others and then paint themselves as the victim. I turned and walked back to them. Mark and Ian looked mortified by what Betsy had said, but she was her usual smug self.

"Thanks, Betsy. Your support means so much to us," I said, putting on my fakest nice voice.

I watched her arrogant smile fade and droop with disappointment, twitching slightly when she realized I wasn't going to react the way she had hoped. The only way to shut down a drama whore like her was to not give her what she craved the most—a reaction. I walked away before I said something I would regret. This was not the time nor the place to pull Betsy's extensions out or break her new nose.

John came out shortly after, followed by James. He looked beat, so we decided to head home. The younger kids were distracted by their iPad, and James continued to stare out of the window as the rain started up again. I reached for John's hand and held it the entire way back. Today, more than ever, I was incredibly grateful to have him by my side, regardless of not seeing eye to eye at the moment.

FIFTEEN

JOHN

I FIRST MET SALLY WHEN SHE WAS IN HER EARLY TWENTIES. SHE had been so young then, and yet it seemed like she had already lived a thousand lives. Her brown hair was tied back in a ponytail, her fingernails were cut short, she had no makeup on, and her clothes hung loosely off her petite figure.

I was living in an apartment, a bachelor pad of sorts, and never really had the time to clean or take care of it. I was only starting out in my field and was working very long hours. The pay was good, though, so I hired a maid from one of those cleaning services. I had seen an ad for it, examined my dump of an apartment, and knew it was time to let the professionals handle it.

Trevor had just died, and Sally was working as a maid since she had never been to college and barely made it through high school, which meant she didn't have the proper qualifications for most other jobs. She took what she could get out of desperation.

When I first saw her, she looked absolutely exhausted. Dark circles under her eyes, lips pursed, slight frown lines on her forehead. Yet her face had so much youthful beauty. She was much too young to be this exhausted. I noticed that even though she looked tired, her eyes always sparkled. And when she smiled, the whole room got brighter.

I was supposed to go out with friends that day—that's why I had asked her to come over to clean. But after one look at her, I decided to stay in. We chatted a bit, and she told me she had just moved to a new apartment downtown with her son because her boyfriend recently passed away.

Although I sympathized with her situation, a small part of me was glad because that meant she was single. A very tiny part of me, I swear.

We talked about her financial situation once, but she seemed closed off, shutting down the conversation as soon as it started. Which was fair. She was there to do her job and owed me nothing more. And I didn't want to come on too strong or be too intrusive, so I let her get on with it. Soon, I was hiring her twice a week, even though I had initially planned for it to be once a month.

Slowly, I kept prying, and she opened up more. She told me a bit about her past, how she had met Trevor, and that she no longer spoke to her mother. And I told her about my parents, who had recently passed away in a tragic accident. Mostly, we talked about her son, James. She always smiled and lit up when she spoke about him. I could tell she adored him.

Eventually, talking turned to flirting. The small things mattered most—laughing together, making inside jokes. She would occasionally touch my arm and I hers. One day, I finally plucked up the courage to ask her out. Unfortunately, I was quickly turned down. She said she was no longer interested in relationships because her son was her priority.

I knew the only way to her heart was to show her that I would be a good stepfather to her son. Maybe someday he would even see me as a father figure. So, I kept bugging the people she worked for and finally got her number. That helped me get her address. And I showed up at her door with roses and children's toys. She would either think I was crazy or a romantic, but I knew I needed to take the chance and go for it.

Thankfully, she thought it was romantic and let me in. James was such a well-behaved child. So quiet, adorable, and friendly. I grew to love him pretty quickly. We got married soon after that. I knew she was the woman I wanted to spend my life with. I loved her, and she loved me. So why wait?

There was a bit of an age difference between us, a decade to be exact. We knew people wouldn't understand—they would think I was taking advantage of her. Or that she was a gold digger. But we didn't care. We loved one another, and that was enough for us.

Early on, I noticed Sally had trouble sleeping. In fact, she would wake up almost every night terrified after having vivid nightmares. I tried to console her, talk to her, comfort her, but she didn't respond well to any of it. She kept pushing me away, refusing to talk about what was bothering her.

When she finally revealed the truth, I was horrified by what she had gone through for years. It broke my heart to imagine, and it hurt even more knowing she would have to live with those memories for the rest of her life.

It explained a lot more about her behavior. How she reacted when I raised my voice even slightly, the way she seemed to flinch at loud sounds, her slightly hunched posture, as though she was carrying the weight of the world on her shoulders. But we tried our best to move on from it. I always held her tight when she woke up crying, and eventually, the nightmares stopped.

A few months after we got married, I legally adopted James. We became a real family, and after a few years, we decided to grow that family. Sophia and JJ came one after the other. James was a loving, doting older brother, and Sally was an incredible mother, as she had always been.

Everything was perfect. Until it wasn't. You may think it all crumbled when Lily was murdered, but it began years before that. When James started acting… different. Sally hated me for keeping it all from her, but how could I tell the woman I loved that her worst nightmares were slowly coming to life? I had promised to protect her no matter what, and that's what I would do. *Till death do us part.*

SIXTEEN

SALLY

"WHY THE FUCK DO WE HAVE A LAWYER, THEN?" I ASKED, pacing angrily.

The police had taken James in for questioning again. It had been five hours, and they still hadn't let him go. The thought of him stuck in that room for hours with no one by his side but his lawyer, made my blood boil. This was ridiculous.

"We can't do anything about it, Sal. They can legally keep him there for up to six hours," John calmly tried to explain for the fifth time.

I knew he was right, but as James's mother, I hated sitting around and not being able to do anything to protect him. Instead of *actually* investigating Lily's murder and trying to figure out who *really* killed her, the police were unfairly harassing poor James. Trying to make him confess or say something incriminating that they could use against him. They were wasting everyone's time and traumatizing my son in the process.

I turned my attention toward my other kids in an attempt to distract myself. They were sitting in the living room, their eyes glued to the television. Sophia and JJ had been quiet recently. After Lily's funeral, they seemed to have understood that things were different. They were around James more, playing and trying to make him laugh. They were trying to comfort him the only way they knew how.

I tried to spend time with both of them as much as I could these days. I didn't want them to be neglected and feel like James was getting all the attention. But they weren't as interested in playing with either John or me as they used to be. It broke my heart knowing that this situation probably forced them to grow up faster than they should have.

We were considering family therapy to help understand how they were coping with everything. As someone who had a hard childhood, I knew it was important to resolve things early on instead of letting them manifest. I looked at their sweet, innocent little faces. I didn't want them to end up like me. I wanted to take care of them the way I wished someone had cared for me when I was their age.

I have no memories of my father and only bad ones of my mother and her string of boyfriends and ex-husbands. My mother was an unstable alcoholic. She didn't mention my father much, but I knew that his leaving her was what had really driven her to start drinking excessively. She had mentioned it a couple of times while drunk.

I had been about five when she first mentioned it and blamed me for his leaving. Apparently, he had tried to be a good dad for a few months but had eventually given up and left. Somehow, that had been my fault for crying too much and being a fussy baby.

We moved around a lot when I was younger. Each time she broke up with her boyfriend, she would promise to turn over a new leaf. And we would move to a different city so we could "get a fresh start." It never lasted more than a few days, a few weeks at most.

I can't tell you how many times I came home from school to find her drunk or passed out. By the time I was Sophia's age, I knew how to check for her pulse, call 911 if I couldn't hear it, and put a towel under her neck so that she didn't choke on her own vomit. When I got big enough, I would drag her to her bedroom and get her into bed.

As far back as I could remember, she'd had a new boyfriend every few months. Some lasted longer, and two of them lasted long enough for her to marry and quickly divorce them. Every single time, she would trade in one abusive sleazeball for another. Never once did she even consider how that was affecting me or that she was not the only one being abused by those losers.

I vividly remember the guy she was with when I saw her for the last time. His name was Vic, and I had been only seventeen when he tried to get into my bed as my mother lay unconscious on our living room floor.

I remember his slicked-back, greasy black hair, his pale skin, and acne-covered face. His protruding stomach that he stroked while mindlessly staring at the TV screen. His thick body hair, the cross tattooed at the top of his left arm. And, of course, the smell of his dollar-store cologne.

The craziest thing was that even after all she put me through, I spent years feeling sorry for her. She was so good at playing the victim that she had me convinced that she was. That it was my fault our life was such a mess, that I had ruined her life by existing. I hate to admit it, but for most of my life, I blamed myself for her hate and abuse. I blamed myself for ruining her life and driving her to drink.

But then I had James, and I realized that she wasn't the victim. I was. As a mother, it's your job to protect your child no matter what. To make sure they have the best life you can provide them with. And she failed to do that. She failed to do the *bare minimum* and somehow still found the audacity to lecture me about not being grateful.

Once I understood that, I no longer felt any guilt. In fact, I didn't feel anything for her anymore.

I BREATHED A SIGH OF RELIEF AS I HEARD JAMES'S CAR IN OUR driveway. He walked into the house with heavy steps, like he was weighed down by it all. John and I asked him how it went, and then let him go up to bed. He didn't tell us much, but we could tell from his demeanor that it had not gone well.

I was starting to get more and more nervous. They clearly thought James did it, and he was clearly their primary suspect. They kept interviewing those around him and calling him in for questioning, too. James continued to deny the accusations, but I could see how much all this was affecting him.

For the first time in a long time, I got on my knees and prayed that night to a God I didn't even believe existed.

SEVENTEEN

I WAS A QUIET CHILD AND GREW UP TO BE AN EVEN QUIETER teenager. I never had any proper friends because we moved too much. Every time I finally made a friend or two, it was time for us to leave again. When I was younger, I thought that was normal. That everyone moved around. But as I got older and observed my classmates, I realized that there was nothing normal about my life.

I grew envious of my classmates, who all had loving parents. Seeing them hugging and kissing their parents when they were picked up after school felt so foreign to me; my mom had never once done that. I usually just stood there, praying she remembered to pick me up this time. Often, she didn't, and I ended up walking home on my own, only to be greeted by her passed out on the couch, the bottle beside her empty.

I became desperate, wanting their lives. Looking back now, I was desperate to have their happiness. That's when I first began using my imagination to escape my reality.

At first, I imagined having loving parents. I daydreamed that one day my real dad would come back and kick whoever my mother was dating at the time out. He would hug us both and apologize for leaving. And we would be one happy family, living in a nice home, having barbecues, and swimming in our pool in the summer. My mother would change. She would stop drinking and finally love me.

Eventually, I realized that was never going to happen. Even in my daydreams, it felt too far-fetched. As I got older, I honestly just didn't want anything to do with my mother anymore. My new daydream was to get as far away from her as possible.

I would meet the man of my dreams, and he would save me from her and this awful life we had. He would take me away, and we would be happy together. We would have lots of kids and a big house where they could run around and play. It would be *perfect*.

And my mother would be so envious of our life and sorry that she hadn't treated me better. One day, she would show up at my doorstep begging for my forgiveness. And I would tell her that although I forgave her, I no longer wanted anything to do with her. She would leave crying, knowing that she fucked up. It would be so satisfying.

I was desperate for that dream to come true, but I had no friends, and none of the boys in high school ever looked twice at me. They only wanted to get the attention of the popular girls. With my skinny, flat body and greasy brown hair, I was practically invisible to everyone around me. Always the ugly duckling, never the swan.

That was until I started working part-time at a store, trying to make some extra cash. I was hoping I could use it to buy more stylish clothes and some makeup. Then maybe the boys would notice me, and I would find *the one*. I knew my mother would never buy those things for me. We only got our stuff from thrift stores and Goodwill.

Unfortunately, I didn't meet *the one*. I did, however, meet

Trevor, *disguised as the one.*

I was sixteen when we first met, and he told me he was twenty. I later found out he had actually been twenty-four. We worked some of our shifts together and began talking. He was extremely extroverted and chatty. The exact opposite of me. But I liked him. And I loved the attention. He was the first person to really see me and genuinely take an interest in me.

And he was so good-looking, too. He had brownish hair with a little bit of blond in it and these big grayish-blue eyes that would stare at me intently when we were together. It made me feel like I was drowning in them, like I would fall so deep into them that I would never see the surface again. He wasn't too tall or too athletic, but was still much taller and larger than I was. I had always been pretty petite—people often assumed I was much younger than I actually was.

At first, we would talk at work, but soon, we were hanging out outside work as well. He would take me out for dinner or milkshakes. We would talk for hours. He always made me laugh, and it had been so effortless to fall in love with him. He was handsome, funny, witty, and intelligent. He made me feel like I could tell him anything, and I naively did. I told him about my mother and her boyfriend at the time, Vic. How he always stared at me when he thought I wasn't looking, how he would sit too close to me when my mother wasn't around.

Trevor swore to protect me and told me to call him immediately if that creep tried anything. I promised him I would. He told me he didn't like my situation and that I would be safer living with him. His apartment wasn't that big, but at least we would be happy there. I told him I would think about it, but knew deep down I was too much of a coward to do that.

We saw each other almost every day, and I could feel myself

falling more and more in love with him. In all my life, I had never felt loved or even wanted, so when I finally did, I clung on to it for dear life, terrified he would eventually see me as the world saw me and lose interest.

My mother and Vic both hated how much time I now spent outside the house. My mother, because it meant she would have to step up and actually do some of the housework. Vic, because I assume, it gave him less time to be a creep. Either way, I remember having a number of arguments with both of them about staying out so late.

They kept badgering me, asking me where I had been going. I told them I had taken more shifts at work. I knew they didn't believe me, but I also knew that they were both too lazy to check up on me to make sure I was really at work. Or so I thought.

EIGHTEEN

When I turned seventeen, Trevor got me the most beautiful bracelet I had ever seen and the first birthday present I had ever received. He told me it was real gold (it wasn't—I tried to pawn it after he passed and was told it was fake). And I was young and stupid enough to believe him.

He was still badgering me to move in with him, and I was genuinely considering it this time because Vic had been getting worse. He had lost his job a few weeks prior, which meant he was home all the time. It was awful. I couldn't leave my room without him lurking somewhere nearby, watching me with a beer in his hand.

I had kept my bags packed, just in case. Not that I had much stuff. It was only two backpacks, but I wanted to be ready if I ever needed to flee. And Trevor had promised to come pick me up, no matter what time or day it was.

I was so thankful I did that because there did come a day when I needed to flee. It happened about three months after my seventeenth birthday. I had gone to bed early, pretending to have a headache, but in reality, I was sick of my mother and Vic bickering on the couch again.

I got into bed and was trying to fall asleep when I heard my door creak open. I could tell it was Vic by the sickly sweet smell of his cologne mixed in with the stench of alcohol. I kept still, hoping he would think I was already asleep and go away.

But instead, I heard him walk closer and then take off his shoes and get into my bed. I could feel the warmth of his body, and the smell of his cologne was even stronger now. I kept my eyes shut, my heart beating faster than it had ever beaten before. I couldn't believe this was happening.

I felt his breath on my neck—I could almost taste the beer on it. The gold cross he wore on his neck daily was currently pressed against my skin. The icy metal felt like it was burning its mark onto me. He lightly stroked my hair while his other hand caressed my thigh. I recoiled at his cold, dry fingers touching my bare skin.

"Get the fuck away from me," I told him, moving away from him to the edge of my bed.

"C'mon now, you know you've been flirting with me all this time too," he whispered.

"I have literally no interest in you, get the fuck out of my room," I tried to sound firm.

"That's no way for a pretty little thing like you to talk …" He smiled at me. Seeing his smile, his exposed, browning teeth, made me sick to my stomach.

"*Go away!*" I said, whispering more loudly.

"You're old enough to know the consequences of flirting. What are you, like, eighteen? You know what happens to pretty young things that tease." He continued to grin.

"I'm *seventeen*, and you need to leave, or I'll tell my mom," I warned him.

"Oh yeah? And maybe I'll tell her you've been sneaking around to go see some boy after work," he threatened.

My heart dropped at his threat. How did he know about Trevor? He must have followed me at some point.

"Fuck you," I said, trying to get out of bed.

He grabbed my wrist and pulled me back onto the bed, holding me down while trying to get on top of me. He had a deranged spark in his beady eyes—his pupils looked almost black, and a shiver went down my spine. I screamed for my mother and then for help, but no one came. I had naively hoped that at least this one time, she would protect me, act like a real mom, but as always, she was too preoccupied with destroying her liver.

I kept trying to shove him away, but he was so much larger than me and continued to easily hold me down. I cried for him to stop. I was terrified at that moment. I still remember it like it was yesterday.

Finally, I was able to twist my leg enough to kick him off me. I kicked him once more for good measure, right in the crotch. He fell off the bed and onto the floor, clutching himself, doubled over in pain.

"You fucking slut!" he screamed, his sweat-covered face redder than I had ever seen it. "You're going to fucking pay for this!"

I wasn't about to wait around for that. I grabbed my bags and ran. I saw my mother passed out on the couch in the living room and glanced at her one last time. This was how I would always remember her—unconscious and not there for me when I needed her most. I left the house and kept running till I was a few streets away, my heart still beating hard. I went into a convenience store and begged the person at the front to let me use their phone. I dialed the only number I could and waited in the parking lot, shivering in my pajamas. Trevor was there a few minutes later.

I calmed down as I got into his car. I could finally breathe, knowing I was safe now. He asked me if I was okay, and I instantly burst into tears. I couldn't seem to stop. He was so kind and comforting. He held me till I stopped crying and then drove me to his apartment. It felt so good to be there, to no longer be scared and anxious.

If I had known then what I know now, I would never have gotten into his car. I would have kept running till I was far away from them all.

NINETEEN

"Shut the fuck up. You had this coming—I saw how you kept looking at him last night!" yelled Trevor, pointing his finger in my face.

"We were just talking. I was being polite because he's your friend," I told him, praying he believed me this time.

"I told you I don't want you talking to anyone but me!" he continued yelling.

"I'm sorry ... it won't happen again, I promise!" My voice cracked, and my heart was racing.

"Yeah, I'll make sure it fucking doesn't," he swore as he advanced toward me, his eyes filled with hate and unjustified anger.

MY NIGHTMARES HAD BECOME FREQUENT OCCURRENCES ONCE more. They were mostly memories I had pushed down, hoping I would never have to revisit them again. Our minds have a way of attacking us when we are at our lowest. At least mine did.

I tried everything to get my anxiety under control—meditation, breathing exercises, ashwagandha, and chamomile tea. But it continued its unwavering assault on my mind. Everything else was falling apart in my life, and my mental health seemed to be going in that direction, too.

The rest of the family wasn't doing great either. Between

James being worn down from the constant questioning and the younger kids having a hard time understanding everything that was currently going on, John and I were quite exhausted. We tried our best to be there for all three kids, but it wasn't easy.

We had a few meetings with James's lawyer to make sure we were still on the same page about everything and had a plan on how to move forward. For now, we were focused on keeping James out of prison, or I guess juvie, and making sure that the real killer was found.

WE WERE ALL SEATED QUIETLY AT THE DINNER TABLE, FOCUSING on our food. I was mostly moving my food around the plate—my appetite had been barely present lately. I just didn't feel like eating anymore. And I could tell James hadn't been eating much either; his cheeks were sunken, and the clothes that used to fit him snugly now hung loosely off his body.

I was about to ask the younger kids how their day was when we heard a knock at the door. I got up to open it and was not surprised to see multiple police officers, including Officers Smith and Jones, at my doorstep. Along with two squad cars parked outside our house. Some of our neighbors were watching from their windows or standing at their front door.

"Good evening, Ma'am. We have a warrant to search the property," said Officer Smith, shoving a paper in front of my face.

I could hear John hurriedly walking to the door as I simply stood there, too exhausted to deal with this right now.

"What's going on?" asked John, standing beside me.

"As I was explaining to your wife, we have a warrant to search the property," repeated Officer Smith.

John grabbed the warrant from him, frowning more deeply as he read it.

"This is ridiculous," John muttered, but moved out of the way and grabbed my arm so I would move too.

We both knew there was little we could do at this point. As the officers entered our home and immediately began making a mess of it, John told me he was calling our lawyer. I nodded and continued to stand there, not knowing what else to do with myself. I didn't know how to react, and my brain was taking a minute to process what was happening.

I could hear John shouting on the phone in the other room, something he rarely did. I could hear James trying to comfort Sophia and JJ, eventually bringing them to me. They all seemed as scared and confused as I was. My heart was beating in my ears, and time seemed to slow down as I watched them tear apart our home. Drawers flung open, couch cushions everywhere. Even our rug was turned upside down.

Seeing the kids' terrified faces—Soph tearing up—helped me snap out of it. And suddenly, all I could feel was rage. My maternal instincts to protect my children kicked in, and I wrapped my hands around the youngest two as we all stood by our front door.

I frowned and occasionally tsked as I heard the clanking of glass from the kitchen and things being thrown around carelessly in our bedrooms. Of course, they wouldn't care about the damage. Not just to our house but to our family. All they cared about was pinning this on James. They had made up their mind that he was guilty, and now they wanted to confirm their bias. It was ridiculous, and this was why people had become frustrated with the legal system these days.

After what felt like over an hour, they finally left, having found no real evidence. All they found was one of Lily's sweaters that she had left behind at some point when she had come over to see James. We put the younger kids to bed, making sure they were okay first. Then we sat down to talk to James about the situation. He was shaken up, too, his bloodshot eyes dark with worry.

It hurt to see him this way. It hurt to know this situation was tearing our family apart. And worst of all, it was a situation I had no control over. I wanted to make things better, to make all the bad things magically disappear so that my kids could be carefree and happy again. But I finally realized that repressing everything wasn't doing us any good. It was easier to run from the problems, the bad memories, the bad experiences. But they were always only one step behind, and at some point, we had to face them.

TWENTY

Having our house searched helped me come to a few conclusions. First, all this time I had been keeping the truth from James because I wanted to protect him. But eventually, it did more harm than good.

I also realized that not telling James the entire truth meant that James didn't truly know himself. The first few years of his life were missing. Of course, he was acting out, getting angry, and blaming himself for Lily's death. He wasn't a monster, like some of the people he and I were related to. He was simply confused.

He was a good boy who happened to be in a bad place and in a bad situation. And the only way to fix that was to tell him the full truth. If he reacted badly to it, that would be his right. But at least he would have the full story. At least he would know where his anger and frustration were stemming from.

Another reason to tell him the entire truth was one I had been trying to avoid thinking about. It was something I genuinely didn't want to admit to myself. It had been bugging me since this whole thing started, but I went into denial mode like I always do.

The thing was, I didn't know James as well as I thought. And I did, unfortunately, know his father well, which led me to believe that there could have been a chance that James hurt Lily.

Of course, I would continue to support him until they found undeniable proof that he did something. But I had to admit to myself that there is always a possibility. Statistically, you're much more likely to be abused or murdered by someone close to you—someone you already know. If James was indeed guilty, I wanted him to know about our past because I thought that might make him want to admit to the truth. That is, if there was something to admit.

"Your father and I wanted to check up on you and see how you were doing with this whole situation," I explained, standing in his bedroom once more.

I couldn't help but notice the mess the police officers had left in their wake and made a mental note to do some cleaning and organizing tomorrow.

"I'm okay. Kinda exhausted," admitted James.

"We understand. This can't be easy for you," John sympathized.

His demeanor was somber as he stood beside me.

"James, I trust you and love you, and that's why I think it's time you know the real truth about your childhood," I finally said after a few seconds of awkward silence.

"What do you mean the *real* truth?" James asked, an inquisitive expression on his face.

"When I told you about your biological father, I may have… left out a hefty chunk of information regarding our relationship and your relationship with him as a young child," I admitted.

"Okay…" James seemed mystified, but he didn't appear annoyed or resentful, which I took as a good sign.

"Before I tell you the full story, I want to make it clear that the reason I didn't tell you everything before wasn't because I didn't trust you. I had a very hard childhood, something you already know, and because of that, I sometimes end up not knowing how to communicate things properly. I tend to shut down instead of communicating as I should. But I want you to know that none of this is your fault. This is all me," I clarified.

James nodded his understanding. I took a deep breath. I didn't even know where to start or how many details to share. I was just going to do it. And if he asked any questions, which I was sure he would, I would answer them honestly. My hands were simultaneously freezing cold and clammy from the sweat. Even after everything I had been through, this was the most scared and nervous I had ever been.

This was a mistake. I shouldn't tell James anything. Studying his young, innocent face, I knew he wasn't guilty. I thought of those little eyes gazing up at me for the first time after a grueling twenty-three-hour birth. This was my baby.

Just as I was freaking out and second-guessing my decision, I felt John squeeze my hand, and I peeked up at him. He smiled and nodded, silently assuring me that he thought I was making the right decision by telling James the truth about our past. That was the only assurance I needed. I trusted John with every fiber of my being. I knew he would never steer me wrong.

It was time to tell James the truth. And tell him the truth, I did. I told him about how I met his father when I was too young to know any better, how everything had been amazing between us until it wasn't. How he got abusive, and eventually the abuse got worse. Worse than I ever thought it could be.

James's expression grew increasingly horrified as I continued. My heart broke for him, knowing that his biological father was a monster, must be so difficult for him to learn. I wanted to comfort him, to tell him he was nothing like Trevor, but I didn't know how to. I didn't know the right words to say, and I knew saying the wrong thing would be detrimental in these circumstances.

"One night, he got so drunk that he was barely coherent. He accused me of emasculating him, and for some reason, he thought that fixing the light I had been complaining about would prove me wrong. I begged him not to climb the ladder in his state, but he refused to listen. You were crying, and I went to check on you in the other room. That's when I heard the sound of the ladder falling. I ran to see what had happened and found him on the floor. There was a pool of blood around his head. I rushed to call 911, but it was too late. He was already dead by the time they got there," I said in a low voice.

I bit my lip, trying to fight the tears. Reliving these memories, thinking about it all over again when I had tried so hard not to, was much more difficult than I had anticipated. I was barely holding it together. Deep down, I wanted to collapse on the floor and cry. But I had to keep going. I had to be strong for James.

"Soon after, I began working again since he had left us nothing but debt. We moved to a different city, and eventually, I met John, and he helped me pay off the debts," I explained.

"It wasn't much money to me. My parents had left me a generous inheritance, and I wanted our relationship to be a new start for Sally." John shrugged.

"And in all the ways it matters, it *was* a new start for me. You were so happy with John. You had never been that happy with Trevor. You always used to cry and fuss. But with John, you were relaxed and cheerful." I smiled, memories of James's happy little face as he played catch with John consumed my thoughts.

TWENTY-ONE

"I SEE... THAT'S A LOT TO TAKE IN," JAMES SAID SLOWLY.

We had talked for quite a while, and he had a lot to process, so I understood. His shoulders were hunched over, and his face was a concoction of emotions. I had wanted to protect him from the hurt and pain. I had wanted him to have a different life than me, but the universe had other plans.

"I know. It's a lot," I agreed.

"But I do understand now why you didn't tell me earlier. And I guess I also understand more about myself," continued James, deep in thought.

He was such an understanding person. I was truly grateful for that. Most teenagers would have had a different reaction to learning this information. They would have been angry and upset. His response to all this was why I was sure he could never be the monster his biological father had been. James was understanding, kind, and sweet. Despite his temper, or whatever other issues he may have, he was inherently good. I knew in my heart that he was.

"Is there anything you want to talk about or...?" I asked.

"No, I think... I think I need some space right now," James told us.

"I understand," I responded.

"Do you mind if I spend the weekend at Ian's? I need to get away from everything and clear my head," James said.

"Of course, as long as his parents are fine with it." I nodded.

"I'm sure they will be. They're always telling me to come over more," James told us.

"Okay, that's fine then. Just be careful with Betsy. You don't want to give her too much information about what's happening right now," I warned him.

"I know," he said, smiling slightly for the first time since this conversation started.

With that, he packed some things into a backpack and left. It was drizzling outside, and I reminded him to take an umbrella.

Soon after, John and I decided to head to bed. As we sat beside one another, the blanket covering our legs, he told me he was proud of me for being more honest with James and that I had done the right thing. Hearing that made my heart swell. The pride was evident on John's face.

I was much lighter now than I had been before our talk with James. I had been carrying a heavy burden with me all this time. I was so used to the weight on my shoulders that I hadn't even realized I had been slouching. I promised myself I would be more honest from now on and that I needed to stop treating James like a child and more like the young man he was.

I also needed to be honest with John about everything I was thinking and experiencing. Communication hadn't been my strong suit in the past because no one around me knew how to communicate well. But John did, and I no longer had an excuse to hold everything in.

It wasn't going to be easy, of course. I didn't expect it to be. But I was going to try my best. And that meant we had to have an open and honest conversation about James and what Lily's murder meant for him and our family. And the best way to move forward.

We also needed to be on the same page about Lily's murder. And James, being the last person to see her alive.

"So, I'm just going to say it," I breathed, gazing into John's eyes.

"Okay…" he said, slightly confused.

"Do you think… Do you think there's any possibility that James did it? That he killed Lily and is lying about it?" I blurted out.

James had been confiding in John more than me over the last few years. Whether I wanted to admit it or not, that meant John knew James a lot better than I did.

John sighed, took off his glasses, and rubbed his temples. He looked both exhausted and defeated. I could relate. That's why I had been avoiding this conversation till now. It hurt deeply to even think about.

"Honestly, I don't think he did," he finally replied.

"You don't?" I raised my eyebrows in surprise.

"No, I don't," he said more firmly.

"Why not? He had an intimate relationship with Lily, he was the last person to see her alive, and he had a motive. Not to mention his past behavior," I probed.

John thought about it before answering, his frown emphasizing the lines on his forehead. It made me realize how much this ordeal had aged him. The fine lines had deepened into permanent creases, and the couple of gray hairs had multiplied into a noticeable streak.

"That's true, but I've known him for years, and I truly don't think he's capable of murder and vehemently deny it this way. Whenever he did something bad before, he would always tell me the truth about it, and I could see he was remorseful about his actions. He was genuinely remorseful about the incident with Brian once things cooled down," John explained.

"Hmm, I didn't know that."

"I think if James ever got that violent with Lily, he would confess almost instantly. I don't think he's the kind of person who could have murdered his girlfriend and then come home and have dinner with us as though nothing happened," John said. "This is the work of a sick person, and I don't think James is a sick person."

"You know, I think you're right," I agreed. "Thanks, hon. Hearing you say that gives me peace of mind."

"Good." John hugged me tightly, kissing my cheek.

I hugged him back. He always knew how to calm my nerves. In his arms, I always felt safe. Eventually, I fell asleep to the sound of the heavy rain outside our window. It was an uninterrupted and dreamless sleep, and I desperately needed it.

TWENTY-TWO

I STRETCHED OUT MY ARMS THE NEXT MORNING, FEELING MUCH more refreshed. After the talk I had with John, that tight knot in my stomach was gone. I was no longer torn between believing James and suspecting him. I had let go of the suspicions and wanted to focus solely on being there for him and the rest of my family.

The sun was shining brightly outside, pouring in through the windows and warming up the house. I smiled at the sound of the birds chirping, their relentless energy contagious. The rain from the last few days had completely subsided, allowing the green grass to display itself once more.

Since the weather was lovely, John decided to take JJ and Soph out for the day, and James was still at Ian's. As much as I loved my family, I was thankful to have the house to myself for a few hours. It was much easier to get everything cleaned and organized again without them in my way.

Opening the storage cupboard under the stairs, I pulled out some cleaning supplies and set about putting the house back together. The police had left quite a mess because, apparently believing they're above the law and what they do doesn't matter. Okay, maybe I was still kind of salty about that and needed to let it go. Today was all about being more optimistic.

I hummed as I picked up items and put them back in their

place. Most people hated cleaning and arranging things, which I understood, but I'd always loved it. Everything had a place in our home, and something just seemed off when things were not in their place.

I cleaned James's room last since that was the room that had taken the brunt of the search. I went to his study table and picked up the small framed family photo he kept there. We were all smiling and waving at the camera. I remembered the day we took it three years ago. We were all bored on a random day in summer and decided to go to the beach closest to us. It had been really fun to relax and enjoy one another's company for a while.

I continued cleaning things up, and before I knew it, his bedroom was back to normal. Well, better than normal because it was usually too messy for my liking. I sat down on his bed and gazed around, lost in my own thoughts.

So much had happened in the past few weeks. So much had happened in the past few days, even. Everything was so different. Yet the same.

I thought about when we had first moved into this house. It was about a year after John and I got married. We knew we wanted a big house because we wanted to have more kids eventually. Money had never really been an issue for John, and he told me to pick the house I liked most. I was beyond excited. It was as if all the daydreams I had as a kid were finally coming true.

We viewed at least a dozen houses, but none of them felt just right. Until we saw this one. It was perfect. The house itself was a fixer-upper, sure, but it had integrity. It had a huge backyard for the kids to play in and for me to garden in, and the rooms were spacious with bright sunlight coming in through every window. But most of all, it didn't feel like a house but rather a home.

As soon as we stepped into it, I knew it was the one. I could see our kids growing up here, playing in the backyard, and having dinner as a family in the dining room. John and I grew old together once the kids got older and went off to college. I could see our whole lives happening here. So, we put in an offer, and a few months later, we were done renovating and moving in. James was most excited to pick his room back then and move all his toys in.

Time really does fly. Those memories were so clear they could have been yesterday, and yet it was years ago. Years of happy memories. So many firsts happened in this house. This house was our new beginning. It was supposed to be our happily ever after.

I sighed and got up. I should probably start working on some of the other housework I had neglected while cleaning everything else up. The dishes still needed to be washed, and I had to prepare dinner and do the laundry, too.

As I walked toward the door, I heard one of the floorboards squeak. That was new. I had been in this room so many times, but had never noticed that. The floorboard looked a little out of place, too. Like it didn't fit properly with the rest of the floorboards.

Before I could think it through, I was already kneeling on the floor, trying to pull up the squeaky floorboard. It was slightly jammed, but eventually, I got it to come out. There were a number of things stashed inside. I froze for a second. Maybe I should pretend I didn't see anything and just leave. I should trust James, like we agreed to do.

I wanted to leave, I really did. But I knew it would kill me to not know what he had in there. It would haunt me forever. I needed to know. So, I slowly sorted through the items. There was an adult magazine, which was weird because internet porn exists now and is free, but whatever. I didn't want to think of *that*.

There were a couple of other innocent things, a test he had clearly failed but was trying to hide. There was a small amount of weed and a lighter. And then I saw something shiny in the corner, hidden below it all. I pulled it out, and my heart skipped a beat.

In my shaking hands was a golden bracelet with a heart pendant, and a phone that was pretty much destroyed. The screen was all cracked, and it had some scratches on it. It looked as though someone had smashed it or perhaps thrown it in anger. Both things were almost instantly recognizable to me because I had seen them in my home multiple times before. These items belonged to Lily.

After James and Lily began dating, Lily was a frequent guest in our home. The younger kids loved playing with her, John would often chat with her, and, of course, she and James were inseparable. They even babysat Sophia and JJ every couple of weeks when John and I had our little date nights.

I had seen Lily use this phone lots of times. I remembered what James had said to the cops about him and Lily fighting because she had been spending too much time on her phone. Could he have smashed it or thrown it at a wall in anger? Could that mean he had physically hurt her, too?

As for the bracelet, James had bought it for her for their three-month anniversary. He asked me to take him to the mall and help him pick out something she would like. I had seen her wear this kind of minimalist jewelry before and thought she would like it. He came home beaming the next day, saying she had loved it and promised to wear it every single day. And as far as I knew, she had done just that. Whenever she came over after that, she always had the bracelet on.

I didn't want to believe my son could be capable of hurting someone. Especially someone he loved so dearly. I thought that raising him right would stop him from turning into his father, but the evidence in my hands seemed to prove otherwise.

What other explanation could there be as to why James had these items? In my mind, I could see clearly what had happened between the two and how it led to Lily's death. Lily had decided to break up with James and told him as much, returning the bracelet he had bought her. He freaked out and got angry. James, being unable to control his rage, threw her phone on the ground, accusing her of having feelings for someone else.

The fight got worse, and he tried to force her to stay with him, but she refused. Overwhelmed by his anger, his fingers wrapped around her throat, and her body went limp in his hands. He hadn't meant to hurt her, let alone kill her. He got scared, so he left the body there. He probably forgot he had the bracelet with him, and he took her phone since it could be used as evidence if it were found.

Eventually, he came home and pretended everything was normal. He denied he had hurt her in any way. Vowed that he loved her, which was technically true. And we believed him—we even got a lawyer to defend him.

I was sick to my stomach and could taste the acid rising to my throat. Tears were streaming down my face as I stayed on my knees, trembling. It was like déjà vu—he had turned into the one person I fought so hard to make sure he didn't turn into.

Eventually, I stood up. I was no longer crying. I went

downstairs, put on my coat, grabbed my purse, shoved the phone and bracelet inside it, and headed to the police station. I knew what I had to do.

It began to drizzle as I drove to the police station, dampening what had started out as a great day. I stared through the windshield, thinking of the day Trevor died and the promise I made to our son.

TWENTY-THREE

IT WAS A WARM, SUNNY DAY. THE BIRDS WERE CHIRPING, butterflies were flying, and everything seemed perfect. That was outside. Inside this apartment was a prison—my own personal hell. I woke up to the sound of a toddler screaming for attention. I rushed to his crib to feed him.

My hand still hurts from last night, and I felt faint. I was worn out from being the only one taking care of James and doing all the housework. Not to mention Trevor coming and going as he pleased. Hurting me every single time he was home.

I knew I needed to get away. If not for me, then for James. He deserved better than this. When I got pregnant, this was not the life I had envisioned for us. I was stupid enough to think that Trevor would do better, that he could actually change. I wasn't that stupid little girl anymore. I was now fully aware that this was exactly how it would always be if I stayed.

I know people think it's easy to leave an abusive relationship, that you can merely report them to the police. Well, I did report him to the police—multiple times. All it did was piss him off. He would be out in a few days, and no matter how far I ran, he would always find us. I even moved to a different city once, but he still somehow found us.

Even if I could get away from him, where would I go? What would I do? No one wanted to hire a young mother who had barely finished high school. And the jobs that were available didn't pay enough for me to survive on my own, let alone for both James and me. Plus, I would have to pay for daycare because there was no one else that I could leave him with.

I finished feeding James and played with him till he was tuckered out. He was a great kid, smart too. He started talking pretty early and hasn't shut up since. He turned three a couple of days ago and was so curious about everything around him. I loved it. He was now my favorite person to talk to, often the only person I talked to for days. He was still innocent and pure. Life hadn't hurt him yet. He saw the world as we do when we're kids. He was wide-eyed and unafraid. No care for the future whatsoever. Just living in the moment.

I wondered if I was ever like that, if I was ever truly carefree. When I tried to think of my childhood, the only memories that came to mind were of me waiting at home alone, anxiously, hoping my mother hadn't forgotten about me or abandoned me. Even at a very young age, all I'd been accustomed to was fear and loneliness.

I never wanted James to feel that way. I wanted him to know that even if he had no one else in the world, he would always have me by his side.

We were both pretty tuckered out by the afternoon, so I put him down for a nap and decided to take one myself. I fell asleep as soon as my head hit the pillow. It was one of those dreamless slumbers where you're out cold. It felt good to not feel anything, to not think of anything, and just rest.

I awoke to someone roughly shaking me, and before I was even fully awake, I found myself on the floor. I blinked in confusion, trying to figure out what was happening.

"You lazy fucking bitch. You're here sleeping while I slave

away trying to provide for our family?" Trevor was yelling in my face, pulling me up by my hair.

My heart pounded in my chest—not out of fear for myself because I knew that this wouldn't end well for me either way— but in fear for James. Please don't let him wake up. I never want him to see me this way. I never wanted him to see his mother as a powerless victim.

"Please, you'll wake James," I pleaded.

I saw something shift in Trevor's eyes and knew that I should have kept my mouth shut.

"What did you say to me? You think you have the right to tell me what to do?" he screamed, slapping me with the back of his hand. I could hear James crying in his bedroom and silently prayed that he would stay there and not come in here. My heart sank when I saw him standing at our door a few seconds later, clutching his stuffed teddy bear, crying.

"Shut the fuck up!" Trevor yelled at James, turning toward him.

"Don't touch him," I warned him, getting up.

But he ignored me and grabbed James by his shirt. James's eyes widened in terror. I knew I had to protect him. Lying his hands on me was one thing, but I would never let him touch my son.

I grabbed the lamp on the nightstand and hit Trevor on the back of his head with it as hard as I could. He fell silently to the ground, twitching a little and then no longer moving at all. James cried even louder, and I stood there in shock, not knowing what to do next. After a few seconds, I realized I needed to get James away from all this. I didn't want him to be scarred for life.

I grabbed his hand and practically dragged him to his bedroom. Kneeling in front of him, I looked him in the eyes.

"I need you to stay here till I tell you to come out, okay?" I instructed. "And I need you to forget what you saw. Nothing happened. Okay, sweetheart?" He nodded, and I picked him up and sat him down on his little bed. He stayed there, still sobbing but silently now.

I hurried back to our bedroom. Trevor still wasn't moving. Slowly, I kneeled down and touched his neck and then his wrist. No pulse. He was dead. The blood pooling around his head had already hinted to me that he was, but I had to make sure.

I knew I had to make this look like an accident. I couldn't lose James. He needed a mother. With no one else to take care of him, he would end up in the system. Or perhaps worse, with my mother.

Suddenly, I had an idea. I ran to our living room and grabbed the ladder that had been there near the couch. I dragged it to my bedroom and put it beside Trevor. I grabbed the telephone by our bedside and called 911. Thankfully, there was a lightbulb close by. I threw it on the ground beside the body, watching it shatter. I examined the lamp. There were drops of his blood on it. I would have to hide that, too.

I remembered the giant stuffed teddy bear we had gotten James—the thing was bigger than I was. Quickly, I ran to the kitchen, grabbed a knife, and headed to James's bedroom. With shaky hands, I started cutting. Soon, the bear was missing a sizable chunk at the back, and I quickly shoved in the lamp. This will have to do for now.

I leaned the bear against the wall, hoping no one would move it around enough to notice. Tomorrow, I will sew it back together. And once this mess was done with, I would discreetly get rid of the bear and, with it, the lamp.

I sat down next to the dead body, and eventually, James came and sat next to me. We both cried, holding one another.

"I will always protect you, James. Mommy will always protect you," I promised him, kissing the top of his little head.

In a few minutes, the ambulance arrived, followed shortly by the police. There were two of them. One was a man, middle-aged and balding. The other was a woman. She was quite young and reserved. They asked me question after question. I could tell they were suspicious. I hadn't done a very good job of making it look like an accident, but to be fair, this was the first time I had ever killed someone.

I never thought I would be capable of murder. I thought I would at least be remorseful at some point. But I wasn't. I didn't feel guilty at all. I just felt... free. Like I could finally breathe again.

"So ... he fell while on the ladder, hit his head, and died?" the male officer asked skeptically.

"He was... intoxicated. He was definitely drunk and may have been on some kind of drug or drugs," I explained.

He studied me for a few seconds and then jotted something down.

"And are you on something?" he asked.

"No, sir." I shook my head.

"I see. Well, we're going to need to examine the body and get back to you. Please don't travel till we've concluded the investigation."

They came over again soon after, confirming that he had been on multiple substances before he died. They still kept asking me questions, though. For days, they badgered me until I was almost ready to break. I was seriously considering confessing when the female officer showed up at my doorstep out of the blue. I invited her in, and we began talking.

"I couldn't help but notice the bruise on your arm and wrist the other day," she told me.

"I... um... fell," I said, lowering my gaze.

"Your son is adorable," she continued.

"Thank you," I told her, not knowing where she was going with this.

"I know what you did, Sally," she quietly informed me.

"Please, you don't understand," I sobbed.

"I do, actually," she said, frowning slightly.

"My best friend, she died a few years ago. She was in an abusive relationship, and I never noticed the signs. The bastard killed her, and they gave him two years in prison. Two fucking years and he's back out. Doing the same thing again." Her nose was flared, and her left hand was clenched into a fist.

"I know you were stuck with him, and I know you did what you had to. If you say he fell off a ladder and died, then he fell off a ladder and died. Case closed."

I sobbed even harder, but this time in relief. She put her hand on my shoulder and squeezed it slightly. I simply sat there, barely hearing her when she got up and left. I hugged James as hard as I could as soon as my mind finally accepted what had happened and what this meant for us. We were free. We were finally free.

I didn't know what we would do, how we would survive, but I knew we would. We would make it somehow. I would do whatever it took.

"I will always protect you," I promised him once more, kissing the top of his head.

The next day, I packed our bags and left the city. It was time for a new beginning for the two of us.

TWENTY-FOUR

I PULLED UP TO THE POLICE STATION AND TOOK A DEEP BREATH. My left hand was in my purse, rummaging around for my phone. There was one last thing I needed to do before I went in.

> I love you

I typed and sent.

I was usually an emotional person, quick to tears. But right now, I felt nothing at all. It was like my heart had suddenly become numb. I couldn't be sure, but I think it was the fact that my body had been in stress mode for too long. It had sort of given up trying. It had accepted that this was our new normal again. Or maybe I was still in shock from what I had discovered in James's room.

I walked into the police station, dripping from the rain. I was hoping to ask for either Officer Smith or Officer Jones, but I happened to see Officer Smith right near the entrance.

"Hi, I'm Sally, James's mother," I introduced myself to him, although I was pretty sure he knew who I was by this point.

"Right, how are you? What are you doing here?" he asked, peering at me curiously.

"I need to talk to you about the case. Lily's murder, I mean," I specified.

He nodded and motioned for me to follow him. He took me to his desk and gestured for me to sit in the chair opposite his. My hands were clammy, and I was no longer as calm as I had been in the car. The anxiety was hitting every nerve in my body. The thunder rumbled outside, the sudden sound making me flinch.

"So, what did you want to talk to me about?" asked Officer Smith, taking a sip of the coffee in his hand.

"It's about Lily's death. I think you need to see this," I told him.

I pulled out her smashed cell phone and bracelet from my purse and put them on his table.

"This belonged to Lily. It's her cell phone and a bracelet my son had bought her," I explained.

"I see… and how did these items come into your possession?" questioned Officer Smith, sitting up and putting the coffee down. He was visibly more interested and attentive now. Staring me right in the eyes, searching for answers.

I swallowed and took a deep breath.

"I had it. I had hidden it in our house under a floorboard. I'm the one who killed Lily," I lied.

He raised his eyebrows in shock and disbelief.

"Why did you kill her?" he asked slowly.

"She wasn't good enough for my James. At first, I thought it was just a fling, and I didn't care too much, but it became more. I was worried she would destroy James's life. I had to protect my son." That last part was true, even if the confession was a lie.

"So, you strangled her because she wasn't good enough for James?" he asked, bewildered.

"Yes, I didn't know they had broken up, and I didn't think

the blame would fall on James since he was always such a great boyfriend to her. I assumed you wouldn't find enough evidence and the case would be forgotten over time," I said, trying to sound calm, but the slight tremor in my voice gave away my anxiety.

"How do I know you're not confessing to protect your son?" he asked, leaning forward.

Fuck. Why would he ask me that? I already confessed—take it and leave James alone.

"I'm not lying. You can ask anyone—Lily and I did not see eye to eye, and I always thought she was wrong for James," I said, hoping he would buy it.

"We've been investigating James for a while now. Why didn't you come forward sooner?"

"I thought it would all blow over, but with the raid and everything, I couldn't risk James being blamed for something I did," I answered as quickly as I could.

"I see. Well, we'll be investigating this further, but for now, you're under arrest for the murder of Lily Johnson," Officer Smith informed me, getting up and handcuffing my wrists. "You have the right to remain silent…"

LOOKING BACK TO THE DAY I TURNED MYSELF IN, I FEEL NOTHING but regret. If I knew then what I know now, I would never have interfered.

What I've realized since is that we have no control over anything in this world. We simply have the illusion of it. And to that, we are absolutely addicted. Constantly fidgeting with everything, thinking we're one tweak away from perfection.

Even though deep down we know there is no magic formula to achieving the perfect life. One without complications, pain, heartbreaks, betrayals, and unexpected life-changing moments. Yet we are caught off guard every single time when it happens.

I don't know if it was fate that led me to the police station or if it was my insistent need for control. But of one thing I am absolutely certain. In the end, I alone was to blame for the destruction of my family.

My mother always told me no one has a perfect marriage. Or a perfect family. Or a perfect life. I guess she was right after all.

TWENTY-FIVE

My mother always told me that I was her *perfect* little boy. I don't think she even realized when she called me that anymore. But hearing her say it made me internally cringe every single time. I hated that fucking word. I hated every single thing about it and the pressure it came with.

I always knew I wasn't perfect. That I was different and not in a good way. There was something about me, something that was off. And I think everyone eventually noticed it, but her. She was constantly preoccupied with perfection to the point that she pretty much closed her eyes to reality. She was oblivious to the things happening right in front of her.

What was off about me? Well, most kids got annoyed when someone took their stuff or teased them. I got irrationally angry. I tried to hurt anyone who pissed me off. I flipped tables, hit them with chairs, scratched, punched—pretty much anything that would make them bleed. And I knew I had the potential to hurt them and hurt them badly enough that they would never piss me off again. And a lot of times I wanted to.

I tried my best to hide that side of me from everyone, my parents and siblings especially. I never wanted them to see that side of me. Hell, I didn't even want to see that side of me. And I certainly didn't want to live with it. As I got older, I got much better at hiding it. Especially from my mom. I always wanted to be the perfect son she thought I was.

But things went south pretty fast once I became a teenager. It was as though the rage inside me grew into a flaming red ball. I had almost no control of myself. Every time I got angry, I had these thoughts. These scary, violent thoughts.

Once I had calmed down, the guilt and regret set in, and I was immediately sorry. But at that moment, all I wanted to do was hurt someone. I could picture hurting them in my head, and I'm ashamed to admit that it felt amazing. Even thinking about it was beyond satisfying.

Despite my problems, I never had a particularly difficult time fitting in at school. I mean, I was a football player and pretty decent-looking. It was easy enough to make friends. Ian was one of my closest friends, probably my best friend. Our friendship had lasted over a decade already, and we were still closer than ever.

We had quite a bit in common, but the main thing was that we were both into all things sports. We joined the football team together, watched sports games together, and rooted for the same teams. No one in my family was particularly interested in sports, not even my dad, so it was nice having someone I could enjoy that with.

He had always been strikingly attractive, and by the time we were teens, we pretty much never went anywhere without some girl or another trying to get his attention. His straight blond hair fell effortlessly, hiding his forehead and accentuating his angular jawline. His toned arms and athletic build made it clear he was a football player. So it was no surprise when he told me he was going to ask out the head cheerleader. And it was also no surprise when she said yes.

Her name was Patricia, and she was beautiful, with strawberry-blonde hair, blue doe eyes, and an incredible body. She was curvy, flirty, extroverted, and insanely hot.

I didn't hate her, but I didn't particularly like her either. I found her to be kind of self-absorbed and controlling. But if he was happy with her, I was happy for him.

Generally, I tried to stay out of her way because she and I had pretty much nothing in common, nor did we enjoy one another's company. Which is why I was surprised when she texted me out of the blue. I instinctively knew she must want something because she avoided me as much as I did her.

Unsurprisingly, she did want something. She wanted to set me up with a friend of hers called Lily. Lily had only moved here a couple of weeks ago, but she and Patricia had already become close friends, from what I could tell. Lily was in a couple of my classes and was sort of the polar opposite of Patricia. She was quiet and introverted, keeping her cautious green eyes lowered most of the time. Lily was pretty too, but in more of a non-traditional way. She had dark hair that was usually tied into a tight ponytail, clear olive skin, and a petite frame. And that was pretty much all I knew about her at that point.

I wasn't sure I wanted to go on a date with her. I wasn't interested in her in that way. I told Patricia as much, but she wasn't the type to take no for an answer. So, instead of confronting me directly, she made Ian reach out and ask me why I didn't want to go on a double date with them.

I told him I wasn't into Lily. But he said it wasn't a big deal —it wasn't serious. We could all hang out, and if I had a good time, I could ask her out again, and if not, we could end it there. Lily, according to Patricia, was okay with that.

I said yes, mostly to get them off my back. After all, it was only one date. No pressure, right? I mean, how could this possibly go wrong?

TWENTY-SIX

Ian and I arrived at the pizza place earlier and waited for the girls. It was a little family-run Italian restaurant that had been around for ages. The decor was kind of tacky, but it had decent food and was nice enough for a date. Despite the cheesy Italian music in the background, of course.

I was suddenly nervous. I didn't date much—I'd never really met anyone I was drawn to enough to date. I often had a hard time connecting with people in general, but especially with girls. It was like they were from a whole different planet.

I didn't tell my parents about the date because I knew they would be weird about it. My mom was already being weird about me getting older, and I didn't want to rock the boat with this. Especially since it wasn't anything serious.

The girls arrived fashionably late, and the first thing I noticed was that Lily looked strikingly different from how she did at school. She was wearing an oversized T-shirt, baggy jeans, and black boots. Her curly black hair was down for a change, covering the sides of her face. It was messier than usual, but she pulled it off. What I noticed most was that she was smiling, and her smile lit up the room as she walked in.

I gazed at her shirt and saw characters from the TV show *It's Always Sunny in Philadelphia* on it. I loved that show, and everyone else I knew hated it, which meant I never had anyone to talk about it with. I needed to know if she was just wearing the shirt or actually enjoyed the show.

"Hey," they both said casually and giggled when they realized they had spoken in unison.

We smiled politely and said our hellos.

"Nice shirt," I mentioned to Lily.

"Thanks. I love *Sunny*," she replied.

"Right? It's literally incredible," I excitedly agreed.

"Absolutely. I don't generally trust men, but if I were stuck in an elevator with the guys from that show, I know I would be safe," she joked.

"I mean, same," I shrugged, laughing.

"Charlie over the bear any day," Lily laughed.

"Again, same," I agreed.

We spent most of dinner talking and making each other laugh. We had tons in common, and our conversation was never uncomfortable or forced. It was a genuinely fun time, and we sort of clicked. We listened to the same music, watched the same TV shows and movies, and we both loved to read. And not only that. She was genuinely the funniest, most intelligent girl I had ever met. For the first time, I was at ease talking to a girl.

I was glad Ian had convinced me to come here tonight. I would never have otherwise met someone I could vibe with like this. After dinner, I told Lily that I had a good time and enjoyed talking to her. I asked her for her Instagram in case she wanted to keep the conversation going, but she told me she wasn't on social media. She did give me her phone number, though, much to my relief.

We said goodbye but kept talking on the phone. At school, we soon became inseparable. We would spend lunch together, along with any other free time we had. Sadly, though, neither of us had a lot of free time, even outside of school. I was busy with football and some of the other extracurricular activities I was involved in. Lily was preoccupied with learning violin.

However, we still tried to make time for one another, and I appreciated how much effort she put into our relationship. For my birthday, she made me these beautiful cupcakes from scratch. They were incredible, and I knew how busy she was, which made me appreciate her effort even more. The days flew by, and I was euphoric. It was like I was in heaven.

She always went out of her way to remind me that I was important to her, and I tried to do the same. I would buy her things when I could, make sure I took her out on dates often, and always let her pick the movie or TV show we were watching. Not that it was ever an issue for us, since we generally loved the same stuff.

I remember our first date, or I guess second, if you count the double date. I had been nervous as hell because I had realized by then how much I was into her. We decided to go to a bookstore since we both enjoyed reading, and it was beyond perfect. As we strolled from one corner to the next, pulling out every book we thought would be interesting, I couldn't help but be mesmerized by her instead of the books.

She was wearing her signature black leather boots, a full-length skirt, and a plain white T-shirt. Her hair was all over the place, but looked perfect anyway. I followed her lovely emerald green eyes. The way they beamed as she scanned book after book, and the way they lit up when her delicate fingers, adorned with silver rings, flipped through the pages. All I wanted to do was take her in my arms and press my lips against hers. But of course, I was a gentleman and held my composure.

For our second date, I took her to dinner at one of the

fancier restaurants in our town. Of course, it was probably nothing compared to what she was used to in New York, but she seemed to enjoy herself. As a present, I got her some chocolates and a book I noticed her browsing through at the bookstore.

We stayed as long as we could, and I could tell she didn't want the night to end either. There was a sadness about her when she had to go back home, and I took that as a good sign. She enjoyed my company as much as I enjoyed hers. All our dates had been amazing so far; I could tell I was falling head over heels for her.

Tonight, we were watching a classic, *The Silence of the Lambs*. A murderous cannibal, a serial killer on the loose, a brilliant detective with a troubled past. What could be better?

It was just the two of us this evening, and we were seated on the couch, holding one another. I was gently rubbing Lily's arm, our eyes fixed on the television screen. I loved how she would flinch and hold me tighter when she got scared, gazing up at me to gauge my reaction.

"You know, I almost always prefer the book more than the movie, but they did a fucking great job with this one," Lily told me when the movie ended.

"For sure. I mean no shade to the book, but this movie is an absolute classic," I agreed.

We had decided to read the trilogy before watching the movies, as we usually did. I know, a jock who loves to read, I was anything but a cliché. The truth is, my parents, especially my mom, got me into reading pretty early on. By the time I was eight, I was reading at a much higher level than any of my classmates and finishing multiple books a week.

Lily was similar. She devoured books with a passion, even with her busy schedule. She even stayed up most of last night finishing *Hannibal,* the final book of the trilogy. I knew that because she texted me every few minutes with her reaction to something in the book. It was adorable. Sure, I didn't sleep most of the night either, since I was busy responding to her texts, but it was worth it.

"What do you think it's like?" asked Lily.

"What?" I responded, confused by her sudden change of tone.

TWENTY-SEVEN

"WHAT DO YOU THINK DEATH IS LIKE, I MEAN," LILY elaborated.

It was such a random question that it threw me off. To be honest, I didn't think about death a lot. At least I tried not to. Because when I did think about death, I thought about what it would be like to watch someone die. See the life leave their eyes.

And sometimes, I would think about what it would be like to be the person taking their life. To press down on their neck till they stop struggling. Or push a knife into their flesh again and again till the life drains from them.

Of course, I couldn't tell Lily that. She would think I was crazy. Even I thought I was crazy sometimes. But I couldn't stop thinking about that stuff. Especially when I got angry. My mind went to dark places, no matter how much I tried to control it.

"I don't know. I haven't really thought about it that much," I said.

"I think about it a lot," Lily confessed, glancing up at me.

"Really?" I asked her.

But I sort of knew why. Her real dad had died not too long ago, and as much as she tried to act strong, I knew it affected her deeply. I saw the sadness in her eyes when she talked about him, the reminiscent look she got when she thought about the memories they had together. And I think the whole situation was even worse because she was constantly butting heads with her stepdad, Paul.

"I don't know. Sometimes I just feel like death would be so much more peaceful than being alive. Being alive is so boring. There's never any real excitement," Lily said quietly, fidgeting with her hands.

"What do you mean?" I asked, raising my eyebrows in surprise.

This was sort of confusing to hear. I was aware that Lily was unhappy with her living situation because of how strict her mom and stepdad were, but I never realized that she was *bored*.

"I don't know, I just… sometimes I wish there was more to life. My life is so stagnant right now. It's like I've been stuck in purgatory. At this point, I would pick hell over purgatory. I'm just so sick of it," she explained, sighing.

"We're still young, Lil. We'll have a lot more adventures when we get older and have our own lives," I tried to comfort her.

It was difficult not to take this conversation personally— was she saying that our relationship was boring? That I wasn't exciting enough for her?

"I guess. I don't know, everything is mundane right now. I wish life were like the movies or books," she continued.

"Are you saying you're bored with me or something?" I flat-out asked her.

"Oh no, not at all—if anything, you're the only good thing in my life right now," she reassured me, giving me a peck on the cheek.

I smiled down at her, and she smiled back. But her eyes were distant. As if she were lost in another world.

"Do you believe in heaven?" she asked me.

"No, do you?" I asked back.

"Yeah, maybe… I'm not sure. I used to believe in heaven and hell. But I don't know if I still do." Lily frowned.

"We never went to church or even talked much about religion," I said.

"You're lucky. It's kind of a fucking mess. It puts all these thoughts into your head that make you feel scared all the time. You sort of become a decent person because of the fear of hell, not because you care or genuinely want to be good. And then you question your faith as you get older, and suddenly you have no more reason to be good." Lily shrugged.

I ran my hand through my hair, digesting what she had said.

"My parents never used religion to teach us right from wrong. They just taught it to us, but I still don't think I'm a good person. I don't know if any of us are truly good," I admitted.

"I don't think we are. I know I'm not, even though my mother shoved religion down my throat without ever bothering to answer the questions I had about it," Lily said.

"What kind of questions?" I asked, curious now.

"I don't know, the usual ones. Like, if we have free will, why are we punished for exercising it and not doing exactly as God wants us to do? Why do religions cause all the problems in the world? Stuff like that."

"Well, I wouldn't say *all* the problems, but I see where you're coming from," I agreed.

"Do you believe in God?" she questioned, studying me curiously.

"No, not really. You?"

"Maybe, probably. I've never known anything else. Right now, though, I believe in God, but I don't like God. If that makes any sense."

"It does. That's sort of the reason I *don't* believe in God. He sits there judging us, but he's the one who created us imperfectly and gave us free will and then gets mad at us for it. He created us imperfectly but expects perfection from us. What kind of bullshit is that? It's like we're some sort of fucked up science experiment."

"That's exactly it… you get me," Lily told me, squeezing my arm and putting her head on my shoulder.

I thought about our conversation as I lay in bed that night. God, religion, morals. Were any of us inherently good? Or were we all different levels of fucked up? Were we just one bad thing away from being a monster?

TWENTY-EIGHT

Things went back to normal with Lily after our talk. We didn't mention that conversation or speak about anything that serious again. Everything seemed good between us, or so I thought.

"My parents aren't going to be home on Friday night and want me to babysit. Wanna come over and chill?" I asked Lily as we sat in my car at lunchtime. "It would just be the two of us…"

She took a drag of the joint in her hand and closed her eyes, blowing out the smoke.

"Sure, sounds fun," she said, handing me back the joint.

We sat in the car for a while, enjoying one another's company. It was a nice day, bright and sunny. Eventually, we went back inside when we heard the bell. I saw her head to her class with Brian. She never even talked to him before, and I had never seen them hang out together. But today they were laughing and talking like they had been friends forever. It was weird. I decided to let it go and walked to my math class.

"Hey." Ian nodded as I sat next to him.

"Hey, man," I replied.

"So, did Lily tell you about Saturday?" he asked.

"No, what about Saturday?" I questioned.

"The music students are going on some trip. My dad's

going, and I heard Lily was going too. And my mom's away for the weekend, visiting my aunt. Do you wanna come over and hang out? I'm probably throwing a party," suggested Ian, enthusiastically.

"Sounds awesome. I'll be there… Lily didn't tell me that, though. Is that weird?" I asked him.

"Maybe she forgot," replied Ian, shrugging.

Usually, Lily and I were pretty in sync. We always told each other about stuff like this. I mean, I had even invited her to come over on Friday, and she still didn't mention that she wouldn't be around on the weekend. It could be that she had simply forgotten. Although this wasn't the sort of thing I would expect her to forget about.

Instead of asking her about it directly, I decided to wait till Friday and see if she brought it up herself. If she *had* forgotten to tell me about the trip, she would probably remember and tell me sooner or later. And if not, I would have to figure out how to confront her and ask her why she hadn't mentioned it.

The rest of the week went by pretty fast, but Lily still hadn't spoken a word about the trip. I even hinted at it, asking her if she had any weekend plans. She shrugged and said she didn't have any solid plans yet.

"Do you know who else is going on the trip?" I asked Ian on Friday during lunch.

Patricia was out sick. Apparently, she had an awful cold. And Lily was spending lunch in the music room, something to do with the talent show. So it was just the two of us at our table.

I was still pretty hung up on why Lily was hiding this trip from me. Not only was she doing that, but she had also grown distant over the last few days. I noticed that she had been spending more time with Brian, though, much to my disappointment. I had tried to probe her about that, but she kept insisting it was because they were both helping with the talent show.

I asked Ian about who else was going on the trip. As much as I trusted Lily, I was really hoping Brian wouldn't be going. I was not comfortable with the idea of them spending that much time together.

"Um, not too sure, but I think it's Lily, Fiona, Jack, Tommy, and Brian," he told me.

Damn it. Fucking Brian. He was really starting to get on my nerves.

"Fucking Brian," I muttered.

"What?" asked Ian, glancing up from his food.

"It's just… that guy's been hanging out with Lily a lot recently."

"Yeah, I noticed that too, but Patricia said they were just friends and were vibing because they both love music," he explained, shoving some more tater tots into his mouth.

"Seriously? Everyone loves music. That doesn't make him fucking special," I responded, still irritated.

"Chill, man. Lily's a nice girl," Ian told me, putting his hand on my shoulder.

"I know she is. It's him I'm worried about."

"He's some rando music nerd. He's not going to fuck around with a football player's girl unless he has a death wish," Ian laughed, rolling his eyes.

I chuckled too and knew he was probably right. Brian was no more than 5'8", his braces were painfully noticeable, and he weighed like a hundred pounds soaking wet. But deep down, I still had a weird feeling about him.

TWENTY-NINE

"Hey, babe," said Lily when I opened my front door for her.

"Hey," I said, giving her a quick kiss.

"Come in," I told her, opening the door wider.

She looked beautiful today, and for a second, my anger evaporated as I gazed at her. Surprisingly, she was wearing a tight red crop top, a short skirt, and sneakers. She usually dressed much more casually and rarely wore this much makeup. A thought crept into my mind that made me mad again. Could the sudden change in style have something to do with Brian?

"Hey, Lily," my mom said, coming out of the kitchen to greet Lily before she and my dad left.

She was wearing a navy-blue dress and high heels and had a tight, forced smile on her face. It was obvious she didn't like Lily. Although she would never tell me that to my face, she had hinted at it a few times. She thought I could do better. But I didn't want to do better. Lily was not perfect, but it had always been her imperfection that had drawn me to her.

As soon as my parents left, we went into the living room and sat down on the couch. Soph and JJ were playing in the backyard, so we would be able to relax before the annoying parts of babysitting started. Although my brother and sister weren't too bad. They were good kids and pretty independent, which thankfully meant that there wasn't much we had to do except check in on them every once in a while.

I wanted to talk to Lily about the trip before they took up most of our attention. She was staring intently at her phone, a small smile on her lips.

"Who are you talking to?" I asked.

"Just Brian," she told me casually, but I noticed her angle her phone away from me, so I couldn't see what was on the screen.

"Oh… speaking of which, I heard the music students were going on a trip this weekend," I said, trying to get the conversation going.

"Oh… yeah…" Lily said, still intently staring at her phone.

"You didn't tell me about that," I mentioned.

"Oh, didn't I? My bad, I thought I told you on Monday," she replied.

"Nope … it's kinda weird that you didn't," I said.

"What do you mean? Obviously, I forgot. Why would I hide it from you?"

"Why *would* you hide it from me?"

"Are you fucking serious right now?" asked Lily, glaring at me.

"Yeah, why the fuck are you lying to me about shit?" I asked her, getting irritated too.

She had this look on her face, like this conversation was an inconvenience to her. Like I was an inconvenience to her, and it was getting on my fucking nerves.

"So now I'm a *liar*? All I did was forget to tell you one fucking thing, and I'm suddenly being treated as if I'm a criminal?"

The fact that she thought she could gaslight me and get away with clearly lying to my face was crazy.

"I brought up this weekend a bunch of times all week, and you didn't say anything," I pointed out.

"This is ridiculous. Did you seriously invite me over to argue with me? You are so petty sometimes!" Lily yelled.

"I'm petty? Okay, well, you're a lying, gaslighting bitch. How about that?" I yelled back.

"Wow, I'm really starting to see the real you, James."

"And I'm starting to see the real you, too, Lily. It's too bad Brian doesn't see this side of you, or he'd have run for the hills instead of hitting on you."

"Oh my God, not this again. I told you, Brian and I are just friends. I'm not allowed to have male friends now?"

"Of course, you can have whatever friends you want. But I don't want them to take up all your time."

"You are such a spoiled brat. Everything is always about you, isn't it? Guess what, James? The world doesn't fucking revolve around you!" shouted Lily. "If I want to talk to Brian, I will."

"No, you fucking won't."

"You can't tell me who I can and cannot talk to." Lily crossed her arms across her chest.

Her face was flushed, and I could see in her eyes that she was as frustrated with this conversation as I was. And the logical part of my brain was signaling to me that we needed to de-escalate the situation. But the logical part wasn't in charge right now.

"Looks like I just did," I said, raising my eyebrows in just as much defiance.

"Yeah, well, fuck you."

"You clearly lied to me and are still lying to me. This little victim act of yours is not working," I informed her.

"You're right. I did hide it from you. Are you happy now?"

"No, because that's such a fucking weird thing to do. Why would you even do that?"

"*Really*? You don't know why?" she asked sarcastically.

How the fuck was I supposed to know why she had suddenly changed into a whole different person? I wasn't a mind reader.

"No, I don't!"

"THIS IS WHY! You're so weird about me being friends with Brian. I knew you would be weird about the trip, too!" Lily screeched. "I am sick and fucking tired of everyone trying to control me and tell me what to do and how to live. I'm sick and tired of your weird obsession with Brian. I can't do this anymore. I can't have the same fucking conversation every day."

Lily got up from the couch and began walking toward the front door.

"Where the fuck are you going? You can't just leave in the middle of our conversation," I said, following close behind her.

"Yes, I can. I'm done. Don't call me," she said.

I grabbed her arm and yanked her away from the door and toward me. Our faces were only an inch or so away, and I saw her eyes widen in terror. I wanted to stop. I wanted to let go of her, but something took over me.

"You are not fucking breaking up with me," I whispered menacingly.

"James, you're hurting me," she cried, tears falling down her flushed cheeks.

Her eyes silently pleaded with mine, quietly begging me to

stop. She had the same look on her face that animals have when they know they've been cornered. Her arm felt surprisingly tiny in my hand. If I squeezed even slightly harder, I could do some serious damage. Maybe even break it.

No, fuck. What the fuck was I doing? I was suddenly more afraid of what I would do to her than she was.

"I'm sorry. I'm so sorry, Lily," I apologized, taking a few steps back.

"Stay the fuck away from me," she warned, her voice heavy with emotion.

She slammed the front door behind her, and just like that, she was gone. I sank to the floor, my face in my hands.

THIRTY

I REALLY DIDN'T WANT TO GET OUT OF BED SATURDAY MORNING, but forced myself to. The birds were chirping loudly, I could hear kids on their bicycles outside, and even the bees seemed less annoyed than usual. *It was awful.*

The first thing I did was check my cell phone, my heart pounding. Still nothing from Lily. I had texted her a few times last night, apologizing profusely for my behavior. I even tried calling her, but she didn't pick up. It really sucked. I hated that she was mad at me, and I hated how I had behaved. In the end, I decided to give her some time to calm down and talk to her when she was ready.

I walked into the kitchen and saw my mom making pancakes for us. I wasn't in the mood to eat, but I knew she would ask a million questions if I didn't, so I grabbed a plate from the drawer and walked toward her.

"Hey, sweetie. You sleep okay?" she asked.

She looked well-rested and comfortable in her sweatpants and hoodie. Her hair was tied into a messy bun that sat slightly crookedly at the top of her head. She smiled as she put a pancake on my plate with a generous helping of butter and syrup.

I nodded, giving her a small smile. I was in no mood to have a conversation right now. I took my plate and sat down at the table beside my family. I would have preferred a quiet morning, but that was nearly impossible with two energetic younger siblings.

"Morning, James," my dad said, smiling.

I nodded at him and continued to play around with my pancake.

"Everything okay?" he asked.

He always knew when something was wrong. Even when I was younger, he could always sense it and tried to comfort me. I usually appreciated that, but today, I just wanted to be left alone.

"Yeah, I'm fine. By the way, I'll be staying over at Ian's tonight, since his parents are out of town," I said, trying to change the subject.

"Oh, yeah, sure. No big parties or anything though, right?" he asked.

"Nah, it's just a couple of us hanging out and playing D&D," I lied.

"No alcohol or anything?" He raised his eyebrows at me.

"Of course not, Dad."

Ian's parties were legendary for a reason. My parents didn't need to know that reason.

I spent most of the day trying to distract myself from thinking about Lily. But I couldn't stop myself from checking my phone on the way to Ian's to see if she had responded. Still nothing. My heart sank.

"Hey, man," grinned Ian as he opened his front door.

"Hey." I nodded and walked in.

A few people from school were already there when I arrived and were clearly less than sober. The speakers were blaring, and I could barely hear myself think. I wasn't in the right mood for this shit right now.

"Whoa, what's up with you, bro?" asked Ian, looking me up and down.

"Lily and I sort of had a fight," I explained.

"Damn, sorry about that. Wanna talk about it?" he questioned.

"I'm good," I replied, my hands in my pockets.

"I know what you need, man—you need to get fucking wasted," Ian told me, leading me to the table full of booze, among other things.

"Fuck yeah, I do," I agreed, grinning.

I grabbed one of the shot glasses and chugged it down. I needed this today. I needed to forget about Lily and blow off some steam.

"Hey, James," said Candice, touching my shoulder.

Candice was in the same year as us, and I recognized her from some of my classes. Her blue eyes, curvy body, long legs, and bleached blonde hair made her hard to miss. She was wearing a sparkly silver dress that was so short she had to keep pulling it down every few seconds to make sure she didn't flash anyone. It reminded me of that episode of *The Office* where Meredith wore an inappropriate dress for casual Friday.

"Oh, hey, Candice," I said loudly, trying to speak over the music.

"It's Candy, actually," she giggled.

"Candy it is then," I chuckled.

"Good boy," she told me, biting her lip.

"Umm… can I get you something to drink?" I asked her, quickly, glancing away.

She was definitely flirting with me, but I wasn't ready to flirt back tonight. I still had hope for my relationship with Lily and had no interest in flirting with anyone else.

"Yeah, thanks, I'd love a drink." Candy nodded, giggling again.

I smiled back politely this time, handing her a beer and quickly walking away with mine. I searched for Ian but didn't see him around.

I saw Jake, another guy on our football team, in the living room, and was told that Ian had gone to pick up Patricia. I decided to get some fresh air outside until they came back. I needed some peace and quiet. I glanced at my phone and saw that there was still nothing from Lily. I ran my hand through my hair. Was she thinking about me at all right now? Or was she too preoccupied with Brian and their stupid trip?

"There you are!" squeaked Candy, her high-pitched voice hitting my eardrums like shards of glass.

"Here I am," I joked, slightly slurring my words.

The alcohol was hitting me harder than it ever had before.

"What's wrong?" she asked me, sounding concerned.

"What do you mean?" I asked back.

"Nothing, you just... seem sad today," she explained, rubbing my forearm.

"Lily, my girlfriend, and I had a fight, and I think it's over between us," I confided in her.

The alcohol was making me extra blah.

"Oh no... well, it's her loss," Candy said.

"No, it's mine. I love her, she's amazing. I fucked up bad," I admitted, shaking my head.

"You poor baby," Candy rubbed my arm, trying to comfort me.

"Whoa," I said, suddenly lightheaded. My hands were shaky, and my vision was blurring.

I leaned against the wall for support and shook my head. I

was dizzy, which was weird—I had barely had anything to drink. Someone must have spiked the drinks. God fucking damn it.

"Um, why don't we go upstairs and lie down? You don't look so good," Candy suggested, leading me into the house and up the stairs. I followed her the best I could, slightly stumbling. Thankfully, she held onto me tightly till we got to Ian's room. I lay down on his bed, the messy white bedsheet cool on my skin, and closed my eyes till the dizziness began to subside.

THIRTY-ONE

I SLOWLY OPENED MY EYES A FEW MINUTES LATER, BLINKING AS they adjusted to the brightness. I had been in Ian's room so many times that I could probably point out each thing with my eyes closed. His lampshade, the bookshelf, the guitar in the corner, posters of his favorite football players stuck on the wall, and his school books sprawled all over the room.

"You know, I think there may have been something in the drinks," stated Candy, playing with a strand of her blonde hair.

"Ya think?" I asked sarcastically.

"Yeah, I do," she giggled.

For some reason, that made us laugh uncontrollably for a minute. As the laughter faded, we just lay on the bed, gazing into each other's eyes. She leaned forward, and our lips locked. A few seconds later, my hands were on her hips, pulling her body closer to mine. Her fingers were intertwined in my hair, tugging just the slightest bit.

We continued kissing for a while, and it felt good. Like really good. Lily and everything that had happened between us sort of evaporated from my mind. At this moment, it was Candy and me. It was pure, physical lust, and nothing else mattered. Heat radiated from her skin as she leaned her body closer, practically lying on top of me.

Things became more intense, and my fingers fumbled with her bra. Although I had done some things with girls before, I didn't have that much experience. Most guys I knew had already lost their virginity, bragging about it to anyone willing to listen. But I had wanted to wait till I found the right person.

I thought Lily would be that person. That we would be one another's first, but that seemed like less of a possibility now. I shook my head. I didn't want to think about her anymore. I wanted to forget about her and our stupid fight and stupid fucking Brian.

"Are you sure you want to do this?" I asked Candy as her hands began undoing my belt.

"More than anything," she growled seductively in my ear.

She kissed my neck, my chest, and kept moving lower till she found the object of her desire. She smelled so good, and her lips were like heaven. My breathing got heavier, and my fists clenched the bedsheets. I moaned louder, focusing solely on her lips. A few minutes later, I was lying on the bed trying to catch my breath.

"That was amazing," I sighed, running my hands through her hair as she lay down beside me.

"It was—we should do it again sometime." She winked.

"Hmm," I replied, not wanting to disagree out loud.

There were a few blissful minutes of heaven, but as my pulse slowed, the weight of what I had done began to dawn on me. I felt sick as the guilt settled in my stomach.

Fuck. Lily would kill me if she ever found out about this. I should never have kissed Candy or even gone upstairs with her. This was all a huge mistake. Ian and Patricia were on their way back. If Patricia found out I hooked up with Candy, she would absolutely tell Lily. And that would be the death of any chance I may have had of getting back together with her.

"Candy, this was great… but I love Lily," I admitted, hoping Candy wouldn't be too mad.

To my surprise, she threw her head back and laughed.

"Look, James, you're cute and all, but I have a boyfriend. I'm not interested in anything serious," she told me.

"You have a boyfriend?" I asked, incredulously.

Why the fuck wouldn't she tell me that before? I was angry at her for not clarifying that before, but deep down, I knew that it wouldn't have stopped either of us had she told me.

"Yeah, Brian Banigan—he's on some lame school trip this weekend," she said, pushing strands of her bleached hair out of her face.

"Wait, Brian is your boyfriend? What the fuck?" I was beyond shocked.

"Yeah, why?" she asked.

"Maybe because you just fucking blew me?" I angrily pointed out.

"So? We're not like super exclusive or anything. And aren't you the one who's hung up on that Lily chick?"

"Look, let's just keep this to ourselves, okay?" I sighed, defeated.

She was right—what I did was equally as fucked up as what she did.

"Duh," she said, rolling her eyes and hopping off the bed.

"This convo is officially lame, I'm going to go downstairs. I'll tell everyone I was helping you because you were dizzy and then you fell asleep, okay?" she told me, a bored expression on her face.

I nodded my consent to her lie, and she left. I sat on Ian's bed, feeling stupid and humiliated. Out of all the girls in the world, why did it have to be Brian's girlfriend? How in the world did he even get a girl like that? I had to make sure Lily never found out about this, or she would never speak to me again. These had to be the worst few days of my life. Everything was going downhill.

THIRTY-TWO

As I continued to lie on Ian's bed, what had just happened between Candy and me kept playing over and over again in my head. So did every possible scenario of what would happen if Lily found out. After a few minutes, I heard the door creak open and turned my head.

"Hey, man. You okay?" asked Ian, walking in and sitting at the edge of the bed.

He looked concerned, but also another emotion I couldn't quite figure out. Pity?

"No, I fucked up," I admitted.

"With Lily and the fight you guys had?" he asked.

"Yeah."

Among other things.

"Hey," said Patricia, walking in.

"Hey," I replied, sitting up.

"Lily told me what happened between you guys," she informed me.

Of course she did. Here comes the lecture about how I messed up and how amazing Lily is. I did not need this right now.

"She really fucked up," Patricia continued, shaking her head.

Wait, what?

"What?" I asked, confused.

"She fucked up, and I told her as much, and now she's kind of pissed at me too."

"What do you mean *she* fucked up?" I asked again.

"Well, you're a great guy, and you've been good to her. She's the one who's been acting so weird recently. She never wants to hang out anymore, and she's always on her phone," she explained. "It's like she's only around physically."

"I mean, I'm not cool with you yelling at her and shit, but, like, I get where the anger is coming from," Patricia clarified.

"She *has* been acting fucking weird," I enthusiastically agreed.

I was so relieved I wasn't the only one who noticed something was off about Lily recently. It wasn't all in my head, and I wasn't being crazy and paranoid. She had been acting odd, and even Patricia had noticed. Vindication. Sweet, sweet vindication.

"It still kind of sucks, though. We were so in sync, and then I don't know what happened all of a sudden," I explained to Patricia.

"I have no idea either, but it could have something to do with her mom and stepdad—they're, like, really weird," Patricia remarked.

"What do you mean?"

They always seemed normal to me. A little strict, but they were quite conservative, so that was sort of expected. Also, to be fair, most people in this town were extremely conservative- it wasn't anything out of the ordinary.

"I don't know, they're just weird about everything, and I think Lily doesn't like living with Paul since he's so creepy," she whispered the last part like it was a big secret.

"What do you mean weird?" I asked Patricia.

He seemed okay to me. An awful person, but in the usual way. Was there more to him than Lily had let on?

"Let's just say there's a reason I don't stay overnight at their place…" she shuddered.

"He didn't try anything with you, did he?" Ian chimed in, instantly defensive.

"No, I'm fine—he just has that vibe, you know?"

"Hmm, I guess." I had never gotten that vibe from him, but maybe that's because I wasn't a hot teenage girl.

"Anyway, chill here for tonight and talk to her when she gets back tomorrow evening. Her parents aren't going to be home till later because they have a dinner thing. Go talk to her in person, and I'm sure you guys can sort it out," Patricia assured me.

"Actually, I'm not in the mood to party tonight. I'm gonna head home. But I will be talking to her tomorrow when she gets back. Have fun, you guys," I said.

"Alright, man. See you at school," Ian told me. I nodded and headed out.

I avoided Candy, who was seated on the couch in the living room, laughing at something Jake said. That girl had issues, and I needed to stay as far away from her as I possibly could for probably the rest of my life. I was lucky she wanted as little to do with me now as I did with her. I didn't want to push my luck by being anywhere in her vicinity ever again.

I thought about Lily as I drove home. I once more wondered if she was thinking about me, too. Patricia was right, I would go see her tomorrow and sort all this out. I needed to know what was going on with her. I wanted the truth this time. And if she wasn't going to tell me, maybe I didn't want a relationship with her anymore either. This wasn't the Lily I had fallen in love with.

I walked into my house, trying to be extra quiet, assuming everyone had already gone to bed, but saw my parents seated on the couch, laughing. They were intently watching *Police Academy,* but turned their heads as I walked into the living room.

"James, I thought you were staying over at Ian's," my dad commented.

"Yeah, I decided to come back early." I shrugged.

"Wanna watch *Police Academy* with us?" asked my mom, patting the empty space on the couch next to her.

"Why not?" I sighed, settling down beside her.

She put her arm around my shoulder and kissed me on the cheek, to which I half-heartedly protested. It always felt amazing when she hugged me. But I couldn't have her knowing that.

As we watched the movie together, and I saw them smiling and laughing, I knew this was what I wanted. A real, honest relationship. No games, no drama—just happy moments. It's what I thought Lily's and my relationship would blossom into, but now I wasn't too sure. I wasn't too sure about anything anymore.

THIRTY-THREE

Sunday passed pretty quickly, and at about six p.m., as I was sitting in bed scrolling through TikTok, I finally received a text from Lily. She told me she was back and wanted to talk. She asked if I could go over to her place since her parents weren't home. Immediately, I agreed and headed over there. Thankfully, she didn't sound angry.

I was still feeling guilty about what had happened at Ian's party with Candy and had spent most of the night tossing and turning. I kept thinking about what would happen if Lily ever found out. My entire future with Lily depended on Candy keeping her mouth shut, and after my last experience with her, that did not seem to be her strong suit.

I knocked on the door when I reached Lily's house, but no one answered, so I rang the doorbell.

"Hey," Lily breathed, opening the door.

"Hey," I mumbled.

I nervously fidgeted with my fingers. I wasn't sure how this conversation would turn out. I had gone through a thousand scenarios in my head, but at the end of the day, we can never predict exactly what's going to happen.

"Come in," she instructed.

I followed her upstairs to her bedroom, passing the many pictures of Paul and her mom in the hallway. We sat down on her bed, facing one another. Her room smelled like flowers—it always did. We awkwardly stared at each other for a few seconds, not knowing where or how to begin the conversation. I finally spoke up, feeling like I owed her an apology.

"I'm really sorry about the other day. I shouldn't have freaked out on you. It's just that I've been feeling like you're pulling away from our relationship lately," I confessed.

She looked away, trying to avoid my eyes, but I caught the glimpse of sadness in hers.

"I'm sorry too, James. I've been so overwhelmed recently, and I think it made me kind of neglect our relationship. There's been a lot going on in my life," she admitted.

"Is something wrong at home?" I asked her, thinking about what Patricia had told me at the party.

"Not exactly. It's just been an adjustment moving in with Paul and moving to a new city. And I think Paul and my mom have been having some problems recently."

"What kind of problems?"

"I don't know. They've been going for counseling with the pastor, but Paul's been drinking a lot."

"That sucks. I'm sorry."

"Yeah, it does suck, but I shouldn't have taken it out on you. It's not your fault, my life is weird right now. You're a good guy, James. Probably one of the few good decisions I've ever made," she finally looked up at me with tears in her eyes.

She reached out for my hand and held it in hers. Her petite, polished fingers felt smooth and warm.

"I love you, Lil." I cupped her face with my other hand.

"I love you too," she murmured.

I was no longer able to hold back and kissed her. Her lips were soft, and I could taste her cherry-flavored lip gloss as the kiss deepened. As soon as our lips touched, it felt so fucking right. Not the rushed and animalistic feeling I had with Candy. This was love. It wasn't just our bodies coming together, intertwining, but our souls, too.

Slowly, our hands began to roam and before we knew it, our clothes were almost completely off. She looked breathtaking in the naturally dim light coming into her bedroom from the sunset outside her window. Her skin was slightly flushed, and her chest rose and fell with every breath.

"Are you sure you want to do this? We can wait if you aren't ready," I assured her.

"No, I'm ready… this feels right," she breathed.

"It really does," I agreed.

And with that, I grabbed her hair, gently pulling her head back and kissing her slender neck. She smelled amazing. It was intoxicating. As I continued to kiss her neck, my hands moved lower and unhooked her bra. I pressed my hands on her chest and felt her moan in my ear.

Soon, I was on top of her with one hand holding her hip and the other gently grabbing a handful of her hair. I could not believe how amazing this felt. I kept thinking about how completely different this was compared to my brief encounter with Candy. I hated that she had been my first sexual experience. This is what it should have been.

Whatever, I didn't want to think about any of that anymore. I wanted to enjoy this moment. Our first time together.

I could hear her moaning louder as I moved faster. Her hips rose to meet mine. Her fingernails dug into my back, and her legs tightened around my waist. And just as quickly as it had all begun, it ended—our bodies shuddering against one another.

We lay silently, both trying to catch our breath. I reached out and held her hand in mine. Her eyes were still shut, but she had a satisfied smile on her face.

A tiny part of me was still dying inside from the guilt and anxiety of what I had done with Candy. What if Lily somehow found out? I'll have messed all this up for nothing.

But for the most part, I was in heaven. Every nerve in my body was alive. My brain was flooded with happy hormones. I was so glad I came over, and I was happier than ever to have *my* Lily back.

"How was that for you?" I asked, rolling over to my side and gazing down at Lily.

"Amazing," she smiled.

"We should probably get dressed in case your parents come back early."

"Oh, yeah, that's a good idea," Lily confirmed.

I got up and began putting my clothes back on, and Lily did the same. Even in this state, with her hair disheveled and not so elegantly putting her clothes back on, she was still the most beautiful thing I had ever laid my eyes on.

"How was the trip?" I asked out of curiosity.

"It was okay. Kinda mid." She shrugged nonchalantly.

"Oh, okay… Again, I'm really sorry about freaking out," I apologized.

"I know, babe, and it's fine. I mean, don't ever do that again, but I forgive you this time," she told me.

I nodded and grabbed her in my arms, giving her a deep kiss. I left shortly after, but was still very much basking in the afterglow.

THIRTY-FOUR

On Monday morning, I was still on a high from the night before. Lily and I had been texting most of the night after I left, and things were finally back to how they used to be. We were cracking jokes, being silly, and mostly enjoying each other's company like we had before. We even decided to rewatch the *South Park* movie together on Friday. At my place, of course, her parents didn't approve of *South Park.* Which is honestly fair.

"You look happy," my mom observed when I sat down for breakfast.

"I am." I smiled.

"Good," she told me, smiling back.

"I take it you had a good time with Lily yesterday?" asked my dad.

"Yeah, we had… a good time," I replied.

I would never tell my parents that I was sexually active now, even though they were pretty relaxed about that stuff. For the most part, I was usually pretty honest with them, but this was definitely something I would be keeping to myself.

"Good, I like her for you—she's a sweet girl."

My dad was always genuinely nice to Lily. Unlike my mom, who was suddenly extremely preoccupied with the pieces of fruit on her plate.

"Thanks, Dad. I like her too."

I rushed to school after breakfast, hoping to spend some time with Lily before class. I walked down the hallway and noticed Patricia putting some books into her locker.

"Hey, Patricia, have you seen Lily around?"

"Um, I think she's in the music room," Patricia informed me.

"Got it, thanks."

"I take it that you two have officially made up after your little lovers' spat?" she asked.

"We have. Thanks for your advice, by the way. I went over to her place yesterday evening, and we sorted everything out. I think we're finally in sync again," I confided in her.

"Yeah, she and I talked too, and she kinda seems back to normal now. Maybe she just needed some time away from home, and the trip helped."

"Yeah, maybe. Anyway, I'm gonna go find her."

I hurried toward the music room, but as soon as I reached the door, I heard Lily talking in hushed tones. I couldn't make out what they were saying, but I assumed she was talking to Brian and wondered what they could be whispering about. For some reason, that struck a nerve with me. I clenched my fists, the anger bubbling up again.

No, I needed to keep myself in check. I had promised to trust Lily, and that's what I was going to do. This whole weekend had been a reminder to me that I needed to have faith in Lily and trust that she would never do anything to betray me.

I took a deep breath. The thing was, I did trust her, that wasn't the problem. It was Brian I didn't trust. If he were dating someone like Candy, he probably wasn't the most moral person out there. What if he tried to steal Lily away from me? Or even worse, what if he was telling her about Candy and me hooking up at Ian's party? Fuck, he was totally the kind of guy that would do that.

And then Lily would break up with me and get with him, which is exactly what he's wanted all this time.

I was going to remind him that she was mine, and he needed to back the fuck off. I barged into the music room, expecting Brian and Lily, but to my surprise, it turned out to be Lily and Mr. Live. They both turned toward me, startled. Damn it, I had overreacted again. What the actual fuck was wrong with me?

"James, nice of you to… visit the music room," said Mr. Live, smiling at me but clearly confused by my sudden appearance.

"Hey, Mr. Live, I just wanted to say hi to Lily before class," I explained, hoping they wouldn't notice how red my face was.

"Ah, I see. Lily, we're pretty much done here—maybe James could walk you to class?" he asked, grinning.

"That would be perfect," Lily confirmed before I could respond. I smiled at her, and she smiled back sweetly.

"Have a great day, you two," called Mr. Live as we walked out of the music room hand in hand and into the chaos-filled hallway.

"So…" I said, awkwardly.

I was hoping Lily had not noticed my more-than-dramatic entrance into the music room. That would not be a good look right after I had promised her I would trust her and give her more space.

"So… that was quite an entrance," she observed.

Damn it.

"Yeah, sorry—" I apologized.

"Don't worry about it. I know the door sticks sometimes. I

almost fell in one time when I first moved here," she chuckled nonchalantly.

Oh, thank God. For a second there, I was sure I was in trouble. I walked her to her math class before heading to my history class. It was nice to have these little moments with her again.

THIRTY-FIVE

"WANNA COME INSIDE? MY PARENTS ARE AT CHURCH FOR counseling. They probably won't be home for an hour or two," Lily told me as I stopped my car outside her house. I loved dropping her off. It meant I had a few extra minutes with her.

"Sounds good," I said.

We headed to her room, and she moved her nightstand to the side to reveal a few blunts in a Ziploc bag stashed behind it. She held them up and wiggled her eyebrows questioningly.

"Nice," I smiled and nodded.

"This will make it extra fun," she winked at me, handing me one of the blunts.

I pulled out my lighter, and we sat on her bed, enjoying the high for a while—the weed was definitely kicking in.

"Oh, my God, the episode where they get sued and Charlie's bird law skills actually come in handy is obviously the best episode!"

Lily was snickering so hard I was afraid she would fall right off the bed. Of course, we were arguing about the best Sunny episode of all time. These were the types of conversations I had missed having with her.

"Nope, the best episode will ALWAYS be the one where Charlie created Nightman. The lyrics for that song alone should have won *all* the awards," I argued, smirking.

"Okay, Nightman, it is—you're right, that episode is the greatest thing to happen on TV," Lily agreed.

"To say the least, Nightman may have somehow changed the course of time." I was exaggerating, but only slightly.

"Are we weird, or is Sunny the best show of all time?" Lily asked, running her fingers through her hair.

"The only weird people out there are the people who don't watch Sunny," I replied with a straight face.

"This is nice," she said, pulling me closer to her.

Our bodies were close enough that I could feel the heat radiating from hers. She felt amazing this close to me. As I lay there admiring her, she lifted her head and pressed her lips to mine. Faster than I expected, our clothes were all over the place once more.

"Oh God," she breathed against my neck, and I knew she was done.

With that, I let myself go and let the pleasure overpower me.

"Fuck," I gasped, pulling her closer to me.

We lay beside one another, enjoying the afterglow. I gazed down at her, and she smiled at me, lost in her own thoughts. I could tell she was far away, even though she was right beside me. And I was okay with that. I knew Lily lived in her own mind, and quite often, I did too.

"So, I hate to hit it and quit it, but my parents are probably gonna be home soon," Lily told me.

"I'll see you tomorrow, though?" I asked her.

She hesitated for a second, and my heart almost skipped a beat. I knew she was busy, but still hoped she would make time for me, for us. Today had been perfect. I wanted every day to be like that.

"Um, I'll let you know… I may have some music-related stuff going on," she explained, staring at her hands.

I didn't want her to feel suffocated again, so I told her that was fine, and I didn't mind at all. I would hang out with Ian if she were busy after school.

I left soon after and headed home. I would probably not see much of Lily for the rest of the week. Between football practice and her violin lessons, we only had a day or two during the week when we could properly hang out. If anything, she was going to be hanging out with Brian a lot more than me.

I shook my head to try to clear it of these negative thoughts. I didn't want to think of Brian anymore. I wasn't going to waste my time with him. Instead, I was going to focus on Lily and our relationship.

I walked into the house and heard my younger siblings shouting in the backyard. It made me want to cover my ears and run.

Ever since I was young, I hated loud noises. Not just the sound itself, but the way they literally made me cringe internally to the point where I would sometimes have to leave the room.

"There you are, sweetie," my mom said, walking toward me and interrupting my train of thought.

"Hey, Mom," I smiled.

"You're back late. Were you at school or something?" she asked me.

"No, I was over at Ian's," I lied.

I didn't want to lie to her, but I knew she would give me that fake smile with the hidden disappointment in her eyes if I told her who I had actually been with. I had a great time with Lily and didn't want my mom's judgment ruining it for me.

"Oh, that's nice. Hope you two had fun," she said with a smile.

"Is dinner almost ready?" I asked her.

I hadn't even been trying to change the subject then—the munchies were just really kicking in.

"It'll be ready in a bit. Why don't you freshen up and come downstairs?"

"Okay, cool," I said, heading upstairs.

The smell of my mom's cooking intoxicated me as I reached my bedroom. All parents have flaws, but cooking was not one of hers. I could tell she had made Thai curry, and my mouth watered thinking about it. It was the vegan version of it, but still tasted great. My parents were vegan, and us kids were by default too.

I understood why my parents were vegan, but I knew I wouldn't remain vegan when I grew up. They cared deeply for animals, but I did not share that feeling. To be honest, empathy was one of the things I struggled with most.

"Dinner's ready!" my mom yelled from the kitchen.

I practically ran downstairs, my stomach feeling like it was on empty.

THIRTY-SIX

"I love seeing you this happy," my mom commented.

I was helping her clean up after dinner while my siblings played with our dad in the other room. I smiled back at her, knowing she genuinely meant it.

"It's because of Lily, isn't it?" she asked, a little cautiously.

"Yeah, our relationship has been great these days," I admitted hesitantly.

I tried my best to avoid talking to my parents about Lily, especially my mom, but it was nice to be honest and let it all out for a change. I mean, she had to accept at some point that I was growing up and wouldn't be her little boy forever. I was almost an adult now.

"I'm glad. She's a nice girl. Although I guess we don't really know too much about her."

"Well, I know what I need to know, and I know that I love her."

"Love... wow, I didn't know you two were *that* serious."

"We are. I think she's the one."

"The one?" my mom gasped.

"Yeah, Mom—the one."

"James, I know when you're young, your emotions are stronger, and you think you're in love, but things change as you get older..."

"Seriously? That's not cool, Mom. I know myself, and I know who I want to be with." I should never have said anything. This had been a mistake. I knew my mom wouldn't be cool about us.

"I know, and I'm not saying she's not the one, James. Maybe she is the one, but you're both still incredibly young, and things change so fast as you get older. Not just circumstances but people, too. People can change in the blink of an eye," she cautioned.

"Maybe they do, but I know Lily. Even if we do change, we'll change together and for the better. We're meant to be together—I feel it in my gut."

I didn't need a lecture from my mother tonight. She was totally killing my buzz. I was finally in a good place in my relationship with Lily and didn't need her getting in my head about it.

"Well, I really hope that happens, but all I'm saying is that you have to be careful with your heart—not everyone deserves it. Lily seems like a nice enough girl, but when you love someone, you give them a lot of power in the relationship, and that can turn ugly sometimes," she warned.

"What would you even know about that? Dad is literally the only person you've ever been with, and you guys never even fight. You have no idea what real relationships are like. I'm fine with being vulnerable around her because I trust her," I snapped, putting down the plates in the sink harder than I meant to.

She flinched at the sudden sound of the plates rattling.

"Look, I'm not trying to start a fight or anything, James. I'm just asking you to please be careful."

"This is pathetic. You're just trying to sabotage our relationship."

"Watch your mouth, James," my mom told me in a quiet but firm voice.

"Whatever. I'm going to Ian's."

"It's too late to be going to Ian's, it's a school night."

My mom crossed her arms over her chest, glaring at me.

"I don't care. It's not like I'm going to bed this minute. I'll be back before midnight."

"Absolutely not—go to your room." My mom pointed at the door.

"No!" I practically yelled at her as I walked out of the kitchen and toward the front door.

I grabbed the keys to my car, along with my jacket.

"James, you need to listen to me!" shouted my mom, following close behind.

"What is going on?" asked my dad, coming out of the living room bewildered.

"Mom won't let me go to Ian's," I explained.

"Because it's late, and you're not allowed to go out late on school nights."

"Why are you going to Ian's all of a sudden? Is it something urgent?" my dad questioned.

"It doesn't matter why. You're not going. John, can you please back me up for once?" sighed my mom, exasperated.

"Look, why don't we meet in the middle? As long as you come back by eleven and finish your homework for the day, you can go to Ian's." My dad was always trying to put out the fires and find the middle ground.

"Fine," I agreed.

My mom huffed and walked back into the kitchen, where

she began to clean up in the noisiest way possible to express her irritation.

"Don't worry—I'll talk to her before you get back and try to smooth things over," whispered my dad, winking at me.

I thanked him and walked to my car. Without even thinking about it, I instinctively drove to Lily's house, and then realized I should probably have called first. Thankfully, I didn't see her parents' cars, and I assumed they weren't home. They didn't like me coming over unannounced.

I called her to ask if it would be okay for me to come over. The lights were all switched off. I wasn't sure if she was even home right now.

"Hello?"

"Hey, Lil, are you home?" I asked.

"No, I'm out," she confirmed my suspicions.

"Oh, okay. Where are you?" I asked, more out of curiosity than anything else.

"Um… I'm—I'm with Patricia… we decided to go out for dinner."

"You're with Patricia?"

"Yeah, we thought it would be nice to catch up—just us girls. I didn't know you wanted to come over again."

"No, it's fine. I'll see you at school tomorrow, then."

"See ya."

Damn it. I was hoping to see her tonight. After a few minutes of contemplation, I decided to call Ian and see if he was home. I didn't want to go back to my place right now and deal with my mom.

"Hey, man, can I come over for a bit?" I asked as soon as Ian picked up.

"Sorry, I'm at Patricia's." I could hear Patricia in the background, asking Ian who he was talking to.

"Oh… is Lily with you guys?" I questioned him.

"No, just me and Patricia. I'd ask you to come over, but…"

"It's cool. I don't want to crash your date—I'll just head home."

"Alright, man."

Had Lily just lied to me about where she was and whom she was with? Why would she do that? We had fun this afternoon. Why was she suddenly avoiding me, and more importantly, why was she lying to me again? Was she with Brian? Was that why she was lying to me?

My head was spinning as I sat in the car, a million thoughts and questions running through my mind. This whole time, she was making me feel awful for not trusting her, but how was I supposed to trust her when she was constantly lying to me?

I would talk to her tomorrow in person. I was too angry and confused right now. I didn't want to snap again. What started out as a great day had gotten a whole lot worse. I drove around in my car for a while, listening to music and trying to calm down. My mom's warnings echoed in my mind.

"People can change in the blink of an eye."

Was she right?

Eventually, I headed home and went straight to my bedroom. I did not want to talk to anyone right now and needed some space.

THIRTY-SEVEN

I was already wide awake when my alarm rang the next morning—my mind preoccupied with thoughts about Lily. Why had she lied to me, and more importantly, who had she been with? That question kept repeating in my head again and again.

I walked to the bathroom and splashed some cold water on my face. I stared at my reflection in the mirror for a few seconds, the icy water dripping from my jawline onto the sink. My eyes were more sunken than I had ever seen them, and my hair was a mess. I barely recognized myself. I was frightened of what Lily was turning me into. I grabbed my hand towel and wiped away the water, avoiding my reflection.

I headed downstairs and was greeted by the smell of freshly made waffles. I walked into the kitchen and saw my mom carefully placing waffles on plates for the whole family.

"Waffles smell good," I told her, trying to sound normal.

I didn't want to fight with her anymore, especially not now that I was no longer as confident in my relationship with Lily as I had been a few hours ago.

"Good—I know they're your favorite…" she explained, looking apologetic. "Listen, James, about last night—"

"I'm so sorry I snapped at you, Mom. I know you were just looking out for me… and you're right. We don't really ever know anyone as well as we think," I admitted, staring at the floor.

"Yeah, but I think I was projecting some of my own insecurities onto your relationship. Lily is a wonderful girl, and if you love her, then that's all that matters."

"Yeah," I said, not knowing what else to say.

I wanted to tell her about how Lily had lied to me for no reason and how I was second-guessing our entire relationship again. But I knew she was the last person I could talk to about Lily. So instead, I grabbed a plate and walked to the table, quickly shoveling down the food without tasting it. I needed to get to school early and talk to Lily before class started.

"Whoa there, James—the food isn't running away, you know," joked my dad, walking in with a plate of his own.

"I know. I gotta get to school earlier today," I responded between mouthfuls.

"Got it… is everything okay?" he asked.

"Yeah, I just need to talk to one of my teachers about an assignment," I lied.

As I drove to school after breakfast, I couldn't help but wonder how it had gotten this bad between Lily and me. We were so happy. Everything had been great. But now, was this relationship even worth fighting for anymore? I flinched at the thought. I wanted to be hopeful, to be more optimistic. But I was tired of being the only one fighting for us, the only one trying to make this relationship work.

Patricia told me Lily was in the music room when I got to school—no surprise there. I headed to the music room directly. Each step I took heightened my anger, and by the time I was at the door, I was practically shaking with rage. I opened the door to see Lily and Brian standing beside one another. They were laughing about something together, and that was more than enough to set me off.

"James, I can explain—" Lily stammered, but I ignored her and walked toward Brian.

All that anger I had been holding in was at the surface now.

"What the fuck is your problem? Why can't you stay the fuck away from Lily?" I yelled into Brian's face, holding him by the collar of his T-shirt.

Time seemed to slow down as I examined Brian's terrified face. I turned to see Lily still standing off to the side, watching me with horror-filled eyes. I let go of Brian's shirt with a shove. He stumbled backward, scrambling away, but I kept walking toward him—slowly, menacingly.

"Look, man, I just got here … I have no idea what you're talking about," he tried to explain.

And then it happened. I lost control of myself, and my anger took over. It was as if my mind and body had completely disconnected. I raised my hand and punched him as hard as I could. He instantly fell to the ground, clutching his bleeding face with a pained expression.

"What the fuck, James! What the fuck is your problem?" yelled Lily, kneeling beside Brian.

"What's *my* problem? What's your fucking problem? Why do you keep lying to me?" I shouted at Lily.

"What the fuck are you talking about?" she asked, her innocent expression angering me even more.

"How about when you said you were hanging out with Patricia when I called you last night, but you weren't because she was with Ian?"

Lily appeared both guilty and frightened, having heard my accusation. She had the same look on her face that my siblings had when I caught them sneaking cookies when they weren't supposed to. She opened her mouth to say something, but before she could, the door swung open, and Mr. Live hurried in.

"What the hell is going on here?" he gasped, bewildered by the sight before him.

"James just attacked me like a psycho," explained Brian, still on the ground, clutching his bloody face.

"James, is this true?" asked Mr. Live, staring at me in surprise.

"I'm sorry, I didn't mean to—"

"Sorry isn't going to stop the bleeding. Lily, please take Brian to the nurse. And, James, we're going to the principal's office. Your behavior is absolutely unacceptable," he instructed.

I silently followed behind Mr. Live while Lily and Brian briskly headed to the nurse's room in the opposite direction. I sat on one of the chairs at the reception with my head down while Mr. Live went into the principal's office to explain the situation. About half an hour later, the reception door opened, and my dad walked in. He silently sat down beside me, the disappointment clear on his face.

I hated disappointing him, especially because he was the one person who believed in me, despite knowing about all the times I had messed up. He truly loved and supported me unconditionally. And I knew it hurt him deeply when I let my anger win, even though he never said it out loud.

"I'm sorry," I finally said.

I wasn't sorry for what I'd done, but I was sorry to have let him down.

"What happened, James? You were doing so well recently," he asked quietly.

"I know. I just… it's complicated," I said.

Before we could continue our conversation, we were instructed to go into the principal's office by the receptionist. Her usually chatty and friendly demeanor was replaced by a grim frown today. She pushed her glasses higher up the bridge of her nose and walked back to her chair. Her full figure was enhanced by her black pencil skirt and blue silk shirt. Her hair, which was in dozens of small braids today, swayed with each step she took. She sat back down and blankly stared at her computer screen once more as we headed into the principal's dimly lit office.

Brian walked in a few seconds later, his face more battered than I had expected. He sat down without looking directly at any of us.

"I need to understand what happened between you two and how it escalated to this," Principal Wilson said, gesturing to Brian's face. "And, Brian, your parents were informed about the incident, but were not able to come in."

Principal Wilson was a thin, small man in stature and personality. Most likely middle-aged. His skin was extremely pale, almost sickly, and his once full hairline was now fighting for its life. Deep lines were visible on his large forehead, a telltale sign of the stress he endured on a daily basis as principal.

"I was chilling in the music room, waiting for Mr. Live, when James walked in and attacked me," volunteered Brian.

"James, what do you have to say for yourself?" asked the Principal, turning his head toward me.

"I wouldn't have attacked him if he hadn't deserved it," I retorted, annoyed.

"James!" my dad exclaimed at my answer.

I didn't want to apologize. I didn't see the need to, but

seeing the dismay in my dad's eyes told me it was the right thing to do, regardless of how I felt about the situation.

"I'm really sorry. It won't happen again," I mumbled, halfheartedly.

"That's it?" Even Principal Wilson was surprised by my disingenuous apology.

I shrugged begrudgingly. What did I have to be sorry for? He was the one who had been hitting on my girlfriend. He was the one who may have ended my relationship. If he hadn't inserted himself into Lily's life, he wouldn't have had a fucked-up nose right now. To me, it was that simple. I had absolutely no remorse for what I had done.

"That's the apology? You're lucky that you're a good student, young man, because I've expelled kids for less than what you've done," he lectured, wiggling his finger in front of my face.

"Um, Wilson… let's not get carried away here," my dad said in a low voice, leaning forward. "I admit that James messed up. We all agree that his actions were wrong, but let's not forget that he's one of your best students… not to mention how generous our family has been with donations. If James were to get expelled or even suspended, we won't be as generous."

Principal Wilson's demeanor changed immediately. I knew this song and dance too well. My parents always gave donations to the schools I attended. My mom assumed it was because of my dad's generosity, not knowing about my anger issues. But the truth was, this was his get-out-of-jail-free card for me. He knew that, at some point, I would fuck up badly enough that I would need it. It irked me at first. I felt like he didn't trust me and expected me to fail. But over time, I understood the necessity of having a backup plan. And I realized he was simply looking out for me.

"Of course, there's no need to be hasty about the punishment. A suspension or expulsion would probably affect his grades," Principal Wilson backtracked, using his handkerchief to wipe away the sweat forming on his forehead.

"Look, I know James—he's usually a great kid. Maybe we can talk it out in the music room and get to the bottom of what happened," quietly suggested Mr. Live.

"Would that be okay with you, Brian?" asked Principal Wilson.

"It doesn't seem like I have much of a choice—" started Brian before he was quickly cut off.

"Great, it's agreed then. Talk it out among yourselves. But I don't want any more incidents, James," warned the principal, glaring at me with his beady eyes.

"We really appreciate you being lenient with James. We'll make sure he does better in the future," my dad promised.

"Yes, I'm sure you will… and I look forward to seeing both you and your wife again when you drop off your yearly donation," hinted the principal, not so subtly.

"Of course. And speaking of Sally… we would appreciate it if you kept this little incident to yourself when she's around. As I've mentioned before, my wife can be much more sensitive than I am, and I would prefer not to ruffle any feathers."

"I understand. She won't hear about it from any of us," promised Principal Wilson, extending his hand to shake my dad's.

That went much better than I had expected. I genuinely thought I would be suspended. This was pretty bad, even for me.

Now that I had some time to think about what I did, I knew I hadn't handled the situation well. I mean, I was still pissed and couldn't bring myself to feel sorry for Brian, but I should have confronted him outside of school or something. It was stupid to have hit him on school property.

"John, thank you for coming, but I think I can take it from here," Mr. Live assured my dad.

"Thanks, Mark. I appreciate you looking out for James. And, James, let's keep this to ourselves, you know how your mom is," he whispered the last part to me, guiding me a little further away from Mr. Live.

He was right. My mom was a sensitive person, and this would break her heart. I needed to continue to hide this part of myself from her. I had to protect her. Just as she had always done for me.

THIRTY-EIGHT

"So, boys, let's talk about what *really* happened here this morning," Mr. Live said as soon as Brian and I sat down in the music room. He was leaning against his desk, his left foot casually crossed over his right, his hands in the pockets of his black trousers.

We both remained silent. I didn't want to explain why I had been angry at Brian, and Brian seemed to be fixated on playing the innocent victim. He sat there stiffly, probably wallowing in his self-righteousness. The thought alone made me regret not doing more damage when I had the chance to make him experience the pain that I felt. I tried to control myself. But the temptation to do more damage was there—it lingered like an addiction.

"Okay… how about I leave you two alone for a few minutes and you talk it out among yourselves?" Mr. Live asked, realizing that neither of us was interested in this conversation.

"And if either of you starts a fight again, I will not hesitate to recommend you both get suspensions," he threatened.

With one last disapproving glance, he left the room, and we continued to sit there in silence. The tension thickened as time passed, and the seconds felt like hours. I took slow, deep breaths, scared that I would snap again and let the remaining anger out.

"What is your fucking problem with me, man?" Brian finally asked.

"What's *my* problem? What's *your* problem? Why can't you stay away from Lily? She may think you're being nice, but I know you're just trying to get with her," I responded angrily.

"What are you talking about? Lily is a friend, I have no interest in being more than that with her," Brian explained.

"Do you think I'm fucking stupid? That I don't know what you're up to?"

"I clearly have no interest in your girlfriend and have never done anything to make you think that I do. You're being paranoid."

I was getting riled up again.

"Never done anything? How about the fact that you're always around *my* girlfriend? It's weird."

"I'm not *always* around her, and when I am around her, it's because she *wants* to hang out with me."

"Yeah, right." I rolled my eyes.

"Seriously, man. I'm not into Lily like that."

"Stop fucking lying!" I yelled, my anger threatening to resurface.

"Chill, dude. You're going to get us both suspended," Brian warned.

"Don't fucking tell me to chill, or I will fucking knock you out this time," I threatened, getting up from the chair but lowering my voice.

Brian raised his hands in defeat, his eyes wide.

"Look… I'm gay, okay?" he confessed.

"What? Aren't you dating that Candice chick?" I asked, confused by his sudden confession.

"I *was* dating her, but we broke up. I guess I was in denial or whatever back then, but I'm gay."

"Why didn't you tell me that earlier?"

"I don't know, maybe because jocks have a history of bashing guys like me? Look at me, man. I'm a black, gay teen in the whitest fucking town. Life is hard enough as it is without people knowing there's one more thing that's different about me."

Shit. He was right. Most of the people here were homophobic as fuck. Even the adults.

I wasn't that way, though. I was taught to love everyone and found homophobia and racism to be beyond ignorant.

"I'm not homophobic or racist. Just FYI," I clarified.

"Good to know," Brian stated with a hint of sarcasm.

I sat back down and rubbed my temples. How do I keep fucking up?

I had to remind myself this wasn't my fault. It was Lily's. Her constant lying was making me crazy. I never used to be paranoid like this. The old me wouldn't have even cared about something as petty as who she hung out with. She was bringing out the parts of me that I had fought so hard to keep at bay.

"I'm sorry, man. I have been acting crazy. It won't happen again. And good luck with the… uh… gay thing," I apologized.

"Um, thanks." He nodded, visibly uncomfortable.

"What happened with us wasn't because of your race or anything. It's just that Lily has been acting weird lately, and it's throwing me off."

"Gotcha," mumbled Brian.

I extended my hand, a gesture of truce. Brian shook it, and we ended up talking some more. I was finally understanding things from Brian's perspective and was feeling pretty guilty about my behavior now.

I was also more confused than ever. According to Brian, Lily knew he was gay and had known since their trip. So why hadn't she just told me the truth? Brian also confirmed he hadn't been the one she was with on Monday night. If that was the case, what had she been up to, and why was she hiding it from me?

"I'm assuming you boys came to some sort of a truce?" Mr. Live asked, entering the music room.

We assured him that we had and would no longer be causing any problems. He seemed satisfied enough with that and let us leave.

I told Ian everything that had happened, and he was as surprised and confused as I was about Lily's lying. We decided it would be best if I talked to Lily in person. I wasn't sure if she wanted to talk to me after everything that had happened. But Ian promised to get Patricia to ask Lily to meet me in my car over lunch. I didn't think she would show up, but I had to try. I needed to know what the hell was going on. I was utterly baffled by the turn our relationship had taken.

I was sitting in my car waiting for her when I got a phone call from my dad. He wanted to talk about what had happened between Brian and me. I told him that Brian and I had gotten into a fight over something he had said because I didn't want my dad to know about the problems Lily and I had been having. I did admit to how guilty I had felt about the whole thing and promised to try my best to control my anger in the future. He told me he was proud of me for that and that I needed to use this as a learning opportunity.

Just as I hung up the phone, I heard a tap on my window. It

was Lily. I opened the door for her, and she got in without a word, crossing her arms over her chest. The irony of her being angry at me after everything she had done to cause this situation was not lost on me. She had no right to sit there on her high horse right now.

"I think we need to have a serious conversation about everything that's been going on," I said.

THIRTY-NINE

"OKAY... WHY DID YOU ATTACK BRIAN? THAT WAS INSANE, James," Lily responded, sullenly staring out of the windshield.

Her eyes were puffy and red, and she was nervously running her trembling fingers through her hair. I wanted to feel sorry for her, but I was still too angry for that right now.

"I acted that way because you lied to me again about where you were on Monday night. I thought you had been with Brian, and that's why I got mad. I'm not angry at Brian anymore, though. He told me he's gay."

"You're not mad at him anymore because he's gay? That's such a giant red flag. You should have trusted me and not fucking attacked him. His sexuality doesn't matter. The fact that you didn't trust me and acted all crazy is what's messed up."

She was clearly trying to weasel her way out of taking any accountability again.

"Don't try to turn this around on me. I've tried to trust you —I've tried so fucking hard. But every single time I try to trust you, every single time I think our relationship is going to be okay, you turn around and lie to me. And now we're just going around in fucking circles because you won't talk to me."

I wasn't going to let her manipulate me this time. I needed a straight answer from her. No more beating around the bush and playing the victim card.

"I know. I'm sorry…"

"I'm sorry isn't enough for me anymore, Lily. I need to know the truth. I need to know what the fuck is going on with you because otherwise, I'm never going to be able to trust you again. I don't want to be with someone who makes me crazy and paranoid all the time."

"Have you ever thought about how hard all this has been for me? I lied to you because I was hanging out with Brian, and I know that every time you hear his name, you get that crazy look in your eye and act weird. I didn't tell you he was gay because it's not my job to out people like that."

"Why are you still lying to me? I know you weren't with Brian. He already told me that. What the actual fuck is wrong with you? Are you a pathological liar or something?"

She looked defeated.

"Fine, you want to know the truth? Here's the truth. I was out alone that night. I just didn't want to see *you* because this relationship is suffocating me and taking up too much of my time. I don't like being around people all the time. I need my space, and you're always there, showing up unannounced and wanting to hang out *all* the time. It's too much for me!"

"You're right. I'm the bad guy for wanting to spend time with someone I love. You know, I remember when you enjoyed hanging out with me. We would spend hours talking on the phone. I guess it wasn't too much then? But now, suddenly, I'm suffocating you?"

"Urgh, I cannot keep having this goddamn argument with you every single day," Lily said, putting her head in her hands.

"Then stop lying to me all the time!"

"I need a break from everything… from us. I need to think," Lily told me.

My heart sank hearing her say those words. I had hoped that she would want to fight for this relationship as much as I did. I thought we loved one another enough to want to be better people for each other. Breaking up had been a possibility for quite a while, but I didn't want to believe it would happen. Not to us. We were supposed to be each other's ride or die.

"You wanna break up?" I whispered.

"I'm sorry, James, but I think it's for the best. I don't know what I want right now or even who I am. I'm tired of dragging you down with me," she continued with tears in her eyes.

"Lil, please—"

"I'm sorry," Lily sobbed.

Abruptly, she opened the door and briskly walked back toward the school. She disappeared into the building, leaving me alone in the car. Leaving me alone, period.

I noticed something sparkling on the car seat beside me. It was the bracelet I had bought her. She had loved it so much that she wore it every single day. I silently shoved it in my pocket, not wanting to look at it right now. I didn't want to believe this was how our relationship had ended. I had so much hope for us; she was supposed to be my forever person.

A tear rolled down the side of my face before I could stop it. I quickly wiped it away with the back of my hand. After taking a deep breath, I started my car and drove away. I didn't want to go back inside. I couldn't go back inside.

FORTY

"Everything okay?" my mom asked me at dinner.

"Yup," I replied, mindlessly playing with the pasta on my plate.

"Do you not like the food?" She was staring at my plate too, concerned.

"It's fine, Mom. I'm not that hungry, that's all. I think I'm going to finish some work upstairs," I said, getting up and heading to my room.

I lay in my bed, Lily's bracelet in my hand. The longer I held it, the more it felt like it was going to burn a hole in my palm. I stared at it for a long time, remembering the good times we had shared. The memories we had made together. The laughter, the inside jokes, the times I held her in my arms, and everything felt perfect in those brief moments. I wondered if she was thinking about me too, hurting the way I was.

Yes, I had messed up, so had she, but this could not be it. We could work on our relationship. We could fix this. We had to. I couldn't lose her. I had to win her back.

Just then, my phone buzzed—it was Ian again. He had been calling me all afternoon. I assumed he knew what had happened between Lily and me. I wanted to talk to him, to tell my best friend everything. But I also knew it would hurt too much to relive what had happened. The wound was still fresh.

After about an hour, I heard a knock at my door. I glanced up, surprised, the bracelet still in my hand. My parents rarely came into my room this late, and my siblings were probably already in bed. I wondered if something was wrong.

"Just a minute," I called.

I hurriedly got up and kneeled down, moving one of the floorboards near my bed. I had been hiding stuff in there for years now. I added the bracelet to my collection of hidden objects, put the floorboard back into its place, and opened the door. My mom was standing there, and behind her was Ian, uncomfortably staring at me.

"Ian's here," my mom let me know.

"Hey," Ian nodded.

"Oh… uh, hi," I replied awkwardly.

I should have just picked up the call.

"Well, I'll leave you two to talk…" my mom said, backing away.

I opened the door fully to let Ian in. He sat down on my bed, and I sat in the chair beside it. There was an uncomfortable silence at first, neither of us knowing how to start the conversation. Even though we told each other pretty much everything, this felt different.

"So… I got you some of the notes and stuff you missed this afternoon…" Ian was the first to break the awkward silence.

"Oh, thanks. Appreciate it."

"Lily told Patricia some of what happened between you guys… are you two really broken up?"

There it was.

"I mean, that's what Lily wants. It's not what I want," I admitted.

"Maybe she's just pissed off right now. You know how it is

with females. One second, they're angry, the next, they love you," Ian tried to comfort me.

"I don't think this was one of those times. I think she was dead serious."

"Man, I can't believe it. I thought you guys were the real deal."

He got up and put his hand on my shoulder supportively.

"I did too. I thought she was my forever, ya know?" I said.

"Yeah, everyone thought that. It's crazy. But you know, maybe whatever happens is for the best."

"I was thinking… Maybe Patricia could talk to Lily for me and tell her how much I still love her? Maybe we can still work things out?"

"I'll ask her, but Lily's been acting weird with her, too. She told me Lily's been dodging her recently."

"She's been doing that to me, too! I just don't get what happened and why she won't tell anyone what's going on with her. I wish I knew how everything went downhill."

I really did. I was still so confused about why Lily had lied. I thought about every moment I could recall before she began acting weird and couldn't pinpoint a single thing that could have caused her behavior to change so drastically.

"I know you don't want to hear this right now, but I gotta be honest, you deserve someone better, man. What she's been doing is fucked up," Ian told me, frowning.

"I know it is, but I also know the real her. Something's up, and if I can fix it, maybe she'll give me another chance," I explained.

"I don't know, James. It kinda sounds like she doesn't want to be with you right now."

"I don't care. I need her."

"I know you love her and think you know her, but if she were a truly good person, she wouldn't be doing what she's doing right now," Ian pointed out.

"You don't know her like I know her, man."

"Maybe I do, maybe I know her better than you because you're too in love with her to see how fucked up she is," Ian said. I just sighed and pushed my hair out of my face. I couldn't do this right now.

"It's up to you, but I think she needs some space right now, and ignoring that won't end well," Ian warned.

I didn't care. I didn't care about anything anymore. All I could think about was Lily. She had consumed my mind, my very being. It was like I was on fire, and she was the only one who could put it out. I needed her in my life—she was *the one*. I could feel it in every inch of my body. I had fucked up, and I needed to win her back.

FORTY-ONE

I anxiously waited for Lily by her locker the next morning, but she never came. I asked around, and apparently, she was skipping school because she was sick. It was hard for me to believe anything she said anymore, which was why I was instantly suspicious. Was she really sick, or was she lying again in order to avoid me?

I sighed, shaking my head. The truth was that it didn't matter. What I needed to focus on right now was talking to her and getting all of this sorted out. I needed to know what went wrong in our relationship. I pulled out my phone and tried calling her again, but once more, there was no answer.

The longer I was apart from her, the worse I felt. The pit in my stomach kept growing, and my chest felt tight. Even when I tried to think of something else to distract myself, my mind eventually wandered back to thoughts of her. Her messy curls, her flowery scent, her smile. She was all I could think about. I knew I wouldn't be able to get my head straight till I talked to her.

"I think I'm going to stop by Lily's today," I told Ian as we sat down for lunch at our usual table in the cafeteria.

He sighed and shook his head with disappointment. I already knew he didn't approve, that he would have preferred I cut Lily off completely because he thought she was toxic. He had told me as much when I texted him this morning, asking if he knew where Lily was.

"You know that's a bad idea," he warned me.

"Yeah, don't go all Joe Goldberg on her—give her some space, dude," Patricia added.

"I just feel like if I talk to her, I can change her mind," I admitted.

"You can't control everything around you. Sometimes people do stuff that hurts us. You have to let it go and move on," Ian advised.

"I can't… I don't want to let it go or move on," I said.

"Do what you want, but I'm telling you now that if you go over to her place, it's not going to end well," Ian emphasized. "You're going to piss her off even more, the two of you will fight, and you'll be back here tomorrow still feeling like fucking shit."

"I know, but I gotta try…" I sighed.

They were right, and deep down I knew that going over to Lily's was a bad idea. More likely than not, she would be mad at me for being there. But I couldn't help it. My anxiety was killing me. I needed to talk to her. I needed to get rid of that awful knot in my stomach. I had to at least try to fight for her. She wasn't just some girl; she was Lily. She was my favorite person in the world. The only person who made me feel whole.

Despite Ian and Patricia's warnings, I drove to Lily's after school. There were no cars parked outside her house, which meant neither of her parents was home. This would give me the perfect opportunity to talk to her privately. Or at least try.

I knocked on her door, but no one answered. I knocked again, louder this time, and heard rushed footsteps. Lily opened the door, and for a few seconds, we both stood there frozen, staring at one another in surprise. She was shocked to see me on her doorstep unexpectedly. I, on the other hand, was shocked by her appearance. She was much paler, and her face was shiny with sweat. Her pajamas hung loosely. I guess she was sick after all.

"What are you doing here?" she asked coldly.

"I wanted to stop by and make sure you're okay."

"I'm fine—now please leave."

"Can we please talk?"

"No," she replied and slammed the door in my face.

I was taken aback by her reaction, but wasn't ready to back down.

"Lily," I called, knocking on the door.

"Come on, open up… I just want to talk to you for a minute," I begged.

"Go away!" she yelled from the other side of the door.

"Please!"

If she would just listen to me for a few minutes, we could sort this whole mess out. I mean, didn't she at least owe me that? After everything we had been through?

"Go away or I'm calling the cops."

"I just wanna talk…"

"I'm not fucking kidding, James. If you don't leave, I'm calling the cops."

"Fine, I'll leave, but this is crazy. We were together all this time, and now you won't even talk to me for a few minutes?"

I waited for a response, but none came. I eventually walked back to my car with my head down. I turned around to study her house one last time. Even though I knew she didn't want to, a small part of me had hoped that she would talk to me. That *my* Lily was still in there somewhere.

Ian texted me in the evening to ask me how things went with Lily. I told him the truth, and although he was sympathetic, he did tell me that I shouldn't have expected any different. She clearly wanted some space. I knew he was right, but it still hurt.

FORTY-TWO

As had become the norm lately, I woke up exhausted and miserable. Lily was still a no-show at school, and every day that I didn't see her, I felt worse. I was numb; my body and mind had given up. I was like a zombie, simply going through the motions.

Getting out of bed was a chore. I would have skipped school completely if not for football practice. The big game was coming up, and I wasn't doing as well as I should have been because of all the distractions in my life right now. Coach had even reprimanded me about it during our last practice, and I knew not showing up for practice would only piss him off more.

I walked through the front doors of the school with my AirPods in and hoodie up, trying to be invisible and get through the day. From the corner of my eye, I noticed Lily standing by her locker. I guess she was finally back. She glanced at me for a second, and it was as though time suddenly froze, but then she turned back to her locker without acknowledging me at all. The color on her face was back, and I assumed she was no longer sick. I wanted to ask her how she was doing, but I refrained. Instead, I ignored her too and headed to my own locker.

I was trying my best to act cool, but my mind was still consumed by thoughts of her. My body craved her. I felt like an addict in withdrawal—empty, broken, and, most importantly, desperate. I kept replaying the last few weeks over and over in my head, trying to think of everything I could have done wrong to make her change and turn into this cold, heartless person.

What could I have done to make her hate me all of a sudden?

The morning went by in a blur, and I was too distracted to even remember most of it. At lunch, I discreetly tried to scan the cafeteria for Lily when I was in line for my food, but she wasn't there. I sat down with Ian and Patricia, both of whom were staring at me pitifully.

"Are you okay?" Patricia finally asked.

"What happened to hello? How are you?" I joked, not wanting to actually answer her.

"I'm serious, James. You showed up at Lily's unannounced, and you look like you haven't slept in days," she continued.

"I'm fine. Don't worry about it," I replied coldly, hoping she would drop it.

"Are you coming to practice today?" I asked Ian, trying to change the subject.

"Yup." He nodded. "Did you finish watching *The Righteous Gemstones*?" Ian asked after a few seconds of awkward silence.

Thankfully, he seemed to get the hint that I didn't want to talk about Lily right now. We continued to talk about *The Righteous Gemstones* until I noticed Ian and Patricia's expressions change mid-sentence and felt a tap on my shoulder. I turned around to see Lily awkwardly standing behind me. She was wearing an oversized sweater, black jeans, and white sneakers. One of her hands was by her side, and the other nervously tucked a strand of loose hair behind her left ear.

"Can we talk after school?" she asked quietly.

"Okay…"

"Cool, I'll meet you out back."

And with that, she turned around and briskly walked away from me and out of the cafeteria. Disappearing as quickly as she had appeared, leaving behind the scent of her perfume in the air. Ian and Patricia stared at me with confused expressions.

"I wonder what that's about?" Ian muttered.

"I have no clue." I was as dumbfounded as they were.

"James... you need to be careful. She's been acting seriously fucking bipolar, and I don't want you to get caught up in her mess again," Ian told me.

"I know, I'll be careful," I promised, nodding.

I was lying. I would take her back in a heartbeat if that's what she wanted. For her, I was willing to do anything. *Anything*.

The day couldn't end fast enough. I was curious to find out what Lily wanted. The rational part of my brain knew it was super unlikely that she wanted to get back together. But that tiny, irrationally optimistic part of me still held a sliver of hope.

I practically jumped out of my chair and walked out the back door as fast as I could when the final bell rang. Lily wasn't there yet. I waited near the trees, hands in my pockets, and slowly paced. My heart beat rapidly as I waited for her. I was more anxious than I had ever been in my life.

I shivered slightly and quickly shoved my hands into the pockets of my hoodie. I wasn't sure if it was the cold air that made me shiver or the thought of finally being alone with her. Of course, I was nervous. This was my one shot to win her back —it had to go perfectly.

A small part of me was afraid she wouldn't show up. That this was another one of the many lies she had told me recently.

I spun around, staring at the trees. My mind was

hypervigilant right now, noticing every tiny detail thanks to my anxiety, and I could have sworn I heard something moving in the woods. Or was it just my imagination? Paranoia brought on by the tension that had taken hold of my nerves.

I turned around again as soon as I heard the door open, and watched her walk toward me. I breathed out. I hadn't even realized I was holding my breath.

FORTY-THREE

"HEY..." SHE SAID, STARING AT THE GROUND.

Her slightly sunken cheeks were flushed, and she was fidgeting with her hair again.

"Hey," I responded, trying to sound casual.

Even though I had been simping for her pretty hard, I was still hurt by how she had treated me recently. I had a lot to apologize for, but so did she.

"I wanted to talk to you about what happened—" she started.

"You mean our relationship?" I clarified.

"No, I mean you showing up at my fucking house like a fucking stalker when I specifically told you I needed space," she spat, frowning.

"I needed to talk to you, okay? You broke up with me with no proper explanation, and you were acting pretty crazy yourself before that. I'm not just some guy you can mess around with and then discard," I snapped back.

I could feel my heartbeat getting faster and took a deep breath, trying to ground myself before I did something I regretted. I knew an outburst was the last thing I needed right now, but her nonchalant attitude toward her own wrongdoings was seriously getting under my skin.

"I don't owe you an explanation or anything, really. How many times have I asked you to leave me alone? You need to stay away from me. What if my parents had been home? I could have gotten in trouble!" Her voice was getting higher.

"I knew they weren't home. I'm not fucking stupid. I checked for their cars and saw they weren't there," I explained.

"Whatever, just stay away from me, okay? I'm fucking done with this drama." She rolled her eyes and started to turn away.

"Wait, look, I'm sorry—I can change, Lil. I love you. I swear I'll be the person you want me to be," I pleaded.

But even I could feel the emptiness in my promises. How many times had I apologized and promised her I would change when she was the one who had fucked up? Why was I the only one always apologizing?

She turned back toward me, her lips curling in disgust as she digested the words I had said.

"You will never be the person I want because you are not the person I want to be with. Get that through your fucking head." Her voice was dripping with contempt, her eyes so filled with hatred that I was taken aback.

She turned around again and began to walk back toward the school building when I instinctively grabbed her by the arm and yanked, forcing her to turn and look at me. Her face was close enough to mine that I could feel her rapid breaths on my skin. Her eyes widened with fear. I was still trying to calm myself down, but I could feel the adrenaline coursing through my veins. And as though to mock me one last time, her phone vibrated, signaling a new text message.

At that moment, something inside me snapped. And snapped like it never had before. It was as if all those moments of frustration hit me all at once. Every single time, she had ignored me to glance at her phone. Every single time she had lied to me about who she was talking to. Every single time, she had undone the love we had for one another, strand by strand.

I could feel my heartbeat in my ears, my nose flared, and my body trembled. My breathing was fast and uneven. Everything suddenly slowed. The rage grew and spread from my toes all the way to the beads of sweat now forming on my forehead. Before I could stop myself, my hands reached out, and she gasped in surprise.

I had yanked her phone out of her hand and thrown it on the ground as hard as I possibly could. I could see the slight cracks on her screen. But that wasn't enough to satisfy the rage that had been brewing inside of me all this time. With my right foot, I stomped on the already damaged phone as hard as I could until I heard the satisfying crunch of the screen fully shattering.

We stood there in stunned silence for a moment, our minds trying desperately to make sense of what I had done. Slowly, I began feeling like myself again. Without the fury controlling my emotions, I realized just how badly I had fucked up this time.

My eyes widened in horror, just as hers had. I glanced down at the shattered phone on the floor and then at her face. She was staring back at me, tears beginning to form in the corners of her eyes.

"What the fuck is wrong with you?" she whispered, sniffling.

I stood there silently, wallowing in my shame, not knowing how to respond. Nothing I said could ever fix what I had done. I had come here prepared to do whatever it took for her to give me a second chance, but instead, I had not only shattered her phone but with it every hope we had of reconciling. It was a final, brutal act of violence, and hidden in that act was everything I wished I had said to her but never could find the words to.

And yet, the anger was still there. Not the rage that had taken over, no. This was different. It was not irrational or intense. The fact that she still refused to take any sort of accountability for the role she had played in the demise of our relationship was what finally made me understand that I didn't matter to her. How I felt, what I did, what I said. None of that mattered to her.

She was not the perfect person I had built her up to be in my mind. No, she was actually awful. She had treated me like I was disposable. She had treated Patricia—her best friend—even worse. And yet, in every single scenario, she still had the audacity to play the victim. I wasn't saying I hadn't fucked up too, but at least I had the balls to admit it, to try to be better.

"Stay the fuck away from me," she repeated. She was trying her best to sound firm, but the crack in her voice gave away her nervousness.

"I *will*. I thought you were the one, but you just… you bring out the worst parts of me," I finally admitted. "I don't want to see you ever again."

She stopped for a second when she heard the final part of what I said. But she didn't turn around. Instead, she continued walking.

For a while, I stood there, watching her walk away. I wanted to scream and put my fist through a wall. To let it all out. But I couldn't. I just stood there all alone. Until this moment, I had some fragments of hope for our relationship, but now I was certain it was over. There was no relationship, no Lily.

Eventually, I bent down and picked up her phone, which

was still lying on the ground. I slipped it into my pocket. I had destroyed it, and it was only right that I get it fixed for her. I would give the phone to Patricia to give back to Lily once I had it fixed. I didn't want to see Lily or be around her again.

I drove around for a bit, knowing I couldn't go home yet. My mom was aware I had football practice today, and if I went back early, she would ask me a million questions about why I hadn't gone to practice. And I was in no mood to deal with that right now. I needed to clear my head.

Eventually, I did go back home and rushed to my bedroom as fast as I could and as quietly as I could in an attempt to avoid everyone.

I locked my bedroom door behind me and moved the loose floorboard. I picked up the bracelet I had put in there earlier and sighed. This was really it. We were really over.

In a strange way, I sort of felt relieved. Relieved that I would no longer have to deal with her constant gaslighting and changing moods. Relieved that I would no longer be letting someone else control my emotions. But more overwhelming than the relief was the emptiness. Like the place I had kept all my love for Lily was now hollow, and I was painfully aware of it.

I stared at the bracelet a little longer. *Should I toss it or keep it?* There was no point in keeping it. All it did was remind me that I had lost the woman I loved. Still, I carefully put the bracelet back where it had been and the phone with it. I'd get it fixed over the weekend, but till then, I needed a place to keep it where no one would find it.

"Dinner's ready!" I heard my mom yell.

I quickly put the floorboard back into its place and headed downstairs, lost in my own thoughts. I was still conflicted about the end of my relationship with Lily. I knew in my heart that this would take me a long time to heal from. But another part of me felt like this was the new beginning I deserved. I wondered if this could be the start of a new chapter for me. One where I could finally find happiness and, more importantly, peace.

FORTY-FOUR

Perfect. My life had been absolutely perfect to a tee. I had the perfect loving family, the kind you see on television. My mom was a stay-at-home mom, and my dad was an engineer. Although he worked hard at his job, he would always make time for me. He would come home and help me with my homework, and when I was younger, we would play together till dinner was ready.

Every Sunday, we would go to church together in the morning and then head to one of our favorite restaurants for lunch. And we would spend the rest of the afternoon together as a family. Even when puberty hit, and all my friends suddenly hated their parents, I loved mine. I wouldn't have traded my life for anything in the world.

It was easy back then to believe in God, to believe in heaven. My life was just about perfect, and I knew how much of a miracle that was. It's easy to love God when you are God's favorite, when the blessings are pouring in.

And then my dad got sick. And he kept getting sicker and sicker. Eventually, he became too sick to work anymore. Although my parents had some savings, they weren't enough for his chemotherapy. My mom began searching for work, and my dad resented himself more and more because of it. I think he believed it was his job to provide for us and hated that he wasn't able to.

Even though my mom did end up getting some part-time work, it only paid minimum wage and did not help much with our debt. We had to move into a smaller apartment—my bedroom was the size of my former closet. But I didn't complain. I tried to be strong for my parents.

One day, when I got back from school, I heard my mom on the phone. My dad was at the hospital, and she probably didn't expect me to come home this early. She was begging someone from our church to help us financially. She begged and begged, but they turned her down, promising that they would pray for my dad but wouldn't be able to do much beyond that.

I heard my mom sobbing in defeat. I walked back downstairs and went to the park. It was the first time I ever questioned the existence of God. It was the first time I ever questioned religion. What could we have possibly done to deserve any of this? As my once picture-perfect life shattered, my faith did too. It became near impossible to believe God loved us when this was our life.

I had always naively believed that humans were inherently good, that there were some bad apples out there, but for the most part, people were good. I always believed that our church friends were kind, generous people who loved one another. How many times had I heard them quote the Bible and say things like "The righteous give generously" or "A generous person will prosper." And yet when we needed them most, they turned us away, pretending they could not spare anything.

I tried not to let it all get to me, to remain positive, especially in front of my parents. I could see how much everything was affecting them, and I didn't want to make it worse than it already was.

My mom's long blonde hair, once the color of sunshine, had become almost fully gray at the roots. Her forehead was filled with fine lines, her mouth stuck in a permanent frown. Her already petite frame was even smaller now, her cheeks visibly sunken. She had always been full of life and joy, but I had not seen her smile once since my dad's diagnosis.

My dad's face was sunken and sad, too. His thick, dark black hair was completely gone. I could see the worry in his deep brown eyes as they filed through reminders of unpaid bills. Even when he tried to smile or make me laugh, it never quite reached his eyes anymore. It was nothing more than a mask. I knew that he thought he had failed his family and blamed himself for our financial debts. It broke my heart to remember what he had been like. Full of energy, full of life.

As for me, I wasn't the same person I had been a few months ago. Something inside me had changed. I had lost a part of myself that I knew I would never get back. This ordeal had broken me beyond repair. The happy little optimist I had once been was gone. She had been replaced by a broken pessimist who had been abruptly shoved into the real world.

Almost two years after my dad was diagnosed with cancer, he lost the battle. We had been preparing for it, but I don't think there's actually any way you can prepare for someone's death. Especially when you are forced to watch them die little by little every single day.

Naively, I thought my father's death would be the saddest thing that would happen to our family. That this was our rock bottom. Of course, I was wrong. My father was gone, but the debt was not. And neither was the void that was left in our lives after he passed. He was the glue that held us all together. Without him, we fell apart.

My mom had no idea what to do, how to move forward. She had a child to care for and was barely making enough for us to survive, let alone live a good life. My dad had always been the breadwinner. He had made the difficult decisions, and my mom had been able to live in blissful ignorance. She was completely lost without him.

Her family no longer spoke to her—they had cut her off for marrying my dad, who was Indian. They thought she could do better, which was a nice way of saying they wanted her to marry someone of her own race. My dad's family had also cut us off, ironically, for the same reason. It hadn't mattered before. The three of us had been happy without them. But now we were painfully alone, and the absence of extended family was devastating.

My mom had lots of friends from church before my dad got sick, but they quickly vanished when they realized she was in need of financial and general assistance. I didn't blame God or religion for their bad behavior. I blamed them and them alone. This whole ordeal made me realize just how many people were only religious when it suited their needs. Or when they wanted to feel morally superior without having any real morals.

The more depressed and overwhelmed my mother became, the more we grew apart. Not that we were that close to begin with. Of course, we had been close to an extent, but not in the same way I was with my dad. It was different with him. It was effortless.

Now that my mom was working longer hours, I barely saw her. There were days when I didn't see her at all because she would leave before I woke up and come back after I had already gone to bed. And when she was at home, she was so busy with the housework and everything else that needed to be done that we barely spent any time together.

This felt like the lowest point of my life. And that's when Paul swooped in.

FORTY-FIVE

Paul Johnson.

Paul was an engineer too and had worked with my dad prior to his death. He was at the funeral—that was the first time I saw him. He was short, visibly balding, with a toothy smile that never quite reached his calculating dark eyes. There was something about him I instantly disliked. Perhaps it was the fake kindness or the way he seemed happy to be at the funeral. Almost giddy, actually.

He had spent a long time talking to my mom and kept finding any excuse to touch her. Rubbing her back and holding her hand as she sobbed. Even then, I had found it bizarre, but I had been so consumed by my grief that I hadn't thought too much of it till it was too late.

He knew my mom was scared and desperate, and soon, he took full advantage of it. Before I even realized what was happening, he was at our apartment all the time. Trying to play house with us. Trying to replace my dad. And to my chagrin, my mom was not only allowing it but encouraging it.

I understood that she was terrified of doing everything on her own for the first time, but I would never forgive her for letting Paul into our lives. I simply could not understand why she picked him out of everyone out there.

My mom did try to talk to me about him when they first

started dating. She promised me it was nothing serious, and she was only going on a couple of dates with him to get to know him better. I wanted to believe her, but I knew this wasn't going to end with only a couple of dates.

Some weeks later, she had invited him over for dinner as a way for the three of us to get to know each other. I was sullen the entire time, trying to get it over with as quickly as possible. Paul kept trying to make small talk with me, asking me about school, my grades, and my interests. He was being extra sweet to me. Too sweet. Sickly sweet. Just seeing him sitting at our dinner table, on the chair where my dad used to sit, was enough to make me nauseated.

Seeing my mom laugh at his stupid, lame jokes made it even worse. I excused myself early and almost ran to my room to get away from it all. I lay on my bed crying, wondering what I could have possibly done to anger God that He made my life this miserable all of a sudden. I cried for the girl I had been, and I cried for the girl I was now.

The next morning, I woke up to the smell of waffles—my favorite breakfast. And that's how I knew something bad was about to happen. My mom was buttering me up for something. I walked into the kitchen cautiously and was greeted by her smiling at me like a maniac. We sat down at the table with our plates, and I silently prayed this would have nothing to do with Paul. She made some small talk at first, but eventually got to the point.

"What did you think of Paul?" she asked, her eyes fixed on her plate.

"He's… okay, I guess," I muttered.

"Do you like him?" she questioned further.

"Not particularly. Do *you* like him?" I asked her, genuinely curious about what she could possibly see in that man.

"Yes, I do, Lil," she admitted.

"Do you love him?"

"I don't know… I think he would be good for us. It would be a new start, away from all the horridness."

"The horridness? Is that how you feel about the time we spent with Dad?"

"No! I—I loved your father. I still love your father… but he's no longer with us, and we have to accept that and move on with our lives."

"Yeah, I can tell you've had no problem moving on before his body was even cold."

"Lily, don't you dare talk to me like that! You have no idea how hard it is to lose a spouse, and you have no idea how hard it is to be an adult and a single parent."

"I have no idea? You're not the only one who lost someone! I lost my dad, too!" I screamed.

"And no one is saying that you didn't. No one expects you to forget your father. I just don't think it's healthy to live our entire lives in mourning. We need to move on eventually and continue living our lives, even if your father can't. We can't remain hung up on the memories of him forever."

"Couldn't you have at least waited before you moved on? Did it have to be this soon? And did it have to be with *Paul*?"

My mom took a deep breath and sighed. She leaned back and stared at me with a more serious expression on her face.

"It's not that I don't miss your father or that I'm in such a hurry to move on. You're a big girl now, and I'm going to be honest with you. The bills are piling up. We still have loans to pay off, and I barely get paid enough to survive. We need someone, and Paul is willing to be that someone."

"So, it's all about the money for you? You know what that makes you right?"

"Don't, Lily. Don't say something you'll regret," my mom warned me sternly.

"A whore. It makes you a whore," I said anyway.

To my complete disbelief, my mom reached across the table and slapped me as hard as she could. I sat there completely flabbergasted. My mom, who was the sweetest and gentlest person I knew, had hit me for the first time in my life. My ears were ringing, and my cheek was on fire. Tears were threatening to fall from my eyes, but I held it together as much as I could. I didn't want her to see me cry. I had too much pride for that.

"Go to your room," she said in a scarily calm tone.

I got up and left, tears now freely streaming down my face as I entered my bedroom. At that moment, all I wanted was my dad. The one person who could fix all this. I slid to the ground, my shoulders shaking as I sobbed.

FORTY-SIX

My mom didn't bother talking to me about Paul much after that incident. In fact, we didn't talk much in general. I had sort of expected her to apologize at some point, but she didn't, and neither did I.

I spent more time outside the house, hanging out with friends and signing up for as many extracurricular activities as I possibly could. I ended up joining the chess club at our school, even though I had never played chess in my life. I needed distractions. I needed to get away from everything.

Paul was still around, though, and he and my mother were getting more serious. I tried to be civil, for my mom's sake. I was hoping that she would eventually realize how awful Paul was. I prayed and prayed to a God I barely believed in anymore. But things only kept getting worse.

One night, Paul and my mom sat me down after dinner. They told me they had some good news to share. They had these stupid, shit-eating grins on their faces. In my heart, I knew what it was, but I didn't want to believe it.

"We've decided to get married," my mom revealed.

They were both beaming, as if this was the best news ever. I was overwhelmed by all the emotions hitting me all at once. It was like my world was slowly collapsing.

"Why?" I finally asked, still stunned.

"Most people say congratulations, Lil," Paul joked, chuckling at his own joke.

"It's Lily," I corrected him for the hundredth time.

"We just feel it would be best for our little family," my mom explained.

"Really? You think this would be best for *our* family?" Was she kidding?

"Yes, we do, and I don't want to hear another negative word about it from you. We're very happy about this and expect you to be happy for us," she said, still smiling.

I got up and went to my room silently. They could stop me from complaining, but they couldn't force me to be happy for them. That was never going to happen for as long as I lived. I could not understand how my mother could betray me this way and, most of all, betray my dad.

She must have assumed I wouldn't notice, but I knew she had been taking down all the pictures with him in them. The family pictures we had in our living room, and the picture she had of the two of them on her nightstand. They were all gone.

I eventually heard footsteps heading toward my room that night and quickly shut my eyes, pretending to be asleep. The door creaked open, and my mom slowly came in. I hoped she would see that I was sleeping and leave, but instead, she sat down on my bed. For a few seconds, I lay there, completely still. And she silently remained there, at the edge of my bed. I felt her hand slowly stroke my hair, like she used to when I was younger.

"I know you're not asleep," she informed me.

She sighed when I didn't respond, but continued to stroke my hair.

"Paul offered to pay off our loans, you know," she stated.

"He's a good man, Lil. You may not like him, and that's okay. But he's not a bad person, and he would take good care of us."

I opened my eyes and looked up at her, unable to hide my disgust.

"I'm not going to stop you from marrying him, but I am never going to like him. And he is never going to be my dad," I said angrily.

"I don't expect him to be your dad, but every child needs a mom and a dad. He could be there for the moments your dad won't be there for."

"I don't want him anywhere near me."

"Please, Lil, we've been through enough. Please don't make this harder for me than it already is," she said with tears in her eyes.

I felt a pang of guilt. It *had* been hard for my mom, too, and I knew that. She had tried to keep it together for my sake, but I had often heard her quietly crying in her bedroom. She did deserve a better life, another chance at happiness. But did it have to be with Paul?

"Fine, I'll be good. But I'm not going to pretend to play happy family with him," I conceded.

"Thank you, sweetie. For at least trying for me." She smiled, gently kissing my forehead.

FORTY-SEVEN

"I DO."

And with those two words, my fate was sealed. I knew nothing would ever be the same again, and I was right. This was only the start. Paul's little nice guy facade was still on display around everyone else, but it was slowly slipping around us. I had initially guessed that it was nothing but an act, but I wasn't in any way prepared for just how bad it would get.

It started with small things here and there. A small comment about my outfit not being appropriate and forcing me to dress more conservatively, more feminine. Then it was about how short hair made me appear too masculine, and I should grow it out. My mom was always on his side and refused to listen to reason, even when I begged and pleaded.

At first, I would get angry and try to fight back. But that would only end with them lecturing me, and Paul would use it to try to convince my mom that I was out of control. He would excuse his controlling behavior by pretending he cared about me, which is why he was strict with me. Eventually, I realized that there was no point in wasting my energy trying to argue with them. It was a battle I would always lose.

As the months went by, the constricting and controlling rules got worse.

One day, out of the blue, my mom informed me that Paul would be legally adopting me, and I would be taking his last name. *Informed me* because I had no choice in the matter.

I begged for days. I sulked. I yelled. I tried everything to stop them from changing my last name. It was the only thing that kept me connected to my dad. But none of it worked.

Soon, my last name became Johnson, and with that, Paul had managed to erase every last bit of my father from our lives. He had succeeded, and my mom had failed miserably to protect the memory of my dad. I thought I had hit rock bottom; I genuinely did. But I wish I had saved my tears because the next change Paul announced broke me.

Paul was not from New York like my parents were. He had only moved to the city a few years ago for work. Originally, he was from a small city in the middle of nowhere. His mom used to still live there, but had passed away recently and left him the house. For a while, he had traveled back and forth to get some renovations done because he was going to rent it out once it was ready.

However, his tune had begun changing as of late. First, it was him talking about how small our apartment in New York was, even though he was paying such a large sum in rent. How it would be way more fun for me to grow up the way he had in a small town. I would be safer and have better friends and influences there.

During his last trip to the house, he told us it was nothing like it used to be now that the renovations were complete. In fact, it looked almost new. And he had such a deep attachment to it that he thought it would be great for us to move there permanently. I could tell that this had caught even my mother off guard. The stunned expression on her face made it clear that Paul had kept her in the dark about this, too.

I didn't say anything or respond in any way. Partly because I was too tired of arguing to say anything, and partly because I knew that saying something would probably make no difference at all.

FORTY-EIGHT

I could hear my mom and Paul arguing in the living room. This was the first time I had heard them argue since they got married. Actually, this was the first time I had ever heard them argue. Period. I had never so much as heard her raise her voice at him before.

I got out my phone and texted my closest friends about what was happening. I waited for their responses to the news, and as I expected, they were as angry and outraged as I was. My bestie, Priya, offered to let me stay with her till I was done with high school. She said her parents would be completely okay with it. But her parents weren't the problem. Mine were.

As soon as I walked into the kitchen the next morning, I knew my mom had not given in because there was a palpable awkwardness in the room. Both Paul and my mom were both seated, silently staring at their plates of scrambled eggs, bacon, and toast instead of at each other.

Neither of them acknowledged my existence as I sat down. A few moments after I sat down, Paul left for work without uttering a single word. To be honest, I preferred this silence and would pick it over his usual annoyingly chatty self any day. The problem I had was with what had caused this silence.

The car ride to school with my mom was as silent and

awkward as breakfast had been. Back before Paul came into our lives, I would have been honest with her about things, and we would have talked openly. But that was back when she had been on my side.

"So… you know Paul has been renovating his mother's house recently, right?" she asked.

I was surprised she had brought up the topic at all. I was used to not having a say in their decisions.

"Yup," I answered, nonchalantly.

I needed to know what she was thinking first and what her strategy was.

"And he's been thinking that it might be a good idea for us to relocate there," she continued.

"Hmmm," I replied.

"It's a beautiful house—it would be a great place for you to grow up… nothing like the city," she explained. "It's a very homey small town—"

"I like it here," I told her firmly.

"I know… I do too," she sighed.

I could tell she was tired; the bags under her eyes were darker than usual, despite her best efforts to cover them up with concealer. And there was a sadness about her.

"Have you told *him* that?" I asked.

"I have… we've been going back and forth about it."

"I see. If you don't want to move either, I don't see why we have to. I mean, if he loves you—loves us—he wouldn't mind doing what makes us happy, right?"

"He does love us, Lil. It's more complicated than that. He wants what's best for us, that's all."

"Do you really believe that, Mom?"

"I do… but I will be talking to him again. I don't think this move is the right thing for us right now, and it's going to be too big of an adjustment for you."

This conversation put my mind more at ease, even if only slightly. As much as my mom was willing to sacrifice to keep Paul happy, I knew moving was something she would not easily give in to.

I came home from school pretty late that evening because I had some extra classes I was attending. I had asked my music teacher to tutor me after school because I wanted to improve at playing the violin before the year ended.

My dad had bought me the violin when I was younger and encouraged me to learn how to play it. A violin teacher used to come to our place once a week to give me lessons, and my dad sat with us the entire time to help motivate me. That was until he got sick, and we couldn't afford the private lessons anymore. But I promised him I wouldn't stop playing, and my music teacher at school was kind enough to help me after school.

Once dinner was done, my mom and Paul sat me down to talk again. My heart was pounding. They were seated together, Paul's arm around my mom's shoulders, and he had this stupid, smug expression on his face. Like he had won, and he knew it. Her eyes were red and puffy, but her lips were curled into a forced smile.

"Paul and I discussed the move, and we think it's best for now," my mom informed me quietly.

"Why?" I whispered.

I thought she was going to talk to him about staying in the city. What happened to that plan?

"I think it could be a great way for us to start over, Lil," Paul smiled, still smug.

I fucking hated it when he called me that. We were not close enough for him to use a nickname.

"I don't want to start over—I love it here! This is where all my friends are, where all my memories of my dad are," I retorted, enjoying the way he flinched when I mentioned my dad.

"It doesn't have to be a permanent move. If you don't like it there, we can move back to the city…" my mom tried to explain.

"Do you mean that, or are you saying that to shut me up?" I asked my mom pointedly.

She sat there fidgeting with the ring on her finger, not knowing how to answer. She knew I had called her out on her bluff.

"Of course we do, Lil—we only want what's best for you," Paul eventually chimed in.

"Sweetie, I'm sorry," my mom said in a low, quivering voice. "I do love you, and I do want us to be happy," she added after a few seconds.

I bit my lip, trying to get a hold of my emotions. I understood that she needed Paul, that he was the financial lifeline keeping us afloat in the sea of debt we had been drowning in. But was moving truly the only option? Couldn't she have fought harder for us just this once?

"This is where I was born. This is where the little deli Dad took me to every weekend is. This is where our favorite hot dog cart is. This is where Dad taught me to ride a bike, and this is where Dad is buried. Do you honestly believe I would be happy somewhere else?" I asked my mom, glaring at her with hate-filled eyes.

"Dad would have hated the woman you've become," I added out of spite.

She stared back at me, defeated. Silently, I got up and walked to my room, slamming the door behind me. I knew nothing I said would ever make a difference, so why bother?

FORTY-NINE

I leaned against the door, breathing heavily. My vision was blurry from the hot, angry tears that were falling down my cheeks.

In my rage, I emptied my school bag and repacked it with some clothes and other necessary items. I couldn't be here anymore. I couldn't take it anymore.

I didn't want to think about moving. I needed some air. I needed to be with someone who genuinely loved and cared about me. So, I texted Priya and headed to her place. I saw her waiting on the pavement outside her apartment building, and she hugged me as soon as she saw me. Her warm brown eyes were filled with worry, her long, straight black hair blowing slightly with the breeze.

The tears fell down my cheeks once again as I followed her to her bedroom. Being next to her, someone who understood what I was going through, already made me feel better. Even though deep down, I knew that this would only be a momentary refuge from the inevitable.

I told her about everything that had happened. She comforted me the best she could and told me I could stay for as long as I needed to. We talked until we tired ourselves out and fell asleep.

I woke up the next day, well rested for the first time in

months. I turned around and noticed that Priya wasn't in her bed, so I went to the living room, expecting to find her there. Instead, I saw her seated on the couch next to her parents, and opposite them were Paul and my mom. My mom seemed genuinely relieved to see me. Paul smiled when he saw me, but I could see the hidden rage behind it.

"There you are! We've been worried sick about you, Lil," Paul exclaimed, a fake smile plastered on his face.

"How could you leave like that, without a single word?" my mom added.

My hands were cold and clammy as I stared at her blankly. I wasn't surprised they were here. I mean, I had dipped without a word, but a small part of me had hoped they wouldn't care enough to look for me immediately.

"We're terribly sorry to bother all of you. We'll take Lily home now and deal with this situation as a family," my mother apologized to Priya's parents.

"Oh, it's no problem at all," Priya's mom said. "She's welcome to stay as long as she wants to. You know the girls are like family."

"Nonsense, we can't leave Lil behind. She's the glue that holds our little family together." Paul smiled, getting up and putting his hand on my shoulder.

"Um, I think it might be best if Lily stays here for a while," Priya chimed in, staring at Paul disgustedly.

"Yes, she could stay here till you're able to settle down in your new place—it's still a while before school starts, right?" asked Priya's mom.

"Thank you for your concern, but we know what we're doing," Paul replied, passive-aggressively, staring daggers at her.

"I don't think you do because it seems like you're pressuring Lily to move when she clearly doesn't want to," argued Priya.

She pulled my arm, so that I was now safely beside her and away from Paul's grip. Paul's cheery smile faded and was replaced with irritation. But as quickly as his performative cheeriness had disappeared, it reappeared to mask the irritation.

"Unfortunately, *we're* her parents, and your opinion doesn't count, little girl," Paul said to Priya in the most condescending tone possible.

"Last I checked, *you're* not her parent, so…" Priya retorted without skipping a beat.

"Priya!" exclaimed her mom, surprised by her outburst.

"We should get going," said my mom, quickly trying to de-escalate the situation.

I didn't want to leave, but I also didn't want to get Priya in trouble. I knew that I had no choice but to go with Paul and my mom anyway.

I turned back to look at Priya. She had a desperate expression on her face, and I knew she wanted me to stay and fight. And I wanted to fight—I so badly wanted to fight. But I couldn't do this anymore, and I didn't want to suck her into our dysfunction. So, I pulled my arm away from hers and silently followed Paul and my mom out of the front door.

They both yelled at me the entire car ride home. They told me how disappointed they were in my behavior, how they expected me to do as I was told, and be grateful for all they did for me. I stayed silent, knowing that saying something would only make the situation worse.

I was about to head to my room as soon as we got back, but Paul asked to talk to me. My mom had left for work, but he had taken the day off, which meant it was only the two of us at home. I reluctantly agreed, not wanting another lecture, and sat down on the couch beside him.

"You know, I just don't understand why you're fighting me at every turn, Lil," Paul told me.

"It's Lily," I interrupted.

He sighed and shook his head. He was trying to play it cool, but his face was flushed in anger.

"I knew it would take some time for you to warm up to me, but this is getting ridiculous. For Pete's sake, your mother and I are married now. You should be happy that I'm here taking care of the two of you," Paul finished.

"I never asked you to take care of me. I never asked for you to be in my life," I reminded him.

"No, you didn't, but without me, you and your mother would be living on the streets," Paul said in a low voice.

His tone had changed, and he was no longer trying to hide his disapproval. In fact, he was sounding more threatening than angry now.

"Maybe that would have been better than this." I leaned back and crossed my arms in defiance.

This kind of manipulation may work on my mother, but it was not going to work on me. I was not going to let him try to guilt me into being nice to him.

"Even if you hate me, you should stop acting like such a little brat for your mother's sake. You have no idea what she's been through because of your dad. She deserves some peace."

"How dare you? Don't you dare bring my dad into this," I warned him, my blood boiling.

"You know it's true. Your mom suffered all this time because of him, and yet you have him up on a pedestal and treat your mom as though her happiness means nothing," Paul went on.

"I'm done with this conversation," I snapped, getting up. "I'm not going to let you manipulate me like you do my mom."

I began walking away when Paul grabbed my arm with so much strength it made me gasp in pain. He spun me around and pulled my arm till his face was right in front of mine. I had never seen him this aggravated before. My brain was yelling at me to get away from him, but he was still holding on to my arm tightly enough that his fingers were digging into my flesh.

"Let's get one thing straight, you fucking little brat. You will do exactly as you are told. God put me in charge of this family. I'm the man in this house, and my word will be the final one. If you don't learn to shut the fuck up and listen when I speak, I can, and will, make your life miserable," he spoke so softly it was almost a whisper.

"Fuck you," I responded, emphasizing every syllable and staring him right in the eye.

His eyes widened in surprise at my response, and while he was momentarily thrown off, I took the chance to spit right in the center of his stupid face. He flinched as my saliva hit his forehead.

The fear I had experienced just seconds earlier seemed to disappear almost magically. Hearing him say all that to me only confirmed that I was right about him all along. He had no interest in our happiness. All he wanted was control.

To my surprise, he let go of my arm and chuckled. He wiped off my spit with the back of his hand. I stood there rubbing the reddening bruise he had left on my arm. Then suddenly, I was on the ground. I grabbed my face. The left side was burning with pain. The metallic taste of blood hit my mouth as my brain scrambled to make sense of what had happened. He had hit me right across the face.

He stood over me, observing, and then slowly squatted beside me as I tried to recover. I cowered, covering my face, bracing myself. But he roughly pushed my arms away and grabbed my chin, forcing me to look at him. I expected him to be angry, but he had no emotion on his face. Even his eyes were eerily blank.

"Don't you ever disrespect me again, do you understand me?" he asked menacingly.

"Do you understand me?" he shouted when he didn't get an answer from me.

I nodded my head as much as I could, sobbing. He let go of me and got up, walking past me and going to his bedroom, slamming the door behind him. I lay there crying on the floor, utterly hopeless.

FIFTY

I STAYED OUT OF PAUL'S WAY FROM THEN ON. NOW THAT I knew exactly what he was capable of, I was not going to go around poking the bear. I talked to my friends about what had happened. Although they were outraged at first, we all knew there wasn't much I could do about it.

No one would believe a "nice guy" like Paul would do something like that. And even if they did, I knew my mother would never leave him. Telling her or anyone about what happened would only make things worse for me.

We agreed that the best thing to do for now was play along. I was almost eighteen. I would wait till I was legal. Then I'd move back to New York for college, and my friends and I would get an apartment together. I had to believe that would happen eventually. It was the only thing that was keeping me going.

In a few weeks, we were all packed up and ready to leave. I said my teary goodbyes to my friends, the little gecko living on my bedroom wall, and the city I loved with every fiber of my being.

As we drove to our new home for the first time, I quickly noticed how strikingly different it was in this town. There were much fewer apartment buildings, barely any. There were, however, lots of expensive and well-maintained houses with lovely front yards.

Our new home was quite beautiful, I couldn't deny it. The classic, old-timey look instantly drew me in. It had hardwood floors, some pretty flowers on the windowsills, and even a swing out front.

The only thing I hated was the decor in my bedroom. It looked like something a five-year-old would enjoy. The walls of the room were covered with bright pink wallpaper, there was a large bed with a pink nightstand on either side at the center of the room, and a matching pink bookshelf in the corner with no books on it yet. There was also a study table by the window with a lamp on it.

The house was lovely, but I didn't get a good vibe from the town itself. It was the kind of place where everyone was in everyone else's business. Where people went to church every Sunday but still found the time to gossip and be the most judgmental versions of themselves, while simultaneously pretending to care.

I walked around the town a couple of times over the next few days, but it gave me the heebie-jeebies with the way people stopped to stare at me. I was the new girl that they would be gossiping about later on.

I noticed young kids rode their bikes or walked around in groups of three or four on the sidewalks daily. I had to duck a couple of times as I tried to avoid a group of them furiously riding their bikes, hopped up on sugar from the ice cream cones in their hands. You don't see that much in the city. There, we learned from an early age the dangers of being young and alone.

I had barely seen anyone close to my age, though. I assumed they were all busy hanging out elsewhere or traveling for the summer. The only people I'd met so far were bored housewives and overly friendly husbands, who were clearly trying to compensate for the cold demeanor of their wives.

Summer was almost over. I had two weeks till school started, and I would have to assimilate with the other kids. I was not too eager to do that. The only thing I was eager to do was talk to the music teacher about helping me with my violin lessons.

I had walked past the school during one of my explorations of the town. It didn't look awful, simply rundown. The paint on the walls was chipping, and the plants were messy and unwatered. I noticed a small Nazi symbol graffiti on one of the walls, and suddenly I was grateful for my green eyes and lighter complexion. This was going to be a long two years.

A couple of days after we had settled in, I had the displeasure of meeting some of Paul's friends from high school. Their personalities closely resembled his own. Self-absorbed narcissists, who had clearly peaked in high school and refused to talk about anything other than the "good ol' days."

After that first dinner, I could tell he was irritated by how aloof I had acted. I had barely said a single word all night. He loudly emphasized to his friends that I was shy and quiet, but I could tell he was embarrassed. Thankfully, my standoffish behavior was enough to make sure I was no longer invited when they hung out again.

It was a relief, really, to have the house to myself, even if it was only for a couple of hours. I could watch things Paul disapproved of, by which I mean literally everything. And I would pretend to be asleep when they got back home, which meant I had little to no contact with them most days.

THE NIGHT BEFORE MY FIRST DAY OF SCHOOL, I HEARD A KNOCK on my door. My mom entered the room and, after a few awkward seconds of standing by the door, she eventually sat down at the edge of my bed. I stared at her suspiciously, putting down the book I was reading.

"How are you liking it here?" she asked.

I shrugged in response.

"Are you excited for school tomorrow?" she went on.

"What do you think?" I retorted, irritated by her line of questioning.

"You know, you might like it here if you gave it a chance, Lil," my mom said.

"Do *you* like it here?" I was honestly curious.

"I… it's different, but I think I could get used to it," she answered.

She was fidgeting with her hands, clearly trying to avoid eye contact.

"But this isn't about me—it's about you. Please try to give this place a chance before you decide to hate it. Make some friends at school, try some activities," she encouraged, trying to steer the subject away from herself.

"Fine," I lied.

I had absolutely no interest in giving this place a chance. But I did want this conversation to be over. She smiled at my answer and left after lightly kissing me on the forehead. I went to bed soon after and barely got any sleep. I kept having nightmares about the new school, and for some reason, all the characters from *Riverdale* were there. Which, honestly, made it way worse.

My eyes opened the next morning before my alarm rang, and I stared out of the window for a while, not quite ready to start the day. Eventually, I got out of bed and got ready for school. I put on my outfit for the day: jeans and a full-sleeved black tee with an oversized half-sleeved T-shirt on top. I decided to go with black boots instead of sneakers.

"Well, don't you look nice." My mom smiled as I entered the kitchen to get my breakfast.

"Thanks," I mumbled, grabbing my plate and heading to the table where Paul was already seated.

"Are you excited for your first day?" Paul asked. "I'm sure you'll love it. Kids here are very different from the kids in the city. Girls are real girls, and boys are real boys. They play football and wrestle and have an all-around good time," he continued before I could answer him.

"The boys here like to wrestle and have a good time with other boys?" I asked innocently.

"They sure do. I know I did when I was growing up," Paul replied, not picking up on my insinuation.

"You may want to hurry up, Lil. I need to drop you off soon," my mom warned.

I knew she had picked up on my comment and was quickly trying to change the subject before Paul figured out what I was doing. I wasn't interested in starting my day with an argument, so I shut up and began shoveling the eggs into my mouth.

"Whoa there, sailor. Young ladies shouldn't eat like that. Slow down and chew your food," Paul instructed.

It took every ounce of self-control I could summon to not spit my mouthful of half-chewed-up eggs right into Paul's stupid, smug, sexist face. Instead, I took a deep breath and swallowed.

FIFTY-ONE

The first couple of days of school were pretty uneventful. I tried to make myself invisible and talk to as few people as I could. It was not exactly easy, considering most of the teachers made me introduce myself in front of the class. The teachers were helpful and friendly, but I didn't know if that was the real them or a facade. The thing with towns like this one was that most people were not who they pretended to be.

The inside of the school itself was not awful, but like most of this town, it looked like it had not been updated much since the 1950s. The textbooks left out a lot of stuff. I wondered what the point of attending school was if we weren't learning anything from this century.

On my first day here, I was introduced to a girl named Patricia, who, according to the slimy principal, was supposed to show me around and help me get settled. She was insufferable. The typical perky blonde who's always had everything handed to her. Every time I tried to get away from her, she would somehow find me again.

The only silver lining was that I was finally able to talk to the music teacher at the end of the week. He was nice and told me he would be more than happy to help me. He also encouraged me to participate in the talent show and join the students who were helping organize it. I agreed, mostly because it meant I would have an excuse to stay after school frequently.

By the time the second week of school arrived, I had pretty much had enough of Patricia. If she didn't leave me alone, I was going to sock her in the fucking face. Almost as though the universe was messing with me, I saw Patricia right on cue, waiting by my locker as soon as I walked into school on Monday morning. She was waving enthusiastically with a huge grin.

"Hey, how was your weekend?" she asked cheerfully.

"It was okay." I shrugged.

"Do anything fun?" Patricia inquired.

"Not really," I sighed.

"Oh… do you wanna hang out after school?" she continued, clearly unable to take a hint.

"No, I kind of prefer my own company, actually," I told her, slamming my locker shut and walking away from her.

I walked into the music room, which was thankfully empty, and sat down. A few minutes later, Patricia barged in angrily. The perky smile was now completely wiped from her face.

"What is your fucking problem?" she asked, her arms crossed in front of her voluptuous chest.

"Right now? It's kind of you," I said casually.

"I have been nothing but nice to you, and this is the thanks I get?" she squeaked.

"I didn't ask you to be nice to me, so leave me alone, okay?"

"Fine, I will. I was just being nice to you because I know what it's like being the new girl," she pouted. "It was hard for me to fit in when I first moved here, and I thought I could make it easier for you."

I kind of felt guilty about my behavior as I studied Patricia's sullen face. She wasn't too bad. Most of the kids here were actually much nicer than I thought they would be, even though they kind of gave me *Children of the Corn* vibes.

"Look, I'm sorry, okay? It's been a big adjustment, moving here and starting over…" I apologized.

"It was like that for me, too. I'm from California, imagine how much of a change this was for *me*," she said.

"Damn, it must suck being stuck here," I sympathized.

"It did at first, but then I met Ian and everything changed. You know, you might like it here if you give it a chance. And you're stuck here anyway—might as well have some fun before you graduate, right?" She grinned.

Maybe I was wrong about her. What she had said made a lot of sense. I didn't have to sit around sulking the entire time I was here. I could have some fun and then dip as soon as I graduate.

"You're right." I smiled back at her.

Over the next couple of days, we got to know one another better. She was actually quite smart, but also really kind. She sort of reminded me of Priya. I ended up spending a lot of time at Patricia's.

If I had thought our new house was big, hers was practically a mansion. It was gigantic. She told me there were five bedrooms, since her stepmom used two of them for her art. Their backyard was huge, and it was even more well-kept than ours. In fact, everything in their house was sparkling clean— practically glowing.

However, the inside of her house was as cold as mine, and once I opened up more to her, I understood why. Although I didn't tell her the extent of how bad things were at home, I did tell her some of it, and she was sympathetic.

Her parents were divorced, and she lived with her dad and stepmom. Her problem was kind of the opposite of mine—neither really seemed to care about her existence at all. That's why her house was so devoid of human touch. But she had learned how to use their lack of interest to her advantage by doing as she pleased.

Staying over at her place was a lot of fun. We binge-watched *Drag Race*, laughing till our sides hurt. And we even tried doing Trixie's signature makeup, which I thought she could absolutely pull off.

In only two weeks, Patricia and I had grown very close. We just seemed to click. She eventually began asking me if I liked anyone at school. I told her I most definitely did not, after which she insisted on setting me up with one of Ian's friends. The only problem was that Ian was a jock, and so was his friend. I didn't date jocks or have anything to do with guys like that. We had nothing in common, and if I wanted to be objectified by a man oozing toxic masculinity, I would simply spend more time with Paul.

But Patricia would not get off my back about it. She told me that it was time for me to get out of my shell and try something new. I didn't have to marry this guy, just had to go on one double date with her and Ian. Eventually, I reluctantly agreed. Mostly to get her off my back because I knew she would not stop till she got what she wanted. And a little bit because she was right—it was just one date.

FIFTY-TWO

THE NIGHT OF THE DATE ARRIVED, AND I WENT OUT OF MY WAY to dress down. The last thing I wanted was for this guy to be interested in me. Or even worse, for him to think that I was interested in him. I was going to go for the date, be polite but aloof (the Lily specialty), leave, and never talk to this James guy again.

I put on my favorite oversized *It's Always Sunny* T-shirt, jeans, and black boots. Casual but cute. I did end up putting on a bit of makeup, even though I had initially thought I wouldn't. Nothing too noticeable, a touch of CC cream, concealer, lipstick, and some mascara.

I gazed in the mirror and smiled. It had been a while since I had been excited for something. It would be a much-needed break from my reality, even if only for a while.

I crept down the stairs, hoping to leave unnoticed. I almost made it to the front door when I heard Paul's voice.

"Going somewhere?" he asked, appearing in the living room doorway.

"Yeah, I'm going out with Patricia. My mom said I could," I replied.

"Oh… where are you two going?" Paul continued to interrogate me.

"Just gettin' some pizza." I shrugged, staring at my boots.

"Nice. We used to do that all the time when I was in high school," he told me, taking a sip of the beer in his hand.

I didn't respond, staring at him blankly instead. I had no interest in prolonging this conversation.

"Anyway, have fun and be back by ten," Paul instructed.

"Mom usually lets me stay out till eleven," I reminded him.

"Well, she's not here right now, is she?" Paul stated.

There it was—he had to do something to ruin my night. He just could not bear to see me happy. I knew he wanted a reaction out of me. Any excuse to stop me from going. But I wasn't going to let him win. I had no intention of giving him the satisfaction.

"Fine, I'll be back *around* ten," I agreed.

"*By* ten," Paul emphasized.

Fucking asshole.

"Fine."

I slammed the door behind me and walked to Patricia's car, which was waiting for me in the driveway. I was still frowning when I got in, but relaxed more as we chatted. Soon, we were rapping along to Doechii and vibing.

The guys were already at the pizza place when we got there. They both stood up to greet us as we approached the table. They were much taller than we were, especially compared to Patricia, who, despite her curves, was a significantly petite person. I had rarely been around Ian, but I could tell why Patricia liked him. With messy, sandy blond hair and a strong jawline, he was quite attractive. Hot, even.

But it was James who caught my attention. A closer inspection confirmed that he was a lot cuter than I thought, and I was taken aback by the fluttering in my stomach as I stared at him.

He had these beautiful gray eyes, which were accentuated by his thick eyelashes. His nose was the kind of attractive, untraditional nose I loved, the kind I assumed Greek gods had. He was wearing his football jacket, which fit snugly around his broad, masculine shoulders. His hand often moved up to push his dark curls back into place.

He was smiling slightly, and at first, I smiled back in response. But to my disappointment, he was pretty obviously staring at my chest. Fun. This night was clearly not going to go well. I was preparing myself for the worst when he spoke up.

"Nice shirt," he told me, nodding his head toward my shirt.

Oh, he had been staring at my shirt, not my chest. *My bad.* I kind of didn't know whether to be insulted or relieved.

"Thanks. I love *Sunny*," I replied.

"Right? It's literally incredible," he agreed.

The rest of the evening went amazingly. We talked almost the entire time. Eventually, we had to call it a night thanks to my early curfew, but we exchanged numbers and decided to keep talking and hanging out with one another.

I didn't know if this would go anywhere or lead to anything, but I could tell James was the kind of guy who would be a lot of fun to hang out with, and I was excited about that. I could tell by the grin on Patricia's face that she was pleased with the results of this evening, too.

I got home a couple of minutes before ten. I figured it was better to be a few minutes early than be late. Paul and my mom were seated on the couch, watching something on TV.

"You're back early," my mom noticed as I swiftly headed for my room.

"Yeah," I mumbled without slowing down.

I assumed Paul had not mentioned his new little curfew at

ten p.m. rule to her. Not that it mattered—she was never on my side anymore.

"I told her she could stay out till eleven, but I guess they were done early," I heard Paul lie to her.

I simply rolled my eyes and shut my bedroom door behind me. I had neither the strength nor the patience to have an argument with him right now.

I was changing into my pajamas when my phone buzzed. It was a text message. It simply said, *"Hey."* My heart beat a little faster. Another text followed.

"This is James, by the way."

I smiled, biting my lower lip. It was sweet of him to text me this soon. I guess he had a good time talking to me, too. I responded to his text, and before I knew it, we had been texting back and forth for over an hour. We finally said goodnight around midnight.

I woke up to a good morning text and grinned. He really did seem genuinely sweet.

FIFTY-THREE

IT HAD BEEN A FEW WEEKS SINCE JAMES AND I HAD GONE ON our first date. We had gone on quite a few more dates since then, and I had even met his family. They were great, just like him. Although his mom was slightly standoffish, I gave her the benefit of the doubt. Maybe she wasn't great in social situations, and it wasn't anything personal. Or maybe she was not comfortable around new people.

Having dinner with them was a lot of fun and reminded me of what it was like when my dad was alive. Everyone was laughing and chatting. His dad asked me about New York, my interests, and how I was settling in. His siblings loved playing with me. I almost didn't want to go back home to that lonely room I was always stuck in.

James asked about meeting my parents, too, and I tried to put it off as much as I could without making it weird. But I knew that eventually I would have to invite him over.

Tonight was the night I decided to tell them about James. I thought I would mention him casually before asking if we should invite him to dinner. Paul seemed to be in a particularly good mood that evening.

My mom placed our dessert in front of us at the end of the meal. It was now or never. As I began mustering up the courage to mention James, my mom asked me if there was anything new going on with me. That gave me the perfect opening.

"Actually, there is something new going on with me…" I mentioned moving the ice cream around with my spoon. I preferred my ice cream room temperature and melted.

"Really?" they both asked in unison.

"This boy at school asked me out, and I said yes," I told them.

They didn't need to know the actual timeline or the fact that we had been dating for almost a month behind their backs.

"A boy?" asked Paul, still visibly surprised.

My mom remained quiet but was staring at me intently. Why was that the part they were surprised about? Was I not attractive enough to find a boyfriend?

"Yup. His name is James, and he's on the football team," I continued, staring at the ice cream.

"That's great!" Paul exclaimed.

"It is?" I gasped, finally looking up.

This conversation had taken an unexpected turn.

"Of course, honey. You're old enough to start thinking about dating now, and we're happy for you." My mom smiled.

Something was definitely wrong. Was I in the *Twilight Zone*?

"We're just glad you turned out okay," Paul exclaimed, beaming.

"I turned out okay?" I asked skeptically.

"Well, you know, with the way you dress and the way you've been hanging out with that Patricia girl… we just thought you might have been… confused," Paul continued to explain.

"Confused about what?" I knew where this conversation was heading, but I kept fishing for a confirmation.

"Well, she's from California, and there's lots of confused people out there living in sin," Paul hinted.

"What do you mean?" I questioned once more.

"We thought you might like girls, sweetie. It's just with the clothes and the fact that you didn't seem too interested in boys till now. And so many kids in your generation are confused like that—easily led astray," my mom explained. "Either way, we're really glad you're normal."

Normal? Seriously? Wow.

"So, when do we get to meet this James? I think it's best if your mother and I get to know him before you two start going out," insisted Paul.

"I guess I could ask him over sometime," I said.

"Why don't you ask him to dinner on Friday?" my mom suggested.

"Um, yeah. Okay," I agreed.

FIFTY-FOUR

"Hello, sir," James greeted Paul, extending his hand.

"Hey there, young man." Paul shook James's hand enthusiastically.

I hadn't seen Paul this happy in… well, ever, now that I came to think of it. He must truly be relieved I ended up "normal." If only he knew.

"Ma'am, I brought these for you. Lily said they were your favorite." James handed my mother a bouquet of lilies.

"They are, so much so that I named her after them," my mom explained, beaming.

"Why don't we talk in the living room and let them handle the cooking?" Paul encouraged, putting his hand on James's shoulder and leading him toward the living room.

I knew that comment probably pissed James off. He was all about gender equality. He told me that it was how his mother had raised him. She taught him to cook, clean, and do other chores pretty early on. I admired that. If I ever have a kid, that's how I would raise them, too.

Thankfully, I had let James know in advance to expect comments like that one because my mom and Paul were a lot more traditional than his family was. He was sweet about it and told me he totally understood. That's how most people here were, so he wasn't surprised.

I went into the kitchen to help my mom with dinner, but could still hear Paul and James talking in the living room. They talked about football most of the time, which was one of the safe topics I had told James to stick to. Soon, we had set the dinner table and ushered them into the dining room.

"So, do you have any siblings, James?" Paul asked, cutting into his steak.

"Yeah, I have two," James replied. "A younger brother and sister."

"That must be nice—siblings are a blessing. I never had any, but I know we would have been so close if I did," my mom interjected.

"Is your brother into sports too?" Paul continued to question James.

"Not really, he prefers reading more," James told him.

"Not to worry, I'm sure he'll grow out of that and get more into sports when he gets older. But you need to make sure you're a good influence on him—toss the ball around with him and such," Paul advised.

I was mortified by his ridiculous comment, insinuating that reading was a gendered activity. My cheeks flushed with embarrassment. James did not seem even slightly phased by it, though, which I was grateful for.

"You know, I could have been a football player myself when I was younger," Paul informed us after a bit of an awkward silence. And with that, it began. A long and obviously made-up story about how Paul could have been an athlete but chose to be an engineer instead because he had strong family values. The man was 5'8" and built like Patrick Star. No one was buying that he could have been an athlete.

"That's interesting. Maybe we can play sometime, and you

can give me some tips," James suggested, with an innocent expression on his face.

I almost snorted with laughter. I knew James was just messing with him for our amusement.

"Oh, yeah… I mean, I would love to, but my shoulder has been giving me some trouble recently." Much to my delight, Paul was now turning beet red.

James secretly winked at me as Paul suddenly became hyper-focused on his food. For perhaps the first time ever, he had nothing to say.

"You didn't tell me about your shoulder—what happened?" my mom asked, genuinely concerned.

This just kept getting better.

"It's nothing, an injury at work, that's all," Paul mumbled.

"At work? Why didn't you tell me about it? What happened?" continued my mom, clearly not reading the room.

"It's nothing—just drop it," snapped Paul.

The table got quiet after Paul's little emotional outburst. I had a feeling Paul would not be mentioning football again for quite a while. If ever.

"We haven't seen your family at our church—do you go to another one?" Paul finally asked.

"Um… we prefer to worship privately," James lied.

I knew his family wasn't religious. Like at all. But James knew mine was and answered accordingly.

"I see," Paul frowned. "Maybe that's for the best. A lot of churches these days allow all kinds of people in. Not my cup of tea, if you ask me."

"That's right, sir. Either follow *all* the rules or don't follow any at all," James replied sarcastically.

James and I had talked about this and the hypocrisy of

people like Paul judging others when they were so far from perfect themselves. Something the Bible specifically forbids. However, Paul didn't get the sarcasm and nodded with a wide grin on his face.

The rest of the night went well, and it was clear that they approved of James.

As I walked James to his car, he told me that he had fun. Especially messing with Paul. I was relieved he felt that way because I had been convinced that this dinner would scare him away. He promised to text me as soon as he got home. I told him I would look forward to it. And I meant it.

FIFTY-FIVE

The next few weeks were amazing. James and I had the most wonderful time with one another. We would watch things we enjoyed together and chat about anything and everything. And best of all, sometimes we would simply quietly enjoy one another's company while doing our own thing.

He took me on the best dates. He bought me little presents all the time, listened to me, and asked questions. And when we touched, when we kissed, it was like heaven.

Which is why I couldn't understand this feeling I had. As though something was wrong. I genuinely enjoyed spending time with James. And I was clearly physically attracted to him. But there was something missing between us.

I tried to be normal around him because I didn't want him to know what I was thinking. I even made an effort to spend time with him whenever I could. Which wasn't easy because I had signed up for a bunch of stuff on my first day of school, hoping to spend as much time away from home as possible. I had even volunteered to help with the talent show as a favor to the music teacher, Mr. Live, for helping me with my violin lessons.

Mr. Live had been great. He gave me violin lessons once a week and was super helpful. And I was actually making good progress thanks to his guidance. He wasn't just the music teacher, though, he was also Ian's dad. So, at first, it was a little awkward. But he had such a calm vibe that made me feel calm around him, too.

He was quite young—something I hadn't expected, considering Ian's age, but I assumed he and his wife had kids early. However, despite his age, he had a mature demeanor. He spoke slowly but confidently in a deep, low voice. His wide blue eyes darted from the music sheet to my violin, but still managed to maintain their serenity.

I had really been enjoying my lessons with him. I could tell he was truly connected with the music, like it was a part of him. And although I had not mentioned why continuing to practice the violin was so important to me, I knew he sensed that I had a personal connection with it and tried his best to improve my skills.

Thinking of my violin, the only connection I had left to my dad, was particularly difficult for me to handle today. It was going to be the anniversary of my dad's death tomorrow.

I was trying my best not to think about it and focus on the present instead. I knew that if I did think about it, I was going to start crying, and I didn't know when or if the tears would ever subside. So much had happened since he passed, and I constantly wished he were still here. I couldn't stop thinking about how my life had been and how it was now, and how it could have been if he were still here with us.

I shook my head, trying to clear my thoughts and focus on the present. I was currently sitting on the couch with James. We were watching *The Silence of the Lambs*. It was one of our favorites.

I was sort of glad we were hanging out at my place tonight, since Paul and my mom had gone out for dinner. Although I enjoyed spending time with his family a lot, I definitely got the vibe that his mom wasn't a fan of me dating her son.

"What do you think it's like?" I randomly asked James, tuning out from the movie despite my best efforts.

"What?" He raised his eyebrows in confusion at my abrupt question.

"What do you think death is like, I mean," I elaborated.

James stared at me in surprise, thrown off by my question. And I couldn't blame him. Still, I appreciated that he thought about it and answered my question the best he could. We talked about our beliefs, and it was interesting to hear about his, considering he had never been raised with any sort of religious influence from his parents.

Despite having such different backgrounds and upbringings, we actually had pretty similar beliefs about good and evil. I couldn't help but wonder if everyone comes to that conclusion eventually—that humans are inherently evil. That we do bad things. And we enjoy doing bad things. It's the bad things that feel so fucking good that make us feel alive.

And that's when it sort of hit me—I finally understood what was wrong with my relationship with James. It wasn't either of us that was the problem. In fact, there wasn't even a problem per se. What was throwing me off was that it was too good, too fucking perfect all the time. And that was annoying.

It took all the fun out of the relationship. It wasn't exciting, or new, or anything really. Instead, it was stagnant. Superficial. James was great, but he would never be able to relate to someone like me. He had always had the house in the suburbs, with supportive parents and loving siblings. He had never struggled the way I did.

I loved our dates, conversations, and time spent together, but when I reflected on them, they seemed mostly mundane. Predictable even. That wasn't the kind of relationship I wanted to be in. I wanted to be with someone who made me feel alive, someone who made me feel seen and heard. I wanted them to see past the mask I put on every day. Someone who saw the darkest parts of my soul and still adored me regardless.

It hurt admitting that as much as I adored James, he was probably not my forever person. Dating James was okay for now. But when I thought about my future and the person I wanted to spend my life with, I knew that it had to be someone who had struggled. Someone who was broken in the same way that I was. And that person was, unfortunately, not James.

FIFTY-SIX

I WOKE UP STILL TIRED AND TRIED MY BEST NOT TO CRY, TO think about how this was the day I had lost the most important person in my life. Instead, I forced myself to get out of bed and get dressed.

My mom drove me to school in silence, never mentioning my dad or acknowledging what today was. When we pulled into the parking lot, she reached over and pulled me into a tight hug. I was surprised, but after a moment, I pushed her away and got out of the car without a word. Too little, too late.

As I sat in the music room at the end of the day, waiting for my lesson with Mr. Live, I got a text from my mom. My fingers clenched around my phone as I read it. She wanted to let me know that she and Paul were going out for dinner to celebrate some promotion he had gotten. The idea of them out at dinner, celebrating, on this day of all days. It hit a nerve.

Before I could get a hold of myself, the tears were already running down my cheeks. I sniffled at first, trying to hold back, but soon it all came pouring out. All the frustration, all the grief, all the sorrow I had tried to hold in all day finally consumed me. In only a couple of seconds, I was crying wholeheartedly, my entire body shaking with every sob.

And right on cue, in walked Mr. Live. I tried to quickly wipe away my tears and compose myself, but I knew it wouldn't help much. My face was flushed, and my lips were still trembling. He was clearly shocked to see me in this state.

"Lily, are you alright?" Mr. Live inquired, walking toward me briskly.

"I'm—I'm fine," I managed to choke out before the tears took over once more.

"You don't seem fine… you can tell me what's wrong, I promise," Mr. Live kindly offered.

"Nothing's wrong, I… it's my dad's death anniversary today," I confided in him.

"I'm sorry to hear that," he sympathized. "You know, it's okay to feel sad about things like that."

He sat down beside me and lightly patted my back as I continued to sit there and silently sob. This was so fucking embarrassing. I hoped he would keep this to himself and not mention it to Ian.

"Feeling better?" Mr. Live eventually asked.

"Yeah." I nodded.

I wasn't lying. That was a pretty good cry. I was still slightly embarrassed, but didn't care as much. It was one of those moments where you cry so hard that by the time you're done, you don't have any more tears left inside you. I could feel the dopamine rushing into my brain, giving the illusion of happiness momentarily.

"You know, Lily, I lost my father when I was young, too," Mr. Live confided in me.

"Really?" I asked, surprised by his revelation.

"Yeah, he was the one who first got me into music. He taught me everything I know," he explained.

"That's nice. You two must have been close," I responded.

"We were. He always told me I would be the one to live out

his dream. He wanted to be a rock star but never quite made it. He told me that I would make it through, that I'd be a rock star someday, and he would be proud."

"What went wrong?" I asked, genuinely curious now. "No offense."

"Well, life happened… My wife got pregnant with Ian when I was in my final year of high school, which made it sort of impossible to pursue my dreams. Instead, we remained here and built a life together."

"Do you regret it? Not pursuing your dreams?"

"I did initially. She wanted to keep it, and I didn't want to be a deadbeat, so I stayed out of obligation. But over the years, I've grown to love and appreciate the life I have now. It might not be the life of a rock star, but it's not a bad life at all. I honestly can't complain." Mr. Live shrugged.

I wondered how he could have let all his dreams go just like that without a fight. He didn't seem regretful; in fact, he seemed satisfied. Or was I mistaking resignation for satisfaction?

"What about your dad? What happened to him? If you don't mind me asking."

"He… well, he killed himself when I was about twelve," sighed Mr. Live.

"I'm so sorry. That's truly awful. I can't imagine what that must have been like for you."

My heart broke for him. What a truly dreadful situation to find yourself in at such a young age. How someone that young would even process a suicide was beyond me.

"It wasn't too bad—my mom was one hell of a woman," chuckled Mr. Live.

He was trying to lighten the mood, but I could tell that he

was still affected by his father's death. Although his lips were curled in a slight smile, his eyes were distant and downcast.

"I'm glad. It's hard being a teenager with no dad," I confessed, trying to comfort him.

"It is, but I want you to learn from my experiences. You're still young and can have a good life if you choose the right path. Things never just magically work out like they do in the movies, but if you work hard, you'll have a good enough life," said Mr. Live.

"Thanks—I think I needed to hear that today. Sometimes … it's hard to remain hopeful," I admitted.

Sometimes I didn't want to remain hopeful anymore. In fact, sometimes I wanted to give up and end it all.

"I know, Lily," Mr. Live studied my face, the sadness still in his eyes. "But you have to keep pushing ahead, and if you ever need to talk to someone, I'm always right here, okay?"

"Okay." A smile formed on my lips.

We sat there after that, silently staring at one another. Our eyes quietly convey our deepest secrets. And in that moment, for the first time since my dad had passed, I truly felt seen. Wholly connected with another human being. Someone who got me, someone who could understand my pain.

My eyes couldn't help but travel down to Mr. Live's lips and then his jaw. He had no facial hair, but I could see a five o'clock shadow forming over his sharp jawline. His skin was smooth, with a few fine lines setting in on his forehead and around his mouth.

I had looked at him so many times. But it was like this was the first time I was actually seeing him. This was no longer the man who awkwardly waved at me when we bumped into each other at church or the grocery store.

I could feel the butterflies in my stomach, and my cheeks flushed once more, only for very different reasons this time. I could smell his cologne—it was intoxicating. Unconsciously, I licked my lips, once more staring into those piercing blue eyes.

"I think it's best if we skip today's lesson… you've had a long day and deserve some rest," suggested Mr. Live, abruptly getting up and walking away from where I was seated.

Did he know? Could he also feel this electricity between us? Or did he think I was just some stupid teenage girl? I hoped it wasn't the latter.

"Um, okay," I agreed, getting up too and heading to the door.

"Hey, Mr. Live," I called from the door.

"Yeah?" he asked, turning toward me.

"Thank you… for today." And I truly meant it.

"Of course, dear," he smiled.

I got into bed as soon as I got home. My knees were weak, and I was too emotionally exhausted to do anything other than lie in bed. I stared at my ceiling, thinking about what had occurred between Mr. Live and me.

I bit my lip, my mind fully occupied with thoughts of him. The way his voice softened when he was speaking to me about his past. The way he smelled like a mix of cologne and aftershave. And, of course, the way his eyes, which were usually so composed, were in that moment filled with raw emotion.

FIFTY-SEVEN

I WAS HOPING THAT MY SUDDEN INFATUATION WITH MR. LIVE would be gone by now, but it was a week later, and there were still butterflies in my stomach every time I was near him. Which was, unfortunately, a lot, considering I was spending the week helping with the talent show and would be alone with him for an hour today for my violin lesson.

The only good thing was that Brian was usually around, and I ended up talking to him much more than usual because I was trying to avoid talking to or thinking about Mr. Live. Brian and I became much better friends through the awkward conversations, though, and it was nice to make another friend here.

Brian was wonderful. He was kind and funny. We instantly got along. And other than me, he was the only person of color I had talked to at this school, which was cool. He wasn't that tall or muscular like James. But he had gentle eyes, clear brown skin, a nice smile despite the braces, and a creative spirit.

He played the flute, among other instruments, and we had very similar tastes in music. We liked a lot of the same bands and artists, and were both currently obsessed with Rage Against the Machine.

Avoiding Mr. Live and everything to do with him was sort of working until Brian told me about the annual trip for music students. I knew it was a bad idea and that I should skip it. But truthfully, I did want to go, knowing Mr. Live was in charge, and this could be a good way to get closer to him.

No, I shouldn't. I couldn't. Poor James—he didn't deserve this. Sure, our relationship wasn't perfect and was missing that spark, but we could work on it. I could try harder to spend more time with him, to try to get to know him better. Maybe the spark would magically appear if I did.

"Are you okay, Lily? You seem to be somewhere else today," noticed Mr. Live.

Damn it.

"I'm fine… sorry," I apologized, shaking my head.

"Maybe we should call it a day—it's been almost an hour anyway," Mr. Live gently suggested.

"Yeah," I agreed, putting my violin away.

"So, will you be coming for the annual trip? I mentioned it to your parents when I ran into them the other day, and they agreed that it would be a great way for you to get to know some of your peers better."

No! Say no!

"Yup, I'll be there," I said.

FUCK.

Everything went by in a blur after that. I started dressing up more for school and no longer wore whatever I could find in my closet. I wore more makeup, too. I styled my hair, enhancing the natural curls instead of combing them out, and my shirts were now cropped and quite tight. Of course, I covered them up with sweaters and hoodies till I got to school.

James didn't show any signs of noticing this sudden change in my appearance, which I was thankful for. Or maybe he did and chose not to say anything. Either way, I was glad to not have that conversation right now.

Unlike James, I sensed that Mr. Live *did* notice these changes in my appearance. I couldn't be sure—I could simply be overthinking everything—but I felt his eyes linger on me slightly longer than they usually would. And sometimes I would catch him staring at me absentmindedly when he thought I wasn't looking. But that could be more out of concern than anything else. I needed to be sure. I needed to know what was really going through his head.

This trip would be the best time to finally figure out what he's thinking—how he felt about me... about us. We were leaving on Saturday morning and would be back on Sunday evening. That would give me two days and one night to get closer to him.

As Mr. Live had already mentioned the trip to them, Paul and my mom were completely okay with it, much to my surprise. I think Paul was only okay with it because Mr. Live was going to be there.

Apparently, Paul knew him from way back because they both grew up in this town, and Paul even went to high school with Mark's eldest brother. They were the cool kids that Paul had admired when he was younger. Even now, he would be all weird around Mark at church. Like he was meeting his favorite celebrity or something. It was super cringey.

FIFTY-EIGHT

"Sure, sounds fun," I said, handing James back the joint we were sharing in his car.

He wanted to hang out on Friday, and I agreed. I was still confused and experiencing a lot of guilt due to my recent feelings for Mr. Live, and I thought that spending more time with James might somehow make me see that James was a much better fit for me. And, hopefully, that would get rid of these unwanted feelings for Mr. Live.

I didn't want this. I would give up everything to make these emotions disappear. But my life wasn't that easy. The more I tried to resist, the stronger they got. It had gotten to a point where I couldn't even concentrate because I was busy daydreaming about Mr. Live all day.

I headed to class with Brian, hoping to find out more about the trip from him, since I knew almost nothing about it when I idiotically agreed to go. I saw James staring at us with a thoughtful expression on his face as I walked away with Brian. I strongly suspected that he thought Brian had a thing for me because he had not so subtly hinted at it.

However, I knew for a fact that wasn't the case because, first, Brian's girlfriend is insanely hot—like Sabrina Carpenter hot. And second, he hadn't shown any signs of wanting to be more than friends.

I had tried to convince James that it was nothing he had to worry about. But I hadn't tried *too* hard because, truth be told, I would rather he be preoccupied with Brian than figure out the real reason why I had been acting so distant and distracted lately.

Friday came pretty quickly, and I was mostly packed and ready for the trip. I was both excited and terrified. I knew another adult would be there too. A female teacher I didn't know well, but who seemed popular with the students, was also joining us. But the thought of being almost completely alone with Mr. Live all weekend was driving me crazy. It was all I could think about.

"Who are you talking to?" James asked as we sat on his couch watching television.

"Just Brian," I told him absentmindedly, hoping that would be the end of the conversation.

In reality, I was on Reddit trying to see if anyone had any advice on how I could spend some alone time with Mr. Live. I obviously did not mention the age gap and the fact that I was technically a minor.

"Oh… speaking of which, I heard the music students were going on a trip this weekend," mentioned James casually.

"Oh… yeah…" I said, still preoccupied with Reddit.

They had some pretty good suggestions.

"You didn't tell me about that…"

Fuck, I knew I was forgetting something! I finally glanced up from my phone, and James was staring at me, much angrier than I had expected him to be. He had sounded laid-back just now. But I guess my not telling him about the trip had frustrated him more than I'd realized.

"Oh, didn't I? My bad, I thought I told you on Monday," I replied, trying to sound nonchalant.

"Nope… it's kinda weird that you didn't," he kept going.

"What do you mean? Obviously, I forgot. Why would I hide it from you?"

"Why *would* you hide it from me?"

"Are you fucking serious right now?" I asked, staring at him.

"Yeah, why the fuck are you lying to me about shit?" he practically shouted at me.

My heart pounded faster because I knew he was right. I had been lying to him and hiding stuff from him. And I couldn't have him knowing why. So, when he accused Brian, I decided to turn the tables on him and tell him I lied because he was being weird and overprotective. I thought he would feel guilty and back off, but all it did was aggravate him even more. I had made the mistake of poking the bear. I could tell this fight was getting out of control.

I got up from the couch and walked toward the front door, hoping to leave before this argument escalated any further. And judging from James's demeanor, I was starting to believe that it might.

"Where the fuck are you going? You can't just leave in the middle of our conversation," he warned me, his voice getting scarily low as he followed close behind me.

"Yes, I can. I'm done. Don't call me," I said, walking faster toward the door.

I was genuinely scared now and wanted to leave before this got even more out of control. But before I could open the door, James grabbed me by my arm and forcefully pulled me back. His face was only about an inch from mine, and the unnerving look in his eyes was startling. I had never seen him like this. Every hair on my body was standing up, a chill going down my spine.

"You are not fucking breaking up with me," he growled, holding my upper arm tightly enough that it started going numb.

"James, you're hurting me," I whispered.

I struggled to pull my arm away from his grip as tears escaped down my cheeks despite my best efforts to stop them. I was taking deep breaths but still felt out of breath, like my lungs weren't filling up, no matter how much oxygen I breathed in.

"I'm sorry. I'm so sorry, Lily," James said, abruptly letting go of my arm and taking a few steps back.

He looked mortified and was staring at me with pleading eyes. But I didn't care anymore. I needed to get away from him as fast as I could.

"Stay the fuck away from me," I warned him, slamming the door behind me.

I lay in bed that night, thinking about what had transpired between James and me. I had never even imagined he could be so violent and angry all of a sudden. He was usually so controlled and calm. Almost overly so, now that I think about it. Had that all been a calculated act to impress me? To hide the cracks beneath the surface.

It had been truly frightening to see this side of him, but I had to admit a small part of me had kind of liked seeing the real person underneath instead of the mask he always had on. In a way, I was relieved that he was fucked up too.

But I was too exhausted to care right now. So instead, I closed my eyes, falling into a restless sleep.

FIFTY-NINE

I woke up pretty early Saturday morning and lay in my bed watching the sun come up. I was still confused about everything, and now I felt even more guilty after what had transpired between James and me yesterday.

Sure, he had blown up at me, but clearly that had been my fault. He was right to be infuriated. I *had* been lying to him and keeping things from him. And the messed-up part was that the secrets I was keeping were far worse than he assumed.

I got up and began getting ready. I noticed some messages and missed calls from James, which I ignored. I did not want to deal with that whole situation right now. I was honestly relieved to get some space from him.

There were some texts from Patricia too, asking about the trip and if I wanted to hang out when I got back on Sunday. I would text her later; I was too overwhelmed right now as it was.

My mom drove me to school and awkwardly hugged me goodbye. I sat down next to Brian on the bus and couldn't help but stare at the back of Mr. Live's head, since he was seated right in front of us. He had a full, thick head of hair. I imagined what it would feel like tangled between my fingers.

"Earth to Lily," joked Brian, interrupting my train of thought.

"Sorry about that. I tune out sometimes," I laughed.

"I was just saying that it'll probably be weird sharing a room with Fiona. She's… um, different," Brian said.

"You mean the girl who I once saw licking chalk is weird?" I gasped with mock disbelief. "Don't worry. I don't plan on spending too much time with her."

"You can always come over to my room," suggested Brian.

"It's the last one before the teacher's rooms, right?" I asked, trying to sound casual.

"Yup, 814, and I think Mr. Live is at 815. But don't worry, I don't think the teachers can hear us—the walls are pretty thick. I went last year, too," he let me know.

"Perfect."

And it was, indeed, perfect. His room was right next to Mr. Live's. I could use that to my advantage. Perhaps knock on Mr. Live's door and pretend I meant to knock on Brian's? Or would that be too obvious? I had to keep thinking. I needed a proper plan.

Thankfully, the day was pretty boring and filled with the usual field trip stuff, which gave me a lot of time to think. The bad news was that I couldn't talk to Mr. Live for most of the day, since Mrs. Spencer was always nearby. I spent most of the day with Brian instead, and by evening, I was getting desperate. It was now or never—I had to find a way to get Mr. Live alone, and I think I sort of had a plan by now.

"You going somewhere?" asked Fiona, casually biting into a tomato like it was an apple.

She was seated cross-legged on her bed with the hotel bathrobe on, her pixie-cut hair still wet from the shower she had taken a few minutes ago. When you first notice her, she's quite pretty in that androgynous, artsy kind of way. Like a young Joan Jett. But then you really notice her, and all you think is, *where did she even get that tomato from? There's no way that was in the mini fridge.*

"Yeah, I'm going to the boys' room to hang out with Brian," I stated, hoping my unfriendly tone would end this conversation.

"Aren't you dating that guy on the football team?" she inquired, clearly not taking the hint.

"Not that it's any of your business, but Brian and I are just friends, and James and I are… well, I don't know anymore," I admitted.

"Hmm… So, do you wanna be more than friends with Brian?" She licked the tomato juice off her fingers as she continued to question me.

"No, I don't. Anyway, I'm outta here—have a good night."

She opened her mouth to respond, but I shut the door behind me before she could ask me any more intrusive questions.

I walked down the hallway with my hands in my pockets. A small part of me was hoping to bump into Mr. Live, but he wasn't around. I knocked on door 814, and Brian let me in. His roommates, Jack and Tommy, had snuck out, which meant it was just us.

Brian sat on a chair beside the beds, and I sat down on what I hoped was his bed. We talked for a bit, but then he suddenly got quiet and looked at me intensely. He got up from the chair and sat down beside me on the bed. For a second, I was terrified that he was going to tell me he was into me or something.

"Lily, I think I need to tell you something," Brian said, slowly.

Shit. Shit, shit, shit.

"Okay…" I cautiously gave him the go-ahead.

"I'm… I'm gay," he revealed.

"Oh… oh, thank God," I blurted out, putting my hand on my chest in relief.

"Thank God?" Brian asked, puzzled.

"Sorry. No, I just thought you were going to say something else. Sorry, this is great though. Thank you for trusting me enough to confide in me, and I hope you know this doesn't change anything between us." I smiled at him.

"Thanks, I thought since you're from New York and everything, you'd probably be cool with it," he explained.

"Yeah, no, I'm definitely cool with it, and if anything, it makes me like you even more," I joked, putting my arms around his shoulders.

He looked so relieved, and I was honored that he chose to come out to me. We hadn't known each other for that long, but the fact that he already trusted me enough to tell me his biggest secret was touching.

"This is the first time I've said it out loud, but it feels good. I was sick of pretending to be someone I'm not," sighed Brian.

"Speaking of which… don't you have a *girlfriend*?" I finally understood why he kept dating her, even though she straight-up sucked as a human being.

"Yeah, I'm going to break up with her when we get home tomorrow. I don't really think she'll care, though. I don't even know why a girl like that wanted to date a guy like me to begin with," he told me.

Daddy issues?

"Are you going to come out to her?"

"No, I'll be keeping this to myself. At least till I go to college," he answered.

"That's fair. Probably best to move out of your parents' house and have your own thing going, just in case."

"Yeah."

We continued chatting, but I wasn't really a present part of the conversation, although I wanted to be. The truth was, I was supposed to have knocked on Mr. Live's door, but I chickened out at the last minute and knocked on Brian's instead. Which I'm glad I did.

Brian did something tonight, even though it was scary for him. And I think I needed to follow suit.

"I should get going. It's pretty late. We'll talk tomorrow, okay?" I promised Brian, getting up.

"Cool, have a good night." He grinned.

My hands were cold and visibly shaking by the time I left Brian's room, but I wasn't going to wuss out this time. I took a deep breath and knocked on room 815. Nothing. I waited for a while and then knocked again. I heard hurried footsteps approaching the door and then the creak of the door handle.

"Lily… sorry, I was in bed. Is everything okay?" Mr. Live asked, looking disheveled.

"Yeah, everything's fine. I was just wondering if I could talk to you? You said I could earlier…" I stammered, barely getting the words out.

"Um… yeah. Of course," Mr. Live said, opening the door wider and stepping aside to let me in.

SIXTY

"So, Lily… what brings you here at this hour?" asked Mr. Live.

He looked concerned, fidgeting with his glasses, not quite meeting my eyes. I couldn't quite tell what he was thinking, whether he was pleased to see me or not. Every bone in my body was telling me this was a bad idea. My anxiety was screaming at me to run back to my room. But I needed to stay strong. I needed to confirm my suspicions once and for all.

"I've been kinda down lately, and I don't have anyone else to talk to that gets how I feel," I lied. "I thought it might be better to talk to you since you know what it's like to lose someone you love."

This was my way in, playing the sympathy card. I sat down on his bed; the bedsheets were still a mess since I had woken him up. Mr. Live sat down on a chair at the other end of the room, appearing nervous. He frowned and pushed his glasses up, something he did quite often. It was really cute, actually.

"I see… well, you can certainly talk to me about whatever is bothering you," he confirmed.

Shit, I should have probably thought about what I was going to say. Fuck.

Not knowing what else to say, I began randomly rambling about my dad and what we went through before he passed. But soon, I found myself spilling the entire truth about my situation and how awful it had been for me since my dad died and Paul crawled his way into our lives. Reliving all that made the tears flow down my face, and soon I was crying uncontrollably with my head in my hands.

Mr. Live got up and sat down by my side, putting his hand on my shoulder in an attempt to soothe me. We sat there for a bit, sort of like we had in the music room. I wiped away my tears when I was done crying, and Mr. Live offered me a box of tissues that was on the nightstand beside his bed.

This had not gone as planned. I was supposed to have seduced this guy, and instead, here I was, weeping like an idiot. *Again!* And I probably looked awful too, with my makeup running from the tears. I needed to stop crying so much around him. But it wasn't my fault—he just made me feel so safe. As though I could tell him anything and everything. And I guess I had done exactly that.

"I had no idea how awful things were for you at home. Truthfully, I never liked Paul, but I had no idea he was capable of such unwarranted cruelty," Mr. Live remarked in a low voice.

I scanned his face, trying to interpret the expression. He was frowning harder than ever, the lines on his forehead deeper now. His lips were downturned, as though the thought of Paul disgusted him.

"Please... please don't tell anyone I told you any of this," I begged, realizing that I may have blabbed way more than I should have. I couldn't have any of this getting back to Paul or my mom.

He lowered his head, his eyes fixed on mine.

"Of course not. And none of this is your fault—I hope you know that," he assured me. "I honestly don't understand how the adults in your life could be this careless… you're such a sweet young thing—you deserve better," he continued, furrowing his brows in annoyance.

"Thanks," I mumbled.

I continued to stare into his eyes, and he into mine. His anger slowly melted away and was replaced by an emotion I couldn't quite deduce. But I knew it was now or never. I took a deep breath, closed my eyes, and pressed my lips onto his. For a second, it was perfect.

And then he got up, taken aback by what I had done.

"I—I think you should leave," he stammered, staring at the ground.

"No, I'm sorry—I just… there's a connection we have. Don't you feel it too?" I cried desperately, walking toward him.

"Lily, you're too young, and regardless of your age—I'm married," Mr. Live reminded me, shuffling away from me as if I had the plague.

"Oh, please," I scoffed. "I've heard all about your wife from Patricia, and we all know you can do better." I went on when he didn't respond. "I mean, she manipulated you into throwing your life away and continues to try to manipulate and control you."

Patricia *had* told me all about Mrs. Live when we first became friends. I hadn't cared back then or even given it much thought. But now it felt like my secret weapon.

And after hearing Mr. Live's story about her forcing him to give up his dreams because of her pregnancy, I disliked her even more. Which was why I didn't feel that guilty about what I was doing.

"You don't know anything about my marriage or my wife.

We need to stop this right now," warned Mr. Live, his face flushed.

"Fine, I'll go, but only if you look me in the eyes and tell me you don't feel anything for me," I countered. "Tell me there's no connection between us, and I'll leave right now."

I stood close to him, suddenly fearless. The anger was evident on his face. But that anger was soon replaced by affection and then lust.

"Damn it," he growled and grabbed the back of my neck, kissing me deeply.

And I kissed him back just as eagerly, wrapping my arms around his neck, breathing in his scent until I was intoxicated. He pushed me toward the bed, and I lay down, my feet still dangling a few inches off the floor. Before I could move, he began kissing my neck, and I couldn't help but moan in response. His hands pushed up my skirt, and his long, slender fingers explored my body. He continued to move lower and lower till he was kneeling at my feet. I lifted my head and watched as he made me feel more amazing than I had ever felt in my life.

"God, you're incredible," he breathed.

"Oh God," was all I could gasp in response, almost at the edge.

A few minutes later, I lay on the bed with one hand in my hair and the other firmly gripping the bed sheet. We were far from done, though. He climbed on top of me, kissing me passionately, till my body was alive again. My heartbeat pounded in my ears. My entire body was flushed and warm.

"Um, be gentle… this is my first time," I confessed.

"I know, and I will be," he assured me with a crooked smirk on his face.

SIXTY-ONE

"That was incredible," I sighed, lying next to Mr. Live with my head on his chest.

He didn't respond, instead he lay there with his eyes tightly shut, still breathing heavily. One of his hands was resting on his pillow, but the other was around my shoulders. I tried to take a mental picture of this moment. This was probably the first time I felt truly happy in a long time. The first time, I didn't feel scared and lost since my dad died.

I waited for him to say something—don't most men say something after sex? And with that, my happy disposition evaporated, quickly replaced by anxiety and panic.

"Did you not enjoy it?" I asked in a panicked tone.

Did I do something wrong? Was I not as good in bed as his wife? I knew I was going to fuck this up somehow. I can never have anything good in my life anymore.

"No, it's not that… of course it's not that," Mr. Live assured me. "But this was a mistake, Lily. We should never have done this, and we are never going to do it again."

He had a stern expression, but I could see the twinkle in his eyes that gave me hope.

"Why not?" I pouted, rolling onto my side so that I could see him better.

"Because I'm married, and you're a child. Do you have any

idea how much trouble I could get into if anyone found out about this?" asked Mr. Live.

I assumed it was a rhetorical question because, duh. Of course, I knew that. But how could he possibly think I would tell anyone? I would never do anything that could harm him or get him into trouble.

"I know, but I would never tell anyone. I don't want you to get into trouble... I care about you," I admitted.

Mr. Live turned too, facing me and lightly stroking my cheek with his thumb. He sighed, shaking his head.

"What am I going to do with you?" he muttered.

"I have a suggestion..." I grinned.

"Absolutely not. You've caused enough trouble, don't you think?" He rolled his eyes. "You need to go back to your room and make sure no one sees you leaving mine. And you will not tell a single soul about what happened tonight."

"Fine, I already said I wouldn't, and FYI, I'll break up with James when we get back," I mentioned, putting on my clothes.

"No, you need to keep dating him and act like everything is okay between you two. We can't have people getting suspicious," instructed Mr. Live in a panicked voice.

"Gotcha. Good night, Mr. Live," I said, heading toward the door.

I needed to play it cool. I couldn't risk messing this up. I would pretend to be good and keep my distance till he was ready to admit he had feelings for me too.

"It's Mark." He smiled.

"Mark." I smiled back.

I headed back to my room, and thankfully, no one was around since it was pretty late. Fiona was asleep when I walked in, which I was grateful for. I headed to the bathroom and changed into my pajamas before getting into bed.

Lying in bed, I thought about everything that had happened tonight. The adrenaline was still coursing through me; all I could think about was the way we had held one another. It had been so right, so perfect. I wondered what Mark was thinking about—was he thinking about me? About us? I couldn't stop smiling.

The only thing that bugged me was staying in my relationship with James. Even right now, when I was at my happiest, there was this feeling gnawing at me. This awful guilt I could not get rid of. I cared about James—I probably always would. That was one thing I was certain about. He was one of the most amazing people I'd met here. He made this move bearable for me.

And was I still attracted to him? Of course. He had that rock-hard football player bod. But the way I felt about Mark was different. It was way more intense, and the fact that it was wrong made it even better. I wasn't comfortable continuing to lie to James. If I had felt shitty about it before, sleeping with Mark had made it a million times worse.

But if Mark thought that staying with James would help us stay under the radar, I guess I would have to trust him for now. It wouldn't be easy to keep pretending with James. I would have to figure out a way to keep my distance for the most part. It would be best if we weren't together too much. That way, I could at least keep the lies to a minimum. Thankfully, both James and I have pretty busy schedules, so it would not be too hard to pull off.

Eventually, I was able to fall asleep despite my mind being preoccupied with this weird love triangle I had gotten myself into. I woke up slightly stiff but much better rested than I had been in a long time. As I was stretching in my bed, I sensed someone's eyes on me. I snapped my head up and noticed Fiona sitting on her bed cross-legged, staring at me intensely.

Her hair was a mess and pointing in every direction; she had probably not been up for too long either. However, she was already out of her pajamas and dressed in black leggings and a black crop top.

"Can I help you?" I asked, irritated.

"You came back pretty late last night," she observed.

"Yeah, and?" I frowned.

I was getting sick of her intrusive behavior. What was wrong with this chick?

"Were you with Brian the whole time?" she asked.

"Yeah, we were just talking," I answered, trying my best not to sound guilty or suspicious.

I had no way to prove it, but something about her demeanor made it seem as though she knew what happened last night. No, that was crazy. How could she possibly know?

"So… did something happen last night?" she said, saying it as though it was a fact rather than her own weird assumption.

"Um, excuse me?" I was taken aback by her statement.

I was now wide awake, my anxiety rising with every word that came out of Fiona's mouth. Did she know something? Did she know what happened between Mark and I?

"It's kinda weird that you would spend that much time with Brian if nothing happened between you two," Fiona declared nonchalantly.

"What exactly are you accusing me of?"

"Well, he has a girlfriend he doesn't like, and you have a

boyfriend you don't like," she explained. "It kind of makes sense that you two would secretly hook up here."

"You don't know what you're talking about. Nothing happened between me and Brian, okay?" I corrected her, getting more annoyed by the minute.

"Sure…" Fiona rolled her eyes.

"I'm done with this conversation." I got up and headed to the bathroom, trying to avoid a fight with her.

The girl was nuts. I was not going to sit around and wait till she figured out who I was, actually with last night.

"'Kay, see you downstairs," chirped Fiona.

I slammed the bathroom door behind me, ignoring her. Eventually, I heard her shut our room door as she left and let out a sigh of relief, finally coming out of the bathroom. Seriously, what the fuck was wrong with that girl? She will most definitely not be seeing me downstairs if I can help it.

I spent most of the day trying to avoid staring at Mr. Live and acting natural. It was difficult, though. I didn't think it was possible, but he was even more gorgeous today than he had been last night. All I wanted to do was run my fingers through his hair once more and stare into his eyes.

But of course, I couldn't, so I tried to keep myself preoccupied. Like the previous day, I spent most of my time with Brian. It was pretty fun, and a few hours later, we were back on the bus heading home. I did notice Mr. Live stare directly at me when he entered the bus, but he quickly averted his eyes and sat down further away from where Brian and I were seated.

I checked the notifications on my phone when I got home and saw a bunch of missed calls from both James and Patricia. I assumed James was still trying to apologize for what had happened at his place. Honestly, I was kind of over it. He was usually such a sweet guy—that was only a one-time fight. I would talk to him when we got back. This wasn't the right time or place for that conversation.

As for Patricia, I was still definitely avoiding her. At first, I was trying to avoid her because she was dating the guy whose dad I had a thing for. Now, I was avoiding her because she was dating the guy whose dad I had *slept* with, which was a million times worse.

Patricia was sharp as a tack. If she were somehow able to figure out the truth, it wouldn't just get *me* into trouble, but Mr. Live, too. And that was something I could not risk.

Paul and my mom weren't home when I got back and probably wouldn't be till much later, as they had gone out for dinner, according to the text I had received from my mom. Paul preferred to hang out with his friends on the weekends and, apparently, also enjoyed drinking excessively, from my observation. I had heard him and my mom whisper-fighting about it when they thought I was asleep a couple of weeks back. Apparently, they were seeing the pastor for counseling, too.

Personally, I didn't think even God could save someone like Paul, but that was the least of my concerns at the moment. I was actually glad they were otherwise distracted and hoped it would stay that way.

I sat on our living room couch and decided that this would finally be a good time to talk to James. I texted him to come over so we could talk about what happened the other day.

SIXTY-TWO

James was nervously adjusting his hair when I opened the front door for him. All I wanted to do was give him a big hug and tell him how sorry I was. The guilt was eating me up inside. I could not stop thinking about how he would react if he ever found out what I did. And with his best friend's dad, of all people.

We sat down in my bedroom, and James began apologizing. He had this adorable deer in the headlights look on his face, and I couldn't help but feel sorry for him. He deserved so much better than me. But at the same time, a part of me still loved him and didn't want to let him go. When I studied his face, I still saw the boy who had saved me from this place. Abandoning him now, with no proper explanation, would be pure evil.

"I love you, Lil," he said, gazing into my eyes and cupping my face with his hand.

"I love you too," I replied, tears forming in the corners of my eyes.

And I did. He would always have a place in my heart.

He began kissing me, and my defenses started to melt away despite having promised myself that I would keep my distance till everything was sorted out with Mr. Live. Deep down, I knew this wasn't right. I shouldn't string him along. But when he kissed me like this and held me close, my brain switched off and a different, more primal urge took over.

I kissed him back, my hands exploring his body. Within a few minutes, he was asking me if I wanted to go all the way, and, fuck, did I ever. Our bodies moved together in a rhythm, faster and faster, till we were both at the highest levels of ecstasy.

It was incredible for a while, but eventually, I couldn't help thinking about Mark again. As much as I was attracted to James and loved him in my own way, it wasn't the same as it had been with Mark. Something was missing. I loved James, but I wasn't in love with him.

I needed to get James out of my house. This had been a giant mistake that I had somehow made even worse. My chest suddenly tightened as I peeked up at James, who was currently observing me lovingly. I swallowed the lump in my throat and quickly made up some excuse to get him to leave. Thankfully, he believed me and left shortly.

I needed to figure out why I had lost control of the situation with James like that. For whatever reason, lying and knowing I was doing something wrong felt irresistible to me. I couldn't seem to stop myself.

As my mom drove me to school the next morning, my mind was preoccupied with thoughts about Mark and James. I needed to somehow save James from this mess. And as for Mark, I truly didn't know where things were headed. Or where I stood with him. But I could not just give up this easily. I needed to talk to him as soon as possible.

As usual, it was a pretty quiet drive, and I was thankful for that. I assumed Paul was hungover because I'd heard him violently throw up and hadn't seen him leave their bedroom since. It had honestly been great for the past few weeks to have Paul too preoccupied with his own life to go around snooping in mine.

Patricia managed to corner me as soon as I got to school, which meant I couldn't head to the music room right away. Instead, I talked to her for a bit and told her about the trip. Of course, I left out the part where I had slept with her boyfriend's dad, and that Brian had come out to me. Instead, we laughed about weird Fiona and her antics. After a couple of minutes, I told her I needed to head to the music room. She narrowed her eyes in suspicion but didn't try to stop me.

As I walked into the music room, the first thing I saw was Mr. Live fidgeting with some of the instruments. He turned to look at me and smiled. I smiled back, nervously tucking my hair behind my ears. God, he was so hot.

"Lily… I hoped you would stop by. I think we have a lot to talk about," he said in a low voice. I nodded and walked up to him.

"About the trip… what happened between us… I've been feeling horrible about it ever since," Mr. Live admitted. "It can't happen again, *ever*."

"Do you seriously mean that?" I asked, trying not to sob.

"I'm sorry, but I do. Of course, I care about you, but you're too young. You have your whole life ahead of you. And James is a great kid. I've known him for years—he could make you very happy if you give him the chance," he continued.

"Why can't you give *me* a chance?" I whispered angrily.

"Because I'm married, Lily," Mr. Live reminded me.

"You deserve better. If you just gave us a chance—" I pleaded when the door suddenly slammed open, and we both turned around in horror.

It was James, and for some reason, he appeared to be as shocked as we were. His face was flushed, and he was breathing hard. Had he run here or something? That was weird, but I was too preoccupied with what Mr. Live had just told me to think about James right now.

"James, nice of you to… visit the music room," Mark said.

"Hey, Mr. Live, I just wanted to say hi to Lily before class," James blurted out.

"Ah, I see. Lily, we're pretty much done here—maybe James could walk you to class?" Mr. Live suggested.

I guess this was it then. He wouldn't even give me a fucking chance. I knew this was his way of telling me that I needed to stick with James. And after our talk, maybe I would. Maybe I was wrong. Maybe I was the only idiot who thought there was something here.

"That would be perfect," I confirmed. If this was what he wanted, then I would play along.

I grabbed James's hand and left the music room without glancing back at Mr. Live. If he wanted nothing to do with me, then I didn't want anything to do with him either.

"Have a great day, you two!" called Mr. Live as we exited the music room and into the chaos-filled hallway.

I was still fuming when James drove me home after school and ended up asking him to come inside. I knew my parents wouldn't be home for a while, and I needed a distraction. James had proven to be quite a good one yesterday, and I hoped it would be the same today. And I was right, he absolutely was. It felt incredible in the moment.

But once we were done, I couldn't stop thinking about Mr. Live again. Something about him telling me we couldn't be together only made me want him more. My mind, which so rarely focused on just one thing, was suddenly hyper-focused on Mr. Live. It was as if I was craving him and nothing would satisfy me except being with him.

And then I remembered something Patricia had told me this morning. Ian's mom was out of town for a few days, and Ian was going over to Patricia's. Which meant Mr. Live would probably be home alone. This would be my chance to get him alone again.

I knew if I could get him alone, I could make him reconsider. I could make him see that there was more between us than just something physical. I could get him to fold the same way I had at the hotel.

"So, I hate to hit it and quit it, but my parents are probably gonna be home soon," I hinted at James.

"I'll see you tomorrow, though?" he asked me in a hopeful tone.

Damn it, why did James have to be such an absolute sweetheart? This was breaking my heart. If something happened between Mark and me, James and I would be completely done. I couldn't drag him along anymore.

"Um, I'll let you know… I may have some music-related stuff going on," I replied, staring at my fingers.

Once James was gone, I quickly took a shower, got changed, and headed to Mr. Live's. They lived close by, so I decided to walk. I knocked on the door, and a few seconds later, I heard footsteps approaching.

"Lily, what are you doing here?" Mr. Live asked, the shock evident on his face.

SIXTY-THREE

"Please don't do this," I sobbed. "Please don't give up on us. I know you're married, but you can't give up on this connection we have."

"Come in," instructed Mark, popping his head out the door to make sure no one else was around.

He was wearing dark blue jeans, a slightly faded AC/DC T-shirt, and sneakers no one younger than thirty would be caught dead in. He looked a lot less put together than he did at school, but in the best way.

I followed him into his living room and sat down beside him on the beige-colored couch. He rubbed his chin, deep in thought. I remained quiet, taking it all in. As much as I adored James, I knew that Mark was different. He understood me. He understood my pain. The pain of losing someone you love, to have your entire life turned upside down.

"Lily, you shouldn't be here," Mark finally said.

"I know, I'm sorry," I apologized. "I didn't know what else to do. You're all I can think of anymore."

Mark put his head in his hands, not saying anything. My heart beat faster—I shouldn't have admitted that to him. I should have played it cool. After what felt like forever, Mark lifted his head and stared at me with a fire in his eyes I hadn't seen before.

"I haven't been able to stop thinking about you either, from the moment you walked into my classroom. Even before you knew we had a connection, I knew. And it tore me apart to see you with James, but I had no other choice," Mr. Live divulged. "And then everything changed. Suddenly, you felt it too. But what could I do? I had to push you away."

I was stunned by his revelation. I stared at him with wide eyes, silently begging him to continue.

"But I can't do it any longer. Every time you're around me, I… I lose control," admitted Mr. Live. "I think about you all the time, every goddamn waking moment."

"I knew it. I knew I wasn't the only one who felt this way," I whispered, gently placing my hand on his cheek.

"No, you certainly weren't the only one…" trailed off Mark.

He sighed in defeat, no longer able to fight his urges. His lips touched mine, igniting a fire in my body. His lips moved to my neck, leaving little love bites. His warm fingers unhooked my bra effortlessly. His touch was like electricity running through my veins. I never wanted this moment to end.

For once, my mind was totally in the present. It was no longer plagued by thoughts of the past or anxieties about the future, about James or Paul or my dad or anyone. I was in the moment and feeling truly ecstatic. This is what I needed—what my body had been craving all this time.

I was no longer in control of my body; my body was in control of me. And it felt amazing to finally shut off my brain and only concentrate on the growing fire, desperate for my attention. Our bodies shuddered in unison, and my soul slowly floated back into my body.

"That was incredible," I sighed, lying on the couch, snuggling Mark.

"It really was," he agreed, lightly kissing the top of my head.

I stretched out my fingers and lightly ran them along his jawline. He was so cute like this, disheveled, with a sheepish grin on his face. I could lie here beside him forever. This was my new happy place.

"How about I make us some dinner?" Mark suggested, stroking my bare arm.

"That sounds perfect," I told him.

He headed to what I assumed was the kitchen, and soon I heard utensils being moved around, and I could smell melting cheese. I put on my clothes and decided to explore the house. I had been quite emotional earlier and hadn't noticed my surroundings much.

I got up and snooped around, making sure to walk as quietly as possible. I wasn't a fan of the decor, but then again, I wasn't a fan of his wife in general, so I was not surprised. There were lots of chunky, sparkly ornaments that assaulted the eye as soon as you walked into the living room. The couches were comfy, but their color was fading.

A faux fur rug lay on the floor beside the mantel, and on the mantel itself stood many pictures of Mark's smiling family, indulging in various activities.

There were pictures of Mark and Ian fishing and the whole family camping, boating, and biking. My stomach felt uneasy. Seeing these pictures made everything real—too real. I had been trying my best not to think about Betsy like this, as a real person whose life my actions could potentially ruin.

And even worse was Ian. Although we weren't particularly close, both Patricia and James adored him. It would ruin his life if it ever came to light that his dad was sleeping with a student.

I was nauseous from the anxiety, but I couldn't seem to tear my gaze away from their happy, smiling faces. Had I been wrong? Was Mark in a happy marriage with a happy life? Was I the villain here?

As though the universe wanted to confirm my suspicions, I saw a wedding photo of Mark and Betsy almost fully hidden behind the rest of the picture frames. I pulled it out and stared at the picture in my hand, running my fingers over the cold, hard glass that covered it. I frowned, imagining them at their wedding.

They were so young. Betsy's glowing face looked nothing like it did now—overfilled and frozen by the Botox. She was radiant in her wedding dress, beaming as all brides do. She had a giant smile on her face, her eyes sparkling with hope and excitement for the future she envisioned with her new husband. Her right hand cradled her bouquet while her left hand rested gently on her protruding pregnant belly.

Mark looked pretty much the same as he does now, except something about him was off. It was his expression—his demeanor. There was a grim look on his face, like he was at a funeral rather than at his own wedding. His lips were tightly pursed, and he was practically glaring at the camera. I guess he wasn't as resigned to his reality back then as he is now.

I knew that this made me an awful person, but seeing him so incredibly miserable in that picture took away some of the guilt I was experiencing. It reminded me that he had been robbed of the chance to have *his* version of the perfect life and was instead forced to live Betsy's.

He deserved happiness. He deserved to be with someone who truly got him. And I was that person.

"Ahem."

Mark was standing right behind me, holding a plate of grilled cheese sandwiches in each hand. He didn't seem surprised to see me by the mantel, examining pictures from his other life. But I was taken aback by his sudden reappearance and needed a minute to gather my thoughts after the internal roller coaster I'd just been on.

"I'm sorry… I didn't mean to pry. It's just—" I tried to explain, my cheeks flushing.

"It's fine, Lily," Mark assured me.

He put down the plates and delicately took the frame from my shaking hands. He lightly ran his thumb over the picture, frowning. He sighed and shook his head a little.

"I had been beyond angry that day… I thought my life was over," he explained. "And worst of all, I felt like I had let my dad down by not pursuing my music and settling down instead. Making the same mistake he had, the one that cost him his life."

I rubbed his arm in an attempt to comfort him. I hated seeing him this disgruntled.

"I'm sorry. It must have been awful," I softly replied.

"Yeah… but that's the thing about life—it goes on, and now I can't imagine my life without my little boy. All those sacrifices were worth it for him."

I hugged him, resting my head on his chest. He was such a great dad, and I loved that about him. But it also worried me. It made me insecure about my standing in his life. If it ever came down to it, would he pick his family over me? And if that did happen, where would that leave me?

I closed my eyes tightly and tried to clear my head. I wanted to enjoy the moment. I didn't need to worry right now—this was one of those times when I would cross the bridge when I got there.

We ended up back on the couch. Mark and I sat cross-legged as we chatted and leisurely ate our sandwiches. It surprised me how comfortable I was around him. I couldn't stand most adults, but something about Mark made me feel all warm and cozy. When I was with him, I felt at home.

Unfortunately, our perfect rom-com moment was interrupted. My phone vibrated, and my heart skipped a beat when I checked to see who it was. *James*. The name flashed across my screen like a slap in the face. Another wave of anxiety hit me, followed by nausea. I hadn't thought about him once since I came here. I truly was becoming an awful person.

"You should pick it up," Mark suggested softly, his eyes fixed on my screen.

Well, this was fucking awkward. Mark appeared collected on the surface, but I could tell from his clenched jaw that he was as panicked as I was. As much as we enjoyed one another's company, we were also aware of the price we would pay if anyone ever found out about us. Considering that I wasn't eighteen yet, that price would be much heavier for Mark than for me.

"Hello?" I said tentatively.

"Hey, Lil, are you home?" James asked casually.

"No, I'm out," I replied.

"Oh, okay. Where are you?" he asked.

"Um… I'm—I'm with Patricia… we decided to go out for dinner." I panicked and blurted out the first lie I could think of.

"You're with Patricia?"

Was it just me, or did he sound kind of suspicious?

"Yeah, we thought it would be nice to catch up—just us girls. I didn't know you wanted to come over again."

"No, it's fine. I'll see you at school tomorrow, then."

"See ya."

I hung up the phone and put it on airplane mode before putting it away, praying that he had bought it. I glanced at Mark to gauge his reaction.

I was done playing games with James. I wasn't comfortable lying to him anymore; it was time for me to set him free.

"I think I need to break up with James," I said.

Mark took off his glasses and rubbed his temples. No doubt thinking of the mess we had created. After a few seconds, he put his glasses back on and rested his hand over mine.

"Yeah, I think you do," he agreed.

Mark tightly hugged me goodbye before I left and reluctantly went back home. I couldn't help but notice the vase full of lilies in their hallway.

SIXTY-FOUR

I was not looking forward to school the next day. I knew I would have to talk to James eventually, and I knew it would suck so much to break up with him. I had to keep reminding myself that it was for his own good, though. I had to stay strong and just rip off the Band-Aid.

I went to the music room first, hoping to find Mark there, but bumped into Brian instead. I hadn't talked to him much recently, so I decided to catch up with him while we both waited for Mark. He was telling me about how he almost got catfished over the weekend, and we were laughing loudly when the music room door swung open.

We were shocked to see James standing there. His hands were balled into fists, and he had this dangerous glint in his eyes. His hair was a mess, and there was something unhinged about his expression. It reminded me of when we got into a fight at his place.

Did he know about what was going on between Mark and me? Was that why he was angry? How could he possibly have known?

James marched toward us, and with every step he took, my heart beat faster. My body was breaking out in a cold sweat, and I was shaking uncontrollably.

"James, I can explain—" I started to say, but he cut me off before I finished my sentence.

"What the fuck is your problem? Why can't you stay the fuck away from Lily?" he yelled in Brian's face, grabbing his shirt.

Wait, what the fuck was going on? Was James seriously still hung up on the fact that Brian and I were friends? I thought he was over that already. Didn't he promise to trust me from now on? I mean, he shouldn't. I've straight-up been cheating on him. But if you're going to get all weird and jealous, at least be angry at the right guy. It was giving toxic masculinity, and I was so not here for it.

My previous dread of being caught disappeared and was quickly replaced by anger.

"Look, man, I just got here… I have no idea what you're talking about," Brian told James, holding his hands out in front of him in surrender.

I was about to speak up when I saw James swing his arm and his fist connect with Brian's face. It all happened so quickly, yet it was like time slowed down. The sound of Brian's nose cracking, the blood and saliva flying out of his mouth, his knees buckling as he fell to the ground. I stood there at first, completely dumbfounded by James's violent outburst.

"What the fuck, James! What the fuck is your problem?" I yelled, running toward Brian and kneeling beside him.

I needed to make sure he was okay, that James hadn't seriously injured Brian. This was my fault. I should have been clearer that I wasn't interested in Brian instead of using him to distract James from what was happening between me and Mark.

Brian was lying on the floor, groaning in pain, his face covered in blood. He flinched as he lightly touched his nose.

"What's *my* problem? What's your fucking problem? Why do you keep lying to me?" James shouted at me.

"What the fuck are you talking about?" I shouted back.

"How about last night, when you said you were hanging out with Patricia, but you weren't—because she was with Ian?"

Fuck, how did he know about that? I had assumed Patricia would cover for me. I should have been smarter about it. I should have said I was with my mom and Paul. Shit. I was trying to think of an explanation when the door swung open once more.

"What the hell is going on here?" Mr. Live asked, walking into the music room, stunned at the sight before him.

Brian was bleeding on the floor. I was kneeling beside him, and James was towering over us both. We were quite the sight.

Thankfully, Mark de-escalated the situation, sent James to the principal, and instructed me to take Brian to the nurse. I did and was super apologetic the entire time. Brian assured me that he was fine and it wasn't that bad, but it did nothing to decrease my guilt. This was getting absolutely out of hand. Innocent people were beginning to get hurt because of my actions. People I cared about.

It was time for me to part ways with James. And this insane fight, paired with his anger issues, may be the perfect get-out-of-jail-free card I had been searching for. As awful as this situation was, I did feel somewhat relieved to finally have an excuse to break up with James.

Once we were done at the nurse's, Brian headed to the principal's office, and I hid in the girls' bathroom. I was not in the mood to go to class right now. I needed to know what happened and was about to text Brian when a message from a number I didn't recognize popped up on my screen.

> It's Mark. Meet me at the staircase.

I left the bathroom and headed to the staircase. Mark was already there, looking irritated.

"What the hell happened?" he asked as soon as he saw me.

"James thought I was with Brian last night—" I tried to explain.

"But you told him you were with Patricia," he cut me off.

"Yeah, but somehow he found out I'd lied to him."

Mark adjusted his glasses and took a deep breath.

"Fuck," he whispered.

"Don't worry, he doesn't know I was with you," I assured him. "What happened at the principal's office?"

"Well, James didn't really get punished. I left him and Brian in the music room to talk it out," Mark explained.

"Wait, James didn't get punished? For punching someone in the face?" I asked, surprised.

"His family is rich enough to keep the principal under their thumb," he clarified. "This isn't the first time he's done something like this, and it won't be the last. That kid's got issues."

"Hmm… do you think it's a good idea to leave them both alone again after what happened?" I wondered.

"They'll be fine. James cools down as fast as he freaks out," he said. "It's you I'm worried about."

"Why?" I questioned.

His eyes darted around to make sure no one was around, and once he was convinced we were alone, he lovingly stroked my cheek with his thumb.

"Because James caught you in a lie—you can't tell him the truth. You're kind of stuck," Mark explained.

"No, I'm not. This fight is the perfect excuse to break up with him," I said.

"That's not a bad idea. Do you think it'll work?" Mark asked, a little skeptical.

"Yeah, I'll make him out to be the crazy, paranoid boyfriend, and after what happened with Brian, I don't think anyone will question it," I added.

"Smart girl." He winked.

I giggled at the compliment.

"I need to head back to the music room to make sure they're okay, and you need to head back to class," Mark said.

"Okay… I'll see you tonight?" I asked, tentatively.

"I'll let you know. I need to make sure Ian won't be home."

I nodded.

"I'll text you," he said.

"Don't save my number though, and delete the messages as soon as you read them," he sternly instructed. I nodded again. I was pretty sure Paul occasionally snooped through my phone, so I had been planning on doing that anyway.

Other than texting Brian to make sure he was okay, I spent the rest of the morning thinking about what I would say to James.

My phone buzzed, and I checked to see who it was, hoping it was Mark confirming our plans for tonight. But it turned out to be Patricia. She told me James wanted to talk at lunch. I asked her why she hadn't covered for me last night, and she sent a sort of snarky response about how she didn't realize she needed to. I decided to let her be for a while. I didn't want to get into another fight right now.

When lunchtime arrived, I walked to James's car and

knocked on the window. The air was cold and sharp against my skin. A part of me wanted to run back inside.

Rip the Band-Aid off. I reminded myself.

"I think we need to have a serious conversation about everything that's been going on," he told me as soon as I got into the car.

SIXTY-FIVE

The distressed expression on James's face when I ended things was devastating. It's something that will forever be etched into my mind. Something I will never be able to forgive myself for.

I had to keep reminding myself why I did it. I needed to let James go. I had to banish him from my mind and soul for his own good, which is why I returned the bracelet he had bought me. I had cherished it so much, worn it daily without fail. But now it just reminded me of my betrayal. It was time to free James from the chaos I had inadvertently brought into his perfect world.

"I know it sucked, but it had to be done. His behavior this morning was… concerning, to say the least," Mark consoled me, softly stroking my hair.

Ian was hanging out with Patricia tonight, which made it possible for me to come over again. We were currently on his couch, and I had my head on his lap. I had been telling him about how awful the breakup had been. I may not be in love with James anymore, but I still loved him deeply.

"Yeah, I know," I sighed, enjoying Mark's gentle touch. "It's just been a shit day."

Mark stared at me intensely, and I wondered what he was

thinking so hard about. His forehead was slightly wrinkled, but the rest of his face was relaxed.

"It'll be okay… I love you," Mark confessed, kissing the top of my head.

"You love me?" I gasped, bolting up.

My hand flew to my mouth, my jaw as close to the floor as it would ever be. I knew I loved him from that first moment together in the music room when he had comforted me. But I hadn't been sure whether he would ever reciprocate those feelings, so I hadn't said anything.

I had pictured this moment happening in my mind a million times, in a million ways, but this was better than anything I could ever imagine. My eyes got teary, and my breath caught in my throat. I wanted to cherish this. I knew I would play it back in my mind again and again. What had earlier been one of the worst days I had experienced was quickly turning into a day I never wanted to end.

"Of course, I love you," Mark told me once more, his eyes crinkling from his smile.

"I love you too," I threw my arms around him, holding him as close to my body as I could.

He pushed my hair away from my face, kissing my forehead, nose, and finally my lips. He ran his fingers up my thigh, and my body shuddered in response. I wanted him. I needed him. I shut my eyes tightly, enjoying this moment.

"I should head home," I whispered breathlessly.

I really didn't want the kiss to end, but we needed to stop before we lost control of ourselves, as we tended to do. I still had a strict curfew, and I could tell Paul was in an awful mood today. He practically bit my head off for leaving my jacket on the couch instead of the coat hanger this morning.

"You probably should. Ian will be back soon, and I'm sure Paul will have a million questions about where you were," Mark joked, rolling his eyes.

He kissed me once more, but not as urgently this time. We said goodnight soon after, and I snuck away before any of his more nosy neighbors spotted me.

Unfortunately, his joke had more truth to it than either of us realized.

I heard the TV blaring as soon as I opened our front door. The smell of alcohol assaulted my nostrils, and I scrunched my face in disgust. All the lights were switched off, and the house was uncannily dark except for the living room, which was illuminated by the light coming off the television screen. On the TV, I heard the voice of a preacher yelling about hell.

I tried to walk to my room as quickly as possible, hoping to avoid a confrontation. But as I tiptoed past the living room, I heard Paul call my name. The happiness I had been wallowing in while walking back home moments earlier vanished entirely as I entered the living room, where Paul was seated with a beer can in his hand. The empty cans littering the floor by his feet gave me an indication of what he had been up to in my absence.

"Where were you?" he asked, barely able to get the words out without slurring them.

"Out with some friends—where's my mom?" I responded, hoping she was home.

"Out with some friends." He smirked. "I know you've been sneaking around lately. Just because I haven't said anything doesn't mean I don't know what you're up to."

"I'm not sneaking around. I always come home on time," I told him.

Technically, that was true.

"You think you're slick, but you're going to slip up one of these days, and when you do, I'm going to be there." He was now standing close enough to me that I was forced to step back.

"Whatever."

I turned around, hoping to leave before this escalated any further, but he grabbed my shoulder and spun me around.

"Don't 'whatever' me. I'm warning you—if you do something stupid and embarrass me, I'll make your life hell," he hissed, leaning in and squinting his eyes.

I pulled myself away from his grip and quickly locked myself in my bedroom. I felt sick—the memory of when he had slapped me across the face played in my head. I took slow, deliberate breaths to calm myself down.

I pulled out my phone and began typing out a message to Mark about what had just happened, but ended up deciding not to send it. I knew he would freak out about it and maybe even confront Paul. I couldn't have that happening—no good would come from it.

I ended up texting Priya instead. I hadn't talked to her much since we moved here. Just as I expected, she was beyond furious but understood there was not much I could do about it at the moment. Instead, she gave me what I needed—a safe space to vent.

As the conversation evolved, she asked me if I was still seeing James, and I ended up saying yes. If I told her James and I had broken up, she would have questions. And she knew me too well to believe my lies. She would instantly know something was up, and I was not prepared to tell her, or anyone, about Mark. I hated lying to my best friend, but I had to protect Mark.

I went to bed, still uneasy.

SIXTY-SIX

As soon as I opened my eyes the next morning, I knew something was wrong. *Fuck, I was going to throw up.* I ran into the bathroom, throwing up more violently than I had ever done before in my life. I didn't even have time to lock the door. I knelt down beside the toilet and hurled. What had I eaten yesterday to make me this sick?

I barely made it back to my bedroom—between the nausea and lightheadedness, I could barely walk straight. I got back into bed but continued to shake because my body remained cold despite the blanket. Both Paul and my mom rushed into my room to see what was going on.

"Are you okay, sweetie?" my mom asked, rushing to my side and checking my forehead for my temperature.

"No, I'm nauseous. I think I must have eaten something bad," I told her.

"Oh, please, she's just trying to get out of going to school." Paul rolled his eyes, exasperated.

"No, I'm not," was all I could manage to say in my defense.

"Get out of bed and get ready. You're fine," Paul said.

"She has a temperature. I think she might really be sick," my mom tried to tell Paul, but he put up his hand, gesturing for her to shut up.

"I said, get out of bed and get ready for school, NOW," he repeated.

"No, she's sick and staying home," snapped my mom.

He moved a few steps back, a bewildered expression on his face.

I was pretty surprised, too, but I guess with everything else going on between them, my mom had finally had enough. She had a fierce twinkle in her eye before it was replaced by the expressionless mask she always had around him.

She cleared her throat and said more calmly but firmly, "I think it's best if she stays home today."

Paul glared at her for a few seconds but walked out of my room silently.

I closed my eyes and went back to sleep.

In a few hours, I felt almost completely okay. Around noon, I heated up some soup and ate it with crackers. I got a text from Mark asking about my absence, and I told him I was sick. He asked what was wrong, and I told him I had a migraine. He didn't need to know all the unladylike, puke-y details. He said he hoped I got better soon and told me he loved me again.

I fell asleep on the couch with a grin on my face. I was enjoying a dreamless slumber when I heard a knock on the front door. I was trying to think of who it could be at this time of day and guessed it might be Patricia checking up on me. I had texted her earlier, letting her know that I was too sick to come to school today, and she promised to check up on me later. I heard a knock again, more aggressive this time.

I went to the door and was surprised to see James standing there looking concerned. Why would he show up out of the blue without telling me, especially when I had made it clear that I didn't want to see him? I was still too weak to yell at him, but I firmly asked him to leave. I would have to talk to him at some point in the future and set stronger boundaries. It sucked that he was so heartbroken, but I couldn't have him randomly showing up like this.

Thankfully, neither Paul nor my mom was home today, but they could have been, and that would have opened a whole can of worms for me. My mom was still working part-time, which meant she worked four days a week, and Paul worked every day except Sundays. And as far as they knew, James and I were still dating.

I thought I would get better in a day or two, but continued to wake up nauseous and lightheaded. It had somehow become a part of my daily routine.

At first, I hoped it was something I had eaten. Then, I *prayed* it was something I had eaten. But by day five, I had to admit to myself that this was probably not just a case of bad food poisoning. I had been having unprotected sex, and these were the most common symptoms of pregnancy. There was no excuse. I had been stupid enough to have sex with not one but two people without protection.

I was diagnosed with PCOS a few years back, and I guess I sort of simply assumed I wouldn't get pregnant because of that. I had last gotten my period two weeks before we went on the trip, and I slept with Mark. I hadn't gotten it since then. Which meant that there was definitely a chance I was pregnant, and if I was pregnant, Mark was most likely the father.

On Saturday, I snuck out and bought a pregnancy test from the pharmacy. I hoped I wouldn't bump into anyone I knew there, which I thankfully didn't.

I got home and did what the box instructed. Which was pretty much to pee on the thing. I waited for the results, more nervous than I had ever been before. If there had been anything left in my stomach, it would have been out by now. My hands were cold and clammy, and I couldn't stop pacing around my bedroom.

Finally, the results were visible. It took me a few minutes to muster up the courage to look at it. When I did, I silently slid down onto my bed. I was terrified. It felt like the walls were closing in on me.

But there was another feeling in my heart. It was excitement, anticipation. Hope? Like this might be my chance at a new life, an escape from this hellhole. Could this be a blessing in disguise? I mean, Mark *had* told me he loved me.

Of course, I wasn't stupid or delusional. I knew Mark was married. I also knew that Paul and my mom would kill me if they found out I was pregnant. And they would definitely kill me if I got an abortion. So, it wasn't looking great on that front. My friends would probably never speak to me again. And most importantly, how would Mark react to the news and be affected by it, considering I was still a minor. I couldn't ruin his life; we would have to figure something out.

But a small, optimistic part of me couldn't help but imagine what life would be like with this baby and Mark by my side. Even if they were empty, meaningless daydreams, I thought about what our life would be like if we were a family.

Physically, I felt better by the end of the weekend and was able to go to school on Monday. But mentally, I was having a nervous breakdown. Most of the time, I would alternate between being terrified and excited. I couldn't eat, sleep, or even think clearly because all I could think about was this baby and how it would change every aspect of my life.

SIXTY-SEVEN

I HAD DECIDED TO TELL MARK ABOUT THE PREGNANCY DURING my violin lesson on Monday. I knew I had no right to be happy, but I couldn't help it. I would finally have someone to love unconditionally, someone that I could raise and cherish. Even if Mark decided he wanted nothing to do with this baby, which I hoped would not be the case, I would still be happy to raise it on my own and give it all the love I had in my heart.

At lunch, I walked into the cafeteria, silently searching for James. I headed to his table as soon as I spotted him. He was seated with Ian and Patricia, both of whom stared at me in surprise as soon as I got to their table. I needed to talk to Patricia at some point, too. I knew she was still mad at me for avoiding her for the last few weeks. But that would have to wait. At the moment, I needed to have a serious talk with James about showing up at my place unannounced. Now more than ever, I needed to be extra careful around Paul.

"Can we talk after school?" I asked him.

"Okay…" he agreed, clearly still surprised.

"Cool, I'll meet you out back," I told him.

I waited till the rest of the students cleared out before I went to meet him. I didn't need any more drama right now. People were already staring and whispering whenever they saw me. Between James's meltdown and us breaking up, we were the talk of the school. At least until something more juicy came along.

The cold air hit me as soon as I opened the school's back door. It was drizzling outside, so I put my hoodie up to protect my straightened hair. Shoving my hands in my pockets, I walked up to James, who was already standing by the trees.

He had been waiting a while. His skin was slightly flushed from standing out in the cold for too long. I couldn't help but feel guilty again, not only for keeping him waiting but for everything I had done recently. But I stayed strong. I tried to be firm about my boundaries and was insistent that he stay away from me.

The problem was, he would not take no for an answer, and it was seriously irking me.

"Whatever, just stay away from me, okay? I'm fucking done with this drama," I finally snapped.

"Wait, look, I'm sorry—I can change, Lil. I love you. I swear I'll be the person you want me to be," he begged.

I didn't want to hurt him, but I had no choice. I needed to make sure he thought I hated him. That was the only way he would move on. It would hurt for a while, but at least he wouldn't be a part of my mess.

"You will never be the person I want because you are not the person I want to be with. Get that through your fucking head," I coldly responded, hoping those words would be enough for him to hate me as he should.

I was about to head back into school when my phone vibrated. It was probably Mark wondering where I was. Just as I was about to check the message, James grabbed the phone from my hands and threw it on the ground.

The screen shattered. But that wasn't enough for him. He

proceeded to stomp on my phone till it was completely destroyed. His hair messily fell over his face, covering the left half of it. He was breathing rapidly, almost like a crazed animal. I stood there, numb, not knowing how to react. Every survival instinct I had was telling me to get away from James as fast as I could.

"What the fuck is wrong with you?" I whispered, my voice cracking.

He stood there silently staring at me, seemingly as upset as I was. I tried to appear unaffected by his tantrum, but in reality, I was petrified. This was not James's first outburst, and now I had more than just myself to protect.

"Stay the fuck away from me," I warned him, turning around and walking briskly toward the school.

"I *will*. I thought you were the one, but you just … you bring out the worst parts of me. I don't want to see you ever again," I heard him say in a low voice.

His words shattered my heart. I almost wanted to go back and hug him. Instead, I bit my trembling lower lip and kept walking. I headed straight to the bathroom—I didn't want Mark to see me like this. My mascara was smeared from the tears, my concealer was creasing, and my hair was getting frizzy from the wind. I was a mess.

I was fixing my makeup in the mirror when I heard the bathroom door swing open. I turned to see who it was and flinched in surprise.

SIXTY-EIGHT

"Oh… Ian, you scared me," I laughed, putting my hand on my chest.

He had caught me off guard. He was pretty much the last person I expected to walk into the girls' bathroom.

"Sorry about that, you probably expected a girl to walk in," Ian laughed too.

"Yeah, are you looking for Patricia or something? I think she went home," I told him.

"No, I was actually looking for you," he told me.

"Oh," I replied, taken aback by his answer. "Why are you still in school?"

"I had—have—football practice today," Ian explained.

"Gotcha…" I said, still confused.

I don't remember ever having a single conversation alone with Ian. I was genuinely taken aback by his sudden appearance in the girls' bathroom. His hands were buried in the pockets of his loose-fitting dark blue jeans. He was casually leaning to the side, his Nike-clad feet crossed. And he was staring at me intently, watching my every move. Something about him seemed off.

"Lily, I need to ask you something," he finally said.

"Okay, shoot," I replied.

"Is something going on between you and my dad?" he asked bluntly.

I froze, my body instinctively stiffening. I was dumbfounded by his question. He knew. How did he know? There was no way he would randomly ask me that if he didn't already know something was up. He needed confirmation.

"Do you mean the violin lessons he's been giving me?" I inquired, trying to sound unaffected by his line of questioning.

"No, not the violin lessons… I think you know what I'm talking about."

He slowly approached me, getting closer and closer to where I was standing by the sinks.

"I honestly don't, Ian." I shrugged, running my fingers through my hair.

"Really? Because I found one of your rings on my couch the other day… My mom was traveling, and I was with Patricia … Why were you at my place?" Ian asked me.

Fuck. Shit, shit, shit. I knew I had forgotten something. I love my rings and wear my favorite ones daily. But for the past few days, I noticed one had been missing. It was silver with a black gem in the center. I had assumed it was somewhere around my room—never in a million years did I think I would be stupid enough to leave it at Mark's.

And now Ian knew. I needed to fix this—quickly.

"I—I had forgotten it in the music room, and your dad was keeping it safe for me," I lied, blurting out the first explanation that came to mind, hoping he hadn't heard the unease in my voice.

"He was keeping it safe for you between my couch cushions?" Ian shook his head in disbelief.

"Don't lie to me, Lily. You can lie to James and even

Patricia, but I'm not as fucking gullible… I need you to tell me the truth," he continued.

"That is the truth! I swear!" My voice quivered.

I began moving away, walking backward until I felt the cold wall tiles against the back of my arms. To my dismay, Ian followed and only stopped when he was standing directly in front of me. He was breathing heavily, and his eyes were clouded with silent rage. My legs felt like jelly as the seriousness of my situation dawned on me.

Suddenly, the ferocity on his face disappeared. He chuckled, shaking his head and running his hand through his messy blond hair.

"Do you think I'm fucking stupid?" he asked, glaring into my eyes. "Do you think this is the first time my dad has tried to fuck one of his students?"

Wait, what? My breath caught in my chest.

"Ian, what are you talking about?" I whispered.

There was a crazed look in his eyes that I had never seen before.

"Tell me the truth. I just want to know the truth, that's all," he told me.

He was so close that I could feel his breath on my face. I knew I had to confess, not that it mattered much at this point. He was clearly fully aware of what had been going on between his dad and me. But I needed him to think I was on his side, that it was just a one-time fling.

"Fine. Yes… something happened," I admitted.

"Seriously, Lily?" He shook his head. "I thought we were friends. How could you?"

"I'm sorry… but it's over between us, I swear."

I was saying what I hoped would get Ian to back off. I needed to get out of this bathroom and away from him.

"Oh, it definitely is. I'm going to make sure of it," promised Ian, grabbing my jaw.

I gasped in pain and shock, trying to push his hand away. Ian had always been quiet and mild-mannered, the kind of person you barely even noticed was around. The sudden violence, the burst of anger—it was terrifying.

I knew I had to act now before this escalated any further. I couldn't put my baby in harm's way. I pushed him away as hard as I could, and he grabbed the sink to regain his balance. I tried to run past him, but he grabbed my waist before I could reach the door. He pushed me down, throwing me onto the floor. I lay on my side, my ears ringing. I grabbed my right foot; my ankle felt like it was on fire. I squeezed my eyes shut, silently praying for the pain to ease.

"You stupid fucking cunt. Do you think you're special? Do you think he loves you? He doesn't love you, or even care about you! He manipulated you because you're a stupid teenage girl, and that's his fucking type!" Ian shouted, standing over me.

"Please don't hurt me!" I begged.

I was in too much pain to even care about what he was saying.

"Why not? At least the other girls were smart enough to keep their distance as soon as they found out what he was. But you? You seriously think this is some kind of stupid love story, don't you?" he sneered.

He moved closer to me, his jaw clenched. I tried to crawl away from him, my sprained ankle hurting too much to stand up. I yelped as a sharp pain exploded on my side, leaving me in the fetal position, clutching my stomach where he had kicked me.

"Please don't!" I pleaded. "I'm pregnant!"

"What?" he gasped, stunned.

"I'm pregnant, and if you let me go, I swear I'll leave, and you'll never see me again. I won't tell anyone about any of this," I spoke quickly, afraid he would hit me again before he heard my full plea.

He stepped back, trying to digest my revelation. His expression softened from fury to distress. And for the first time since he had walked into the bathroom, I saw a hint of sympathy in his eyes.

"I don't want to hurt you, Lily, I—I don't want to hurt you or your baby or anyone. I never wanted it to be this way." He kneeled, tears streaming down his face. "I'm just trying to protect. I was offered a football scholarship last week—that disappears if anyone finds out about this." Ian's voice shook with emotion.

"I know, Ian. That's why I'm moving back to New York—I promise none of this will affect you or your scholarship." I tried to sound calm, but I could hear the urgency in my voice.

Ian continued to kneel by me, a tormented expression on his face.

This was my chance to get away—he was distracted. I ignored the intense pain in my ankle and jumped up, trying to run past him, but he grabbed my foot. My body hit the floor once more with a thud. Tears blurred my vision as I desperately begged him to let me go.

But I could tell from his now resolute stare that no amount of begging would change his mind. He had made his decision. Even though I knew it was too late, I opened my mouth to scream for help. But he quickly wrapped his fingers around my throat, silencing me before I could make a sound.

I tried to scratch him, kick him, push him away. Anything to get him to loosen his grip.

"I'm sorry, Lily, but I can't have you messing up my life. I'm not going to let you destroy my future. Everything I've worked so hard for."

His face was frighteningly blank as he continued squeezing my throat. I gasped for air, my lungs burning. I blinked rapidly. My vision was getting blurry, and I was starting to see spots.

I had read so many theories about what those last few seconds of life were like. Some people said that you'd see a light or the people you love most or memories you cherish. For me, I thought about my baby. They would never get to experience the world, never get to experience life. Maybe that wasn't such a bad thing. I thought about James, about my friends. And finally, I thought about my dad. How deeply I had missed him all this time. Now, I would finally get to be with him. For eternity.

I closed my eyes and stopped trying to fight back, accepting my fate. Letting the darkness consume me.

ACKNOWLEDGMENTS

I want to start by thanking my best friend, Priya, without whom this book would not be what it is today. Thank you for the many times you read and reread each draft, for every word of advice, for every encouragement. I am eternally grateful for you. I could not ask for a more perfect best friend.

Thank you to my family. My parents, in particular, who inspired me to write, read, and be creative from a young age. And who have encouraged and continue to encourage me to pursue my dreams.

To Shreya, thank you for being the person I can always turn to when I'm stressed out or freaking out (which is a lot). Our many conversations have brought me so much joy and comfort. Thank you for being the amazing person that you are.

To my cousins, Veer and Yash. I am so grateful for the many times you dragged me away from my computer and reminded me of the importance of having balance in my life. Thanks to you, I have a never-ending vault of memories in my mind and absolutely no memory left on my phone.

Leah, thank you for the conversations and for taking the time to check in. It means the world to me to have someone who does that (even though I'm awful at replying in a timely manner).

Cindy Georgakas, thank you for taking the time to read my

draft, even though I know this isn't a genre you would otherwise indulge in. I'm so thankful for your support, encouragement, and our many chats that keep me sane. Only a writer fully understands another writer's experience. Thank you for being that person, my writing soulmate.

Thank you, Dr. Rechael, for your support and guidance with both books. I would not be the person I am today without it.

I would be remiss if I did not mention the incredible women who helped me put this book together and bring it to life. Abigail, I am so thankful for you. Neither of my books would have made it to print if it weren't for your help. Maddie, my editor, thank you for your invaluable feedback. It improved the book more than anyone will know. My proofreaders, Brandee and Brandi, thank you for giving the book its much-needed final touches. Brittany, I so appreciate everything you've helped me with, especially with marketing. Kendra, thank you so much for your feedback; it was incredibly needed.

To my Lifesfinewhine family, I am beyond grateful for all of you. I'm thankful every day that I found my online community on WordPress. You are the reason I get to live my dream every single day. You are the reason this book exists. Thank you doesn't feel like enough. You changed the entire direction of my life. You are the reason I have all that I do. None of this would be possible without every one of you. I am forever filled with gratitude for your love, support, and kindness.

ABOUT THE AUTHOR

P. J. Gudka is a writer, blogger and freelancer. Her journey as a blogger began when she created her multi-niche blog, *Lifesfinewhine*, as a teenager, to share her experiencs with the world. She published her first book, a poetry collection, *All The Words I Kept Inside*, in 2024. Her writing has also appeared in bestselling anthologies like *Hidden In Childhood*: *A Poetry Anthology* and *Petal Of Haiku: An Anthology* as well as multiple magazines.

www.ingramcontent.com/pod-product-compliance
Lightning Source LLC
Chambersburg PA
CBHW032216050726
47591CB00001B/136